Guardians Of The Round Table 6
Cursed Harp

Guardians Of The Round Table 6
Cursed Harp

Avril Sabine, Storm Petersen
and Rhys Petersen

Cracked Acorn Productions
Australia

Guardians Of The Round Table 6: Cursed Harp

Published by

Cracked Acorn Productions

PO Box 1365

Gympie, Queensland 4570

Australia

978-1-925941-08-1 (Kindle)

978-1-925941-09-8 (EPUB)

978-1-925941-10-4 (Print)

Genre: Young Adult Fantasy LitRPG

For Adam. Some adventures wouldn't be the same without the right teammates.

Mallory thought tracking down a kidnapped and cursed harp wouldn't be too difficult. After all, the one who'd kidnapped the harp wasn't exactly keeping a low profile. As always things weren't as simple as they first appeared and now she feared they didn't have enough revives to get them through the tasks.

*

This story was written by Australian authors using Australian spelling.

Name Pronunciation

Like many names there is more than one way to pronounce the following ones. These are the pronunciations used in this story.

Characters

Azerron (az-er-ron)

Danae (da-nay)

Deneg (den-eg)

Ehrok (air-rok)

Emica (em-e-cah)

Esben (es-ben)

Hisoki (hiss-oh-key)

Jenet (jen-et)

Jorgen (jaw-gen)

Kruth (kr-uth)

Melsed (mel-said)

Milos (me-los)

Ninette (nin-et)

Pelga (pel-guh)

Remora (reh-more-uh)

Rodina (row-dean-uh)

Sarisa (sa-risa)

Sidree (sid-ree)

Tivon (tiv-on)

Tyne (tine)

Zorlla (zore-lah)

Places

Buckneth (buck-neth)

Delten (del-ten)

Eridell (air-a-dell)

Eswen (es-when)

Jenlea (jen-lee)

Inadon (in-ah-don)

Merrow (mare-row)

Shadville (shad-vil)

Shadhurst (shad-hurst)

Simria (sim-re-ah)

Surith (soo-rith)

Ursen (ur-sen)

Velkden (velk-den)

Wrentville (rent-vil)

Foreword

Opening stats, Mallory's notebook entries recapping the previous adventures and other details can be found at:

www.avrilsabine.com/series/gotrt

The notebook entries will contain spoilers if you haven't read the book they refer to.

Chapter One

Mallory leaned out the back of the wagon, which had a canvas cover draped over arched saplings to provide them with shelter, and took a sack of herbs from Callum. He, along with Jorgen and Ninette, was currently helping Brodie collect herbs. When Callum headed back to Brodie, she faced the interior of the wagon, trying to decide where to put yet one more sack.

Emica, who sat on the front seat next to Danae, driving the wagon, called over her shoulder, "We're about ten minutes from South Point if you want to let everyone know."

Mallory looked in Emica and Danae's direction even though her view of them was mostly blocked by the table and chairs Brodie had taken from Cutthroat Harbour. "I don't suppose the two of you have any more space for herbs up there."

"Not likely," Emica said. "You should drop them where you pick them."

Danae laughed softly. "I doubt Brodie would be happy with that. I hope we can find someone to buy them when we reach South Point."

Mallory's gaze was drawn to the many sacks of herbs, making the space even more cluttered than it had been with only the furniture, timber chests and tall cane baskets. Ryan, Smudge and Jorgen's cousin Esben, who they'd rescued from Cutthroat Harbour, were currently the only ones in the back of the wagon with her. They hadn't all been in the back since they'd left the abandoned farm out from Cutthroat Harbour. That had been several hours, more than two thousand herbs and two bandit attacks ago. There'd been four bandits in the first attack and six in the second. She'd only gained fifteen experience points from the two fights, nowhere near enough to level up since she hadn't collected any herbs like everyone else had. They'd gained twenty-seven copper pieces from the fights and a bright yellow tunic that was badly in need of washing. They'd put the tunic under the wagon seat where the cat, that had joined them at Velkden, had been hiding. He'd shrunk back into a corner and glared at the garment. The coins had been put in the chest with the rest of the ones they'd set aside since they now had too many for her to carry in the belt pouch even with its enchantment to reduce the weight of its contents by fifty percent.

Again Mallory's gaze was drawn to Esben leaning against a tall cane basket, asleep. Two of the traveller's thin plaits, several glass beads in them, had fallen forward to rest across his shoulder and chest. He'd been the only other one who hadn't gathered herbs, everyone else taking turns with Brodie when he took a break every fifteen to twenty minutes. Surprisingly, Esben hadn't complained, but Mallory had a feeling the bumpy dirt road was making his broken arm ache. She wouldn't be able to use rapid mend on it again until nine that night. She'd offered him some health tea, but he'd declined. She supposed it did take a bit of effort to get through a cupful of health tea so it could take effect.

The one who was the happiest out of all of them was Brodie. He was back to earning experience points and had gathered a ridiculous amount of herbs along the way. As well as some vegetables. Her gaze was again drawn to the numerous bags and sacks filled with herbs. The ten minutes everyone else had gathered for during Brodie's breaks meant that Emica had gained a CAS point and was halfway through level two and Jorgen had also gained a CAS point and had mentioned he was nearly halfway through level six. Mallory still didn't know if it was polite to ask him exactly how far through level six, but at least she now had a better idea of his stats.

Ninette had been thrilled to gain another CAS point and had again thanked them for letting her come with them. She'd also mentioned she only needed to earn another sixty-four experience points to be halfway to character level one. Danae had offered to let Ninette have her turn gathering herbs, but Ninette had declined and Danae had gained a CAS point and only had another four to earn before she reached character level three. Callum had also gained a CAS point and only had another forty-eight experience points to earn before he reached character level three. Ryan had gained a CAS point and wasn't far off reaching character level two, needing only eighty-one experience points.

Brodie had been the one to earn the most. Mallory started to open her journal to check what his current experience points were when Emica spoke.

"I can see the village. Are you going to let everyone know it's time to stop gathering herbs?"

Ryan looked up from the book he was reading,

'Lost And Powerful: Myths Of Misplaced Staves'. "Want me to get them?"

Mallory shook her head, jamming the sacks of herbs into an already cramped area of the wagon. "It's okay. I'll let you finish reading the book since I've already had a chance to read it." She jumped out of the back of the wagon, striding towards Brodie who was picking a herb. She brought up the journal as he gained another experience point. He was now four CAS points into character level two with thirty-four of the next one hundred and twenty-two experience points he needed for his next CAS point. It looked like they needed to work on levelling up Ryan and Callum next with how many levels Brodie had gained.

Seeing his sister, Brodie grinned. "Fang levelled up." Brodie paused a moment. "Your companion animal has reached level two. Your companion now has twenty-five percent increased movement speed."

Mallory bent to pat Fang who gave a short, soft bark. Straightening, she faced Brodie again. "We're nearly at South Point. Time to stop gathering herbs." She pushed back the thin plait that had fallen forward over her shoulder when she'd patted Fang, a single dark blue bead with silver swirls plaited into it. Jorgen had done it for her while she'd been reading earlier. He'd also done a plait for Ryan and Danae.

"I can't wait to see what South Point looks like." Ninette strode towards the wagon, Jorgen and Callum following her. "There are so many places I want to see."

When Mallory tried to follow, Brodie grabbed hold of her arm and drew her back. She easily pulled out of his grip. "What's wrong?"

Before speaking, Brodie glanced at the rest of their group who were now well ahead of them. "Why does he make me visit when he hates me?"

She didn't need to ask Brodie who he was talking about. She'd been thinking about needing to stay at their father's for the weekend too. "He doesn't hate you." The words were automatic, ones she'd spoken far too many times over the years.

"Come on, Mal. You don't have to keep lying about it. I got over it ages ago."

Mallory met her brother's gaze, seeing the worry in his green eyes that were the same colour as her own. Clearly he wasn't over it. "He doesn't hate you. He doesn't hate either of us. But I don't think he'd tolerate us if we weren't his kids."

"So he doesn't like us."

Mallory shrugged. "Who knows how he thinks or feels. I certainly don't."

"He's pretty clear on what he thinks. He tells me all the time not to be so weak."

She tried to come up with something reassuring to say to her brother, but nothing came to mind. "He says the same to me."

"Not in the same way he says it to me. When he says it to you he sounds mildly annoyed. When he says it to me, he sounds angry."

"Brodie-" She broke off when Callum called out to them, relieved for the interruption.

"We're coming into the village and will gain new location XP shortly. Or are you finished worrying about earning XP for the day?"

Mallory laughed, glancing at Brodie before she hurried after the wagon, her brother keeping pace with her. "Don't worry about it, Brodie." She kept her voice low as they approached the wagon. "We'll manage. It's only for two days." She tried to tell herself the time would go fast since it was so little time. Unable to convince herself, she didn't bother speaking the words aloud. There was no way she'd be able to convince her brother.

"Yeah. I suppose." He clambered into the back of the wagon to sit beside Callum. "When are you going to use up some of your CAS points? You've got sixteen of them. It's not like they're collectables."

Callum shrugged. "I'll spend them as I need them. Next time we need a skill or ability, like we did with apothecary, I might have the points to get it."

Mallory checked her journal, finding it was a notification letting her know she'd gained ten experience points for discovering a location. She was still a long way from her next level, not that she was that concerned after all the grinding she'd done recently.

"What are you going to put your new CAS points into, Brodie?" Danae asked.

"I can't decide between cooking, brewer or bartering."

Emica brought the wagon to a stop and turned to peer through the furniture. "There are some people here building a cabin if you want to ask them about Deneg."

"We'll wait with the wagon." Jorgen glanced at Esben. "We don't want to overwhelm them."

Chapter Two

Mallory jumped out of the back of the wagon. Ryan, Brodie and Callum joined her. Fang followed Brodie while Smudge remained curled up asleep in the wagon. She glanced around the village, her gaze drawn to the freestanding timber cabin being constructed by two gnomes and a demon. His dark wings were furled at his back, he only wore trousers and his body was covered with demonic rune tattoos, the ink darker than his skin.

The demon spotted them first and, after a glance over everyone, strode towards them. "Were you looking for a cabin?"

"We'd have nowhere to put it," Mallory said.

The demon grinned, revealing pointed teeth. "You're adventurers?"

Mallory nodded.

"Then you set it up beside your wagon when you

stop for the day. We make sure enchantments for stability are added so it can be put on uneven ground."

Callum studied the cabin. "Set it up when we stop for the day? They go on wheels?"

The demon chuckled. "Sounds like you're well and truly not looking for South Point Compact Dwellings."

Mallory eyed the cabin the gnomes continued to work on. "Compact?" It was small, but she wouldn't exactly have called it compact.

The demon nodded. "Ours shrink down to the smallest size possible." He gestured towards a nearby building. "We have three currently available." He led the way to the building, glancing at them as they trailed after him. "A single room cabin with a fireplace, kitchen table and two chairs and a double bed that are all linked to the enchantment for a low hundred and fifty thousand gold. Or if you prefer something for a large party, we have a cabin with two bedrooms upstairs. And of course you can add extras such as storage containers that can be in use when the enchantment is activated." He stepped inside the building and gestured towards three small cabins that looked like children's toys.

Mallory, who'd been about to speak, not having

wanted to interrupt his spiel, finally realised what the demon was talking about. "They shrink? That cabin being built out there will eventually look like these?"

The demon nodded. "The enchantment does of course use the mana of the one activating it, but as long as you have the mana, you can shrink and unshrink them as many times as you wish."

"We need cabins like these." Brodie peered in through a window. "This one has an oven."

"Yes, and the finest clay bricks have been used to make it," the demon said.

Mallory nearly groaned. Brodie was going to be desperate for one of these. "We only stopped to ask if you knew of the bard Deneg."

"He played at the tavern last night. Wonderful talent. I had to drag my workers away or they would have been there till daylight and they'd have done nothing today," the demon said.

Callum took a step towards him. "He's still at South Point?"

The demon shook his head. "Organised a ride on to Delten with a wagoner that was leaving after midday. Once his wagon wheel was fixed. Although I'm guessing things didn't go according to plan because they didn't get away from here until a couple of hours ago. Well after midday."

"We've not long missed him?" Mallory asked.

The demon shrugged. "Seems that way. Why are you looking for him?"

"We were hoping he could help us complete a quest," Ryan said.

Mallory somehow managed not to smile at Ryan's evasive answer. Although she didn't blame him with how enthusiastic the demon had been about Deneg's abilities. She took a step towards the door, ignoring the journal notification that had appeared at the demon's information. "Thanks for your help."

"You're welcome." The demon grinned. "If you ever decide you want your own compact dwelling, you know where to find me."

They thanked him as they headed outside, Brodie glancing over his shoulder several times as they went, talking to Callum about how useful a compact dwelling would be and all the meals he could make with a set up like the larger cabin had.

Ryan entwined his fingers with Mallory's, grinning at her as they approached the wagon. "Sounds like we need to focus on earning money faster than we've been doing."

She sighed heavily. "I don't think we're ever going to earn enough for all we want." At least not with the way they'd been spending it lately. Her gaze was momentarily drawn to her brother who clambered into the wagon, answering Emica's questions about what they'd learned.

"Are we going onto Delten now?" Ninette asked.

"What about dinner?" Brodie asked. "I was hoping we could stay here long enough to have dinner at the tavern."

Ryan glanced skywards as he followed Mallory onto the wagon. "We should arrive at Delten around dinner time. It's only two and a half hours away. Or there abouts."

"Can we have dinner at the tavern there?" Brodie asked. "That's if they do have a tavern."

"Most places do," Danae said.

Esben eyed the furniture at the front of the wagon, the canvas arching over the top of them, touching it in places. "Didn't you want to sell some things? Like the bear pelt. And herbs. Might want to sell the table and chairs too. There's not much space on the wagon."

Brodie looked from the demon, who'd returned to working on the cabin, and the furniture. "I'll be right back."

Mallory leaned against Ryan as she watched her brother. He gestured towards the wagon several times and nodded once. The demon beckoned one of the gnomes over, who raced off after nodding enthusiastically.

Brodie strode towards them with a grin. "He'll take the furniture, the bear pelt and he's sent one of his workers to let the trader know we have a lot of herbs." He turned to Mallory. "And to bring back one of his workers that is currently unable to work because he's injured. He needs you to do rapid mend."

The demon reached them only seconds after Brodie finished talking. "I'm always in need of furniture. And I can have the bear pelt tanned and it'll make a nice option for those wanting more than the basics in their dwelling." He nodded towards one of the timber chests. "Interested in selling that?"

"I don't know," Brodie said. "We might need it."

"What about the four pieces of material from Cutthroat Harbour?" Ryan asked. "We don't need them."

Brodie nodded. "We can sort through all our gear. It's been a bit since we did."

The demon beckoned the other gnome over and let him know what was happening.

The gnome gave a sharp nod of his head. "I'll tell everyone travelling merchants have arrived."

He was gone before Mallory could protest. They weren't travelling merchants.

"Travelling merchant." Brodie spoke the word as if he was savouring it. "I like the sound of that." He clambered into the wagon and opened the chest, holding up a dagger. "Do we need all the spare weapons?"

Night had fallen by the time they'd sorted through all their gear and Mallory had done rapid mend on three people as well as diagnosed and treated several more. She'd been surprised she'd gained experience points not only for healing people, but also when they'd paid her. Including when she'd been paid a basket of eggs by one woman. The rest paid in copper and silver pieces.

They managed to sell the bear pelt, but none of the spider fangs or bear canines. They also sold one of their tall cane baskets, one of the timber chests and the furniture. They kept the packing crate even though the demon had made an offer on it.

Since they'd not needed it up till now, they sold the stamina potion along with one of the deck of cards, the linen sheets Rodina had given them, all the patterns they'd gained from Velkden even though Callum had argued against selling them and the empty salve jar. Callum had been adamant that none of the books were to be sold. Since they could make corpse rot poultices, they sold the corpse rot potions along with the four pieces of material Brodie had taken from Cutthroat Harbour. He also sold all the fruit and vegetables along with the salted venison and the rest of the fresh bear meat, keeping only the jerky, dried venison, flour, oats, oil, rice, honey and maple syrup. He said they'd gather more along the way when Danae and Emica had both questioned his willingness to sell the food.

They sold the seven grey blankets, since they had five other blankets and six bedrolls, and also sold the thin blanket and feather pillow that Mallory had used her mend spell on to repair the damage from Fang. They managed to sell approximately half the herbs including some of the ones that had been sorted for health tea and corpse rot poultices. The spare clothing they sold went the quickest and they handed over three pairs of brown trousers, a grey pair, a light grey shirt, a khaki shirt, all the spare leather belts and boots, the fleece lined clothing and boots and only one of the mage robes. They also sold most of the spare weapons, keeping only the sheathed longsword from the orc mage, the steel longsword from the merfolk and a hunting knife.

Chapter Three

It was well after dark when they drove off with a lantern hung from one of the saplings that arched over the back of the wagon to support the canvas. It swung back and forth with the movements of the wagon as they headed towards Delten.

Brodie sat beside Mallory, watching her count the coins they'd earned, drawing his hand back when she slapped it for the second time. "I can help."

"I'd be finished counting a lot quicker if you'd leave me to it." Mallory stacked the coins into piles of ten to make it easier to keep track of the amounts.

"You could go back to gathering herbs. And vegetables since you sold all of them." Emica glanced over her shoulder from where she sat on the driver's seat along with Ninette and Esben, who had tried to tell them he could take a turn driving.

"Once I find out how much money we earned," Brodie said.

Danae shifted the basket of eggs away from Fang who sniffed them. "Maybe we shouldn't have sold the rest of the bear meat."

"We can share the dried venison and jerky with her," Brodie said. "They won't last forever. Just like the food we sold. We'll get fresh stuff." He studied the basket. "How big are drake eggs?"

"About one and a half times the size of these chicken eggs." Danae set the basket of eggs inside the tall cane basket that still contained herbs.

"We can use the basket, and the other one we have, for collecting the drake eggs. We should be able to take more that way," Brodie said.

"We have two wooden buckets we could use," Callum said.

Brodie glanced at their donkey, Bobbi, who carried some of their gear. "I suppose."

Mallory counted each of the piles of coins. "We made one hundred and ninety-eight gold, one hundred and sixty-seven silver and one hundred and thirty-five copper pieces."

"They should go in the chest with the rest of the money we put aside," Brodie said.

Mallory stared at her brother, wondering if she

should be concerned. Before she could ask him if he was okay, Ryan spoke.

"You sure you didn't get hit on the head rather than shot in the knee?"

Brodie glared at Ryan. "It makes sense. We need money to get to the mainland when Danae moves over there."

Ryan chuckled. "When you put it that way…" He glanced at Danae before returning his attention to Brodie. "We need enough money to pay for everyone who wants to go to the mainland."

"You will pay our way?" Esben asked.

Ryan nodded. "It's only fair."

Esben gestured between him and Jorgen. "Both of us."

"Yeah." Ryan grinned. "Both of you."

"What if I wanted to go to the mainland?" Emica asked.

Ryan again nodded. "Any of you who want to travel with us."

"Are you thinking of going to the mainland?" Mallory asked.

Emica shrugged. "I hadn't been until now." She shrugged again. "I don't know if I will, but travelling with you has been interesting."

Mallory gathered up the coins, a handful at a time,

and hid them in the bottom of the chest. "We aren't travelling over there straight away. We still have a few things to do on Ruby Isle first."

"It'll give me time to think about it then," Emica said.

Mallory reached for the lantern, planning to put it out so they didn't waste oil.

"Leave it." Callum took out the book 'Lost And Powerful: Myths Of Misplaced Staves'. He held it up. "I think the dark forces are going after one of these staves."

Brodie took it from him, flicking through the pages. "How did you work that out?"

"They had two copies of it, snow gear and a silver piece from Eswen. The last known location of the Frost Chain staff is on the Eswen and Ebren border." Callum glanced at Jorgen. "Which Jorgen told me has snow for large periods of the year and areas that are permanently snow covered. Most of the ships they were focused on also travel down there."

Brodie stopped flicking through the pages, staring down at the page he had open. "Chain a foe in place with frost. That could be handy."

Esben angled himself on the driver's seat to face them better. "You're going after it?"

Brodie looked from the book to Esben. "Your name sounds a lot like Eswen. And even Ebren."

"I was named for the town my parents met each other in." Esben gestured towards the book. "Are you going after it?"

Callum opened up the map of Inadon. "It's a long way from anything, but maybe we could let the guardians know what the dark forces might be planning."

"Then they'd get the staff," Brodie protested. "This staff works best against demons. It's just what we need when we go through Hellfire to Cape Barren."

"Since when have you wanted to go there?" Callum asked.

Brodie shrugged. "You want to go there, don't you? For coffee."

Ryan grinned. "Probably been interested in going since the trader at Velkden said there's better profit from travelling to demonic lands."

Brodie glared at everyone when they laughed. "It's not like Callum would let up if we didn't go," he muttered.

Ryan gestured towards the map. "We can't do everything. That's a long way for us to travel. It might even be too great a distance for Danae to travel and still get back to the academy. Either in time to start or in time to keep up with her studies."

Callum folded the map. "We don't have to decide right away. But we can let someone know. A guardian. Maybe they'll have ideas about what can be done."

"They'll steal the staff," Brodie muttered.

"It doesn't matter," Ryan said. "Better that a guardian has it than someone from the dark forces."

Callum rested his hand on Smudge, briefly smiling down at the sleeping river otter. "We should do some more levelling up."

"Whose turn?" Esben asked.

"I think Mallory should gain a few more levels. Take her apothecary up to level fifty so she can use weak increased healing when using potions, salves and ointments. That'd make health potions twice as effective, giving twenty health for only ten mana." Callum faced Mallory. "To heal for twenty health with the spell, it'd cost you sixty mana."

"But it'd mean using one of our health potions," Brodie said.

"Which if we're using one, it'd mean we'd probably be needing the extra health," Callum said.

Brodie continued to argue with Callum who gave him more calculations to prove his option was best.

Ryan jumped out the back of the wagon, taking a hessian bag with him. "I'll start since I have the lowest stats."

Mallory followed him, casting magelight. "Need a hand?" She took the sack from him when he held it out, checking her brother's stats while she picked up the herbs Ryan dropped on the ground. Brodie had added his class point into rogue, but hadn't as yet assigned his five attribute points or any of his CAS points. Having read all the books on the classes, she knew he could now wield an enchanted stiletto. More than likely he'd be pestering her to buy one.

Jorgen and Emica joined them, pointing herbs out to Ryan to speed up the process.

Chapter Four

Mallory recast magelight when it went out after fifteen minutes, wondering if the bright light that followed her scared away any creatures or bandits in the area or if the road between South Point and Delten was quiet. Once Ryan earned the seventy-one experience points he needed to reach level two, he told Mallory to take a turn. She shook her head. "What about everyone else?"

"I'm halfway through level two," Emica said. "I'm not that worried about levelling up at the moment."

"I'm well above that level," Jorgen said. "You don't need to worry about me."

"And the rest?" Mallory asked.

"I don't think Callum will mind since he suggested it. Brodie is probably the only one who'll complain." Ryan took the hessian bag from her, grinning. "Your turn. Again."

"There are herbs over here," Jorgen called out.

Mallory hurried to his side, picking the herbs and letting them fall at Ryan's feet. "What are you putting your attribute points into?"

Ryan put the herbs into the hessian bag. "I probably should level up." He paused a moment. "You have reached level two warrior. You can now wield enchanted short swords and enchanted shields."

"We need to get better weapons before we leave Ruby Isle," Mallory said. "And especially before we go to demonic lands." She picked several herbs, letting them fall to the ground. "What are you putting your attribute points into?"

"Two in both strength and constitution and one in dexterity. That's taken my health up to thirty-three and stamina to fifty-five." After picking up the herbs, Ryan followed Mallory to the next cluster.

As she gathered the herbs, Mallory checked her brother's stats, seeing that he'd finally assigned his attribute points. One each in strength, constitution, dexterity, charisma and luck so that his health was now thirty and his stamina fifty. She also noticed they had two reputation points in South Point. It made her think of their negative reputation in Cutthroat Harbour and of Rass. What level was he now? If they were lucky, they wouldn't run into him again. They probably needed to leave Ruby Isle sooner rather than later so they could put more distance between them and Rass.

They gathered herbs mostly in silence, only Jorgen and Emica calling out where the herbs were. Mallory didn't gather herbs as fast since she didn't have as much help, but she was still managing to gain seventy experience points every ten minutes, the magelight making it easier for her. Callum joined them partway through gathering, along with Danae, and the two of them hunted down a rabbit each, sharing one rabbit between the companion animals and hanging the other one on a pannier with plans to have it for dinner when they stopped for the night.

They were about halfway to Delten, and Mallory only had another five experience points before she gained her third CAS point from gathering herbs and vegetables, when an arrow struck a tree beside her as she stepped away from it.

Ryan readied his bow. "Can you put your magelight out? It's like a beacon for them."

Another arrow came out of the darkness well back from the side of the road, striking Jorgen in the arm. "Retreat to the wagon. I'll go after them."

Mallory smiled. "I have a better idea." She cast

beacon at the ground near where the arrows had come from, lighting up the area.

Four archers lowered their bows and turned to run.

Jorgen raced after them, turning into a crystalline wolf in mid-stride, Emica following him, changing into her fox form. Mallory cast a fireball at each of the archers, relieved when arrows came from three different directions as Ryan, Callum and Danae joined the fight. It was over in seconds and she grinned when she realised Brodie ran towards them, too late for the experience points.

Brodie stopped beside Mallory. "Why didn't you call me? You know I need XP."

"What were you doing?" She hurried forward to help search the archers, also healing Jorgen.

"Ninette is teaching me how to drive the wagon." Brodie crouched by the archer Danae searched, helping her look for items. "It's easier than I thought it'd be." He grinned. "Cool. Got some jerky."

Danae took the four strips of jerky from him. "It's beetle jerky. It's fishing bait, not food."

Jorgen looked up from the archer he helped Callum search. "Goblins eat it."

Emica laughed, looking Brodie up and down. "Goblins will eat nearly anything."

Glaring at Emica, Brodie rose to his feet,

muttering. "I don't eat nearly anything." His words brought laughter from everyone.

Callum finished searching the archer before joining Danae. "Can I see the bait? What's it used to catch?"

Danae handed the beetle jerky over. "Some of the rarer fish can't resist it. Just like goblins can't."

Ryan clapped his brother on the shoulder. "You might as well keep it. Smudge is the one who loves fish. You might be able to catch him some delicacies."

"Some of the fish you can catch with beetle jerky are worth too much to eat. They're used for alchemy and enchanting." Danae handed five copper coins to Mallory, replaced the missing arrows in her quiver and handed five arrows to Callum to replace his.

Mallory glanced over her shoulder as she recast magelight. "We need to catch up with the wagon. Who knows what else is around here." She pocketed the coins from Danae and the silver piece Emica gave her. Between them they also found a quiver, six spare arrows as well as enough arrows to fill everyone's quiver and a night vision potion that would last for three hours.

Callum put the beetle jerky in his belt pouch as they strode after the wagon, nodding towards the potion Mallory slipped inside her satchel. "Looks like they probably would have seen us even if you weren't using the magelight."

Brodie slowed his pace to come alongside Mallory. "Now you've levelled up, whose turn is it to gather herbs? There has to be at least an hour before we reach Delten. Lots of time for gaining XP."

Ryan spoke before Mallory could. "Callum hasn't reached level two yet."

"Whose turn after he reaches level two?" Brodie asked.

Mallory laughed. "Why don't you just come out and ask when it'll be your turn again?"

Brodie glared at Mallory, muttering that he hadn't been trying to ask that.

"We should try and get everyone to character level three as soon as possible," Mallory said. "Alternating between everyone until they are." She stared at the wagon only metres ahead of them, moving to the side of the road and out of the trail of dust it stirred up. "And that includes Ninette." She turned to Callum. "Do you need to take Smudge with you so he gains XP?"

Callum shook his head. "The wagon was close enough that he gained XP from the archers too. It'll be quicker to gather herbs if he waits in the wagon." He smiled at Smudge when he looked out the back of the wagon. "And he probably wants to finish eating his dinner."

Smudge made several soft sounds before he returned to his meal, Fang beside him.

"Want some help?" Brodie asked Callum.

Callum reached for a lantern. "You can carry this."

"I can cast magelight for you," Mallory offered.

Callum lit the lantern before handing it to Brodie. He turned to Mallory. "You can help after you've read the crafting ability books. You're the only one still to read them."

"It won't take me long." Mallory clambered into the wagon.

Brodie looked over his shoulder as he followed Callum. "Make sure you level up your apothecary."

Not bothering to answer her brother, Mallory took out the two books, assuring Ninette when she asked that they were all unharmed. Before reading the books, she put five CAS points into apothecary. The three she'd earned tonight and the two she'd kept in case she needed them. She ignored the notifications about new levels, only reading the one that gave her a new ability. *You have reached level fifty apothecary. You now have the ability to use weak increased healing when using potions, salves and ointments.* She smiled. Not only was she level fifty apothecary, but she was one CAS point off being halfway through level five. Before they left Ruby Isle, they should have the skills and levels to face more dangerous areas. Like Hellfire.

Chapter Five

Opening up the book for enchanting, Mallory read only enough to unlock the crafting ability. *You have unlocked enchanting, a crafting ability that allows you to use mana to enchant items, jewellery, weapons and armour that are of at least good quality.* She set the book aside and picked up weaver. *You have unlocked weaver, a crafting ability that allows you to make thread, wool, rope, material, rugs and sails.* Finished, she put both books away. There were so many useful crafting abilities. It'd take forever to learn all the ones that sounded interesting.

Her fingers brushed across her satchel, which contained the timeless potion. And they should have the time to learn all they were interested in and level up each class they were intrigued by. Eventually. Her lips slowly curved into a smile. There were so many possibilities in this world. Her smile faded as she thought of her own world and needing to stay at her father's for the weekend. She didn't blame Brodie in the least for not wanting to go home. Not with what they currently had to look forward to.

Mallory faced the front of the wagon where Ninette and Esben sat on the seat, everyone else helping Callum. Which, by the amount of experience points he'd gained, looked like he'd level up faster than she had. "I'm going to help Callum."

"Do you need me to help too?" Esben asked.

Mallory hated to tell him no with how hopeful he sounded. "It won't be long and your arm will be healed. I'll do another rapid mend on it when we reach Delten." She hopped out the back of the wagon and headed for the lantern light, trying not to feel bad about the look of disappointment that had washed over Esben's face.

Callum managed to gather enough herbs, as well as some vegetables, that as they came into Delten, the location experience points earned him another CAS point so he was halfway through character level two. Smudge had also levelled up and now had two thousand two hundred and ten experience points needed of the three thousand for level three. He'd also gained twenty-five percent more movement speed.

"What are you going to put your CAS points

into?" Brodie asked Callum as they walked beside the wagon, headed towards a tavern. "Surely there's something you want to put at least some of them into. Don't you have a crafting ability or skill you want to focus on?"

Callum shrugged. "I'll figure that out when I have more information. And like I said earlier, I'll have points if we need a particular skill if another situation we can't deal with comes up. I do know I plan to put my attribute points in strength, constitution, dexterity, charisma and luck." He paused a moment. "You have reached level two archer. You can now use enchanted hunting knives, short bows and arrows."

"You've got twenty-two CAS points," Brodie said. "You could do something with at least some of them. You don't have to save all your CAS points."

"You've got twelve you haven't used," Callum pointed out.

"I can't decide if I should put more in cooking, start levelling up brewer or add some to barter. I just don't have enough points for everything," Brodie said.

"I'll park the wagon around the back of the tavern," Ninette said.

"Will it be okay leaving it there?" Callum asked.

Ninette shook her head. "I'll stay with it."

"Can we set up a fire to cook dinner on?" Brodie asked.

"Not in the village," Ninette said. "If we parked on the outskirts we could. Or if we knew someone here, they could let us set up camp by their house."

"You can't stay on the outskirts of the village by yourself," Ryan said. "We don't know what's in the area."

"We'll stay with her." Jorgen glanced at Esben as he spoke.

"I could stay and guard the wagon too if you need me," Emica offered.

Mallory looked at each of them. "If you don't mind."

Emica grinned. "It's not like we'll be missing out on anything. Every village tavern is pretty much the same."

Ninette changed direction, eventually pulling up on the outskirts of Delten. It didn't take long to get a fire going and for Brodie to add rabbit, vegetables, herbs and water to the cooking pot and place it on the rock Jorgen had put in the middle of the fire pit. He also put extra vegetables along the edges of the fire pit, covering them in a light layer of soil and giving Ninette orders to put coals over them when the rabbit stew was nearly cooked.

Brodie took a step back from the fire, his gaze remaining on the pot. "We need a bigger cooking pot. That one isn't big enough to feed all of us."

"Do you want to stay here and finish cooking?" Mallory looked up from doing rapid mend on Esben. Three more rapid mends and his arm would be healed.

"I'm not staying behind." Brodie turned his back on the fire. "Maybe we can find someone who does have a larger pot for sale. A fourteen litre one would be good."

"We should check the tavern and see if Deneg is still here or has been here." Callum put Smudge in the makeshift sling, patting the river otter on the head when he made soft, contented sounds.

Mallory walked beside Callum, Ryan on the other side of her while Brodie and Danae led the way, Fang trotting at Brodie's side. "Are you sure you'll be okay?" She kept her voice low so that only Callum, and possibly Ryan, would hear her words. While she waited for his answer, she checked that her magelight would last long enough for them to reach the tavern.

Callum smiled briefly. "Don't worry. I'm not about to throw myself at him and beg him not to leave me again."

Ryan chuckled. "You've never been the dramatic type."

Callum smiled again, this one lasting longer than the previous one. "No, that would be Brodie."

Brodie turned, walking backwards so he could face them. "What would be me?"

"The dramatic one," Ryan said.

"I am not," Brodie protested.

Danae grabbed Brodie's arm when he stumbled. "We're nearly at the tavern."

Brodie faced forward. "I'm not the dramatic one." Reaching the tavern, he opened the door, looking from the interior to Fang. "Will she be able to come inside?"

Danae nodded. "Most places allow companion animals." She stepped past him.

Mallory glanced at Callum again, the sounds of music reaching them. She wanted to again ask him if he was okay, but she kept the words to herself. "Come on, let's get that harp back." She followed Danae inside, heading towards Deneg who was seated on a stool, his fingers plucking the strings of a lap harp.

The moment Deneg spotted them, his fingers faltered and he glanced around the room, bringing the music to a close. He smiled at the people seated at a table in front of him, slowly shaking his head.

Mallory and her companions reached Deneg before he could go far. She stepped in front of him, the rest of her party surrounding him. "I'm sure you know why we're here." Her gaze momentarily rested on the harp he clutched.

Before Deneg could say anything, three large men and an equally tall woman joined them, one of the men stepping close to Ryan. "What is going on here?"

Mallory looked from Deneg to the four people. "You're friends of Deneg?"

"You know him?" the woman demanded.

Callum nodded, turning to face Deneg. "You left without saying goodbye."

"I thought it best under the circumstances." Deneg glanced at the harp he held against his chest.

"I thought…" Callum's voice trailed off.

One of the men looked between Callum and Deneg. "A lover's quarrel?" He took a step back. "I'm not about to get in the middle of that."

The woman also took a step back. "Will you still need a lift to Seacoast tomorrow?"

Callum moved so he could slip his arm around Deneg's shoulders. "I doubt it." Smiling, he leaned in close to Deneg, his lips brushing across his cheek before he drew back, his gaze meeting Deneg's. "Isn't that right?"

Chapter Six

Mallory had no idea what Callum had whispered, but Deneg nodded in agreement. She faced the four who'd confronted them. "I'm sure they'll be too busy sorting their misunderstanding out for Deneg to go to Seacoast."

With nods and an offer to let them know before they retired for the night if Deneg changed his mind about going to Seacoast, they returned to their table. Callum waited until they were seated before he spoke. "We want the harp back."

"I can't. I need her," Deneg protested. "I always planned to return her after I earned enough money, but I'm starting to think this wasn't the best plan." He smiled sadly, his sharp canines visible. "I'm not a fighter, but it might come to that if I want to rescue my brother."

Mallory frowned. "Rescue your brother?"

The tavern owner joined them, interrupting Deneg when he started to speak. "I'm not paying you if you're going to stand around gossiping all night."

Brodie stepped forward, Fang remaining close to his side. "Is there anywhere around here I can buy a large cooking pot? One that's about fourteen litres."

The tavern owner looked from Brodie to Deneg. "Well…" His voice trailed off.

"I only have an hour left to play," Deneg said.

Ryan slung an arm around Deneg's shoulders, his arm resting across Callum's, his gaze meeting Mallory's. "We'll stay with Deneg while Brodie and you take care of buying what we need. We should probably top up on lantern oil too."

"My son is the local trader," the tavern owner said.

"Will he be open at this hour?" Brodie asked as Ryan, Callum and Deneg headed back towards the stool Deneg had been sitting on when they'd arrived.

"Not usually, but he's been known to open up for some travellers," the tavern owner said. "Depending on what they want to buy or have to sell."

"We have lots of herbs to sell," Brodie said.

"Well, I'm not sure he'll need many of them, if any. We have no apothecary or alchemist in our village," the tavern owner said.

"We have both with us." Brodie nodded to

Mallory. "Our apothecary. The alchemist is at our camp."

The tavern owner rubbed his chin. "That's a different story. Why don't I send for my son and we'll see what we can do? It's been awhile since we've had either call through." He turned to Mallory. "What level are the two of you?"

"I'm level fifty, but our alchemist can only do poultices and health tea." Mallory sent her brother a look, wishing he'd been clearer about their abilities when he'd mentioned them.

Brodie grinned. "She can recognise and treat up to rare ailments and diseases, do average surgery, do average rapid mend on broken bones and use weak increased healing."

Mallory stared at her brother, amazed he'd remembered all her abilities. Before she could say that she didn't have surgical tools, the tavern owner spoke.

"Where have you set up camp?"

"On the outskirts of the village." Brodie gestured in the direction of where the wagon was parked.

"I'll organise one of my other children to take over here and we'll meet you out at your camp." The tavern owner turned to Mallory. "You don't mind if I let a few people know you're visiting?"

"No, that's okay." When the tavern owner gave

them a nod and strode back to the bar, Mallory followed Brodie from the tavern, looking over her shoulder at Ryan and Callum as she reached the door.

Ryan grinned at her.

She returned his grin as she stepped outside, casting magelight before following Brodie back to the wagon, only half listening to him talk about how useful it was that she was an apothecary. When his steps slowed, and he stopped speaking, she looked over at him. "What's wrong?"

"Why does Dad need us to visit him? He has our fake siblings. He doesn't need us too."

Mallory couldn't resist smiling at her brother's name for Landon and Vincent. "I don't think it's the same. They're his girlfriend's kids, not his."

"They might as well be his. He likes them better than us."

She tried to think of something to tell him. In the end, she sighed. "Once we each turn eighteen, we no longer need to have anything to do with him."

Brodie stopped, grabbing Mallory's arm to drag her back to him. "You better not expect me to visit him on my own during the nine months between when you turn eighteen and when I do."

Mallory didn't have the chance to reassure her brother.

A woman approached them, looking from one to the other. "Are you the alchemist and apothecary who are visiting?"

"I'm the apothecary," Mallory said. "The alchemist is at our camp."

"This way." Brodie strode towards the wagon that was visible ahead of them, the campfire mostly a bed of coals, the smell of cooking food reaching them well before they arrived at the wagon.

They'd barely made it to the wagon before three other villagers joined them, all looking for the apothecary and alchemist. More arrived as Mallory treated the first lot, Danae needing to make up health tea for one of them. The tavern owner and his son, the trader, arrived while Mallory was busy with a patient and Brodie talked trade with them.

Ryan and Callum returned before Mallory was finished treating the patients, bringing with them Deneg who they stayed close to. She didn't blame them. The vampire looked like he'd run at the first chance. Ryan and Callum continued to shadow Deneg, sitting beside him by the fire when the villagers finally left and they all sat around it to have a late dinner.

"I managed to trade that quiver we got today, one of the mage robes and a heap of herbs for a fourteen litre cooking pot and our lanterns and oil flasks refilled." Brodie grinned at Mallory and Danae. "And best of all, we made nineteen gold from you two doctoring all those people. I put the gold pieces with the rest of the coins we've set aside."

"If I had surgical instruments, I could have treated one more villager." Mallory checked their reputation. They now had two for Delten. Would they have had a higher reputation if she'd been able to treat the other villager?

"Shouldn't you and Danni get the money for treating the villagers?" Esben asked.

Danae smiled. "I'm happy for the little bit of money I would have earned to go to the party. I didn't do much."

"Same." Mallory turned from Esben to Deneg. "We need that harp back." She glanced at the harp that was now in a leather travelling case.

Deneg drew the harp closer. "I can't. It's the only way I can think of to earn five thousand gold pieces."

Chapter Seven

Mallory stared at Deneg. The amount seemed impossible to earn. Look how long it had taken them to earn what little they had.

"How will the harp help you earn that much?" Brodie asked.

"You're not planning to sell it, are you?" Callum asked.

"I'd never do that to her," Deneg protested.

"Why would we believe you?" Callum asked. "You used me."

"It wasn't like that. I did enjoy your company. But I'm also willing to do whatever necessary to save my brother."

"That's the second time you've said that," Ryan said. "What exactly do you mean?"

Deneg didn't answer immediately. He stared at the harp he held. "Ehrok had a few financial difficulties and I was travelling at the time so he had no one to turn to for help."

"What has that got to do with the harp?" Brodie asked.

"It's not just a harp," Deneg said. "She does have a name. It's Pelga."

"Why did you kidnap Pelga?" Callum asked.

Deneg sighed. "It made a lot more sense when I first came up with the idea."

"These things usually do," Esben said.

Jorgen laughed softly, glancing at his cousin before returning his attention to Deneg. "How about starting at the beginning? With the reason why you kidnapped Pelga. Her grandaughter is worried about her welfare."

"I have no plans to hurt anyone. And especially not Pelga. I was going to take her to Ruby Peak afterwards and try to break the curse. That is if I could find some adventurers willing to help me. And after I've earn five thousand gold pieces."

"Why do you need that much money?" Mallory couldn't even imagine what that amount of money would look like. Would it fill a chest? Several chests?

"I actually need fifteen thousand gold pieces, but I have the other ten thousand. Ehrok borrowed money from the wrong people, expecting to pay them back well before his loan was up. He would have if he hadn't fallen in love with the wrong woman and her father did everything possible to break them up, including ruining Ehrok financially. The people he borrowed money from sold him to the dark forces as a slave to make back the money he owed them."

Mallory wasn't sure if she should believe him. It sounded rather dramatic and she didn't know if things like that happened on Inadon. "How will fifteen thousand gold pieces help your brother?"

"Is it to buy him back?" Callum asked. "How do you know if those who bought him would be willing to part with him?"

"They aren't," Deneg said. "But there are adventurers who, for a price, rescue slaves. Ehrok was taken to an arena in Hellfire. He's only human. He won't last long there. I need to earn the money as quickly as possible and I don't have anyone I can ask for help."

"Aww, come on," Brodie exclaimed.

Mallory didn't need to check the journal notification in the corner of her vision to know it was a quest. Not after Brodie's protests. "How much have you earned with Pelga's help?" She opened her journal. *Brother Enslaved: Deneg needs help earning five thousand gold pieces so he can pay adventurers to rescue his brother from an arena in Hellfire.*

"Nowhere near enough. I was starting to think I needed to go to the mainland. If I was a warrior, it wouldn't be a problem. I know where there's a treasure waiting for someone to take it."

Brodie leaned forward. "What kind of treasure? And why hasn't anyone taken it before?"

"It's probably cursed," Emica said.

"Is it?" Brodie asked.

Deneg shook his head. "No, but the directions to it were in a cursed book. The one who tried to break the curse ended up with the curse instead. He copied down the details in a notebook before he died, planning to leave the directions to his children."

"This was your father?" Ryan asked.

Again Deneg shook his head. "I overheard some bandits in one of the taverns I played at. I don't know who the notebook originally belonged to since the bandits never said."

"How do you know what you overheard will be enough information to find the treasure?" Ryan asked.

"It wouldn't have been. So I took the notebook from them," Deneg said.

"You seem to have a habit of taking things that aren't yours." Callum glanced at the harp.

"They were bandits. It wasn't their notebook," Deneg protested. "It's like taking things from the dark forces."

"And Pelga?" Callum asked.

"I would have made sure her curse was broken." Deneg held Callum's gaze for a moment before he looked away, glancing at each of them. "I only need five thousand gold pieces. I'm willing to offer the rest of the treasure to any adventurers who can help me find it and escort me to the nearest town or village."

"Finally. A quest worth doing," Brodie said.

Mallory checked her journal again, smiling as she read the quest over. *Treasure Hunt: Deneg has the directions to a treasure he will share with a group of adventurers who can help him reach it then escort him to the nearest town or village afterwards. All he needs is five thousand gold pieces worth of the treasure and the adventurers can share the rest of the treasure between them.*

"What if there isn't five thousand gold pieces or something of that value?" Ryan asked.

"There will be. It's a demonic dungeon," Deneg said.

Mallory couldn't help thinking about the demonic

spider they'd fought in the Velkden mine. "What exactly does that mean?"

"Danger and valuables," Jorgen said. "If no one has been in there before, it could be worth three to five times what Deneg wants."

"Danger," Mallory said.

Brodie spoke at the same time as his sister. "Valuables. Fifteen to twenty-five thousand gold pieces worth of valuables."

Deneg nodded.

"Did you forget the part about danger?" Mallory asked.

"We need to discuss it." Ryan held out his hand to Deneg. "Leave Pelga with us and come back in half an hour."

"Make sure you go far enough away that you can't hear us," Emica warned.

"You're thinking about helping me?" Deneg asked.

Ryan continued to hold out his hand. "The harp."

"But I need her," Deneg protested.

"Whether we help you or not, you don't get to keep her. She's going back to her family." Ryan took the harp when Deneg reluctantly held it out.

"But you are thinking of helping me," Deneg persisted.

"I wonder what sort of compact dwelling we could get for twenty thousand gold pieces," Brodie said.

"You never told us where the demonic dungeon is," Callum said.

"West of Longmeadow." Deneg rose to his feet. "I'll be back in half an hour." He took a step away. "Will that give you enough time?"

Ryan nodded. "Should do."

Callum watched Deneg stride away. "This is probably a bad idea. We trusted him once. I trusted him."

Ryan rested a hand on his brother's shoulder. "We didn't have all the facts."

"Who's to say we have all of them now?" Jorgen asked.

"We wouldn't have to go all the way to the end of the demonic dungeon. There'll be valuables all through it. We could leave as soon as we have enough," Esben suggested.

"Someone will have to stay with the wagon and not just Ninette," Ryan said.

Brodie spoke quickly. "Not me."

Chapter Eight

Mallory sighed as the conversation went back and forth. Brodie voted for the treasure hunt while Callum suggested caution. Esben didn't want to stay behind, Ninette was willing to watch the wagon and Emica only wanted to go if she didn't have to sit around guarding the wagon. Jorgen, Danae and Ryan mostly remained silent. Mallory sighed again. She didn't know what to do. Esben's arm wasn't healed yet, Ninette was a fairly low level and a demonic dungeon sounded extremely dangerous considering how little they had. "We need better gear."

Brodie gestured in the direction Deneg had taken. "His treasure hunt will give us better gear."

"If we survive long enough to buy better gear," Mallory said. "And we can't leave Ninette on her own. Not at her level."

"We should have kept Kruth with us," Brodie muttered.

"We need to know how far Longmeadow is from here." Ryan took the map of Ruby Isle out of his belt pouch and unfolded it.

Callum gave a single nod towards the map. "Want me to figure it out?"

Ryan stared at the map he held. "Not yet. It's at least as far as Delten is from Cutthroat Harbour." He looked up from the map. "We could level Ninette on the way so she's not too low a level to guard the wagon."

"What about the rest of us?" Brodie demanded.

"Ninette will need breaks." Ryan handed the map to Callum. "We can travel through the night, some of us sleeping and some helping Ninette level up. And of course, someone driving the wagon. There are enough of us we should all get plenty of sleep."

"The horses will need breaks," Danae said.

"Okay," Ryan said. "We'll figure that out too."

"We're doing this?" Mallory asked.

Ryan grinned at her. "I vote yes."

"Hell yeah," Brodie exclaimed.

Callum looked up from the map. "I'd like to see how demonic dungeons are different from normal dungeons."

"It sounds interesting. As long as I'm not left behind," Emica said.

"Esben and I can stay with Ninette and the wagon," Jorgen offered.

Esben muttered something under his breath that Mallory couldn't hear properly, catching only the words 'sitting around'. She wanted to protest Jorgen's comment. He was the highest level out of all of them and demonic dungeons didn't sound easy.

"I'd like to explore a demonic dungeon," Danae said.

Ryan turned to Mallory. "Looks like we're doing this. Majority rules."

She drew in a deep breath, pushing aside images of the demonic spider. It didn't help. They reformed in her mind, large fangs clearly visible. She had no idea why she didn't have nightmares after all she'd experienced. "Okay. But only once we get everyone to at least halfway through character level two, including Ninette."

"Hell yeah!" Brodie victory punched the air. "Thousands of gold pieces."

"Where is the closest demonic bank to Longmeadow?" Mallory dreaded the thought of carrying that much money around on them. Maybe the next person who tried to rob them would be better prepared than the frog mage had been.

"There's one in Longmeadow," Emica said. "It's a large village, almost big enough to be considered a town."

Emica glanced at the wagon. "It's less than an hour till midnight. Should we start taking turns to sleep now? And what are we going to do with all the herbs? We're running out of space for them."

Callum ran his finger across the map. "We go by way of Seacoast, up through Jenlea, across to Wrentville and then on to Longmeadow. That way we can sell what we can in each town and village. Although that will probably mean waiting for shops to open in Seacoast since it isn't that far from here."

Deneg walked towards them, his steps silent. "You're going to help me?"

There were murmurs of agreement and nods.

Deneg faced Callum. "You won't need to go into Longmeadow. You turn west just before you reach the turn for Longmeadow."

Callum gave Deneg a single nod before turning to Brodie. "Can you make me a coffee while I figure out the times between the locations?"

While Brodie made coffee and Emica, Ninette and Danae had a sleep, Mallory took out her notebook and finished her entry for that day. It didn't take her long and she looked longingly at the wagon, wishing she could have a sleep too. Instead, she helped Ryan clean up after their meal and pack what few things they had out.

Deneg's coffin and chest were put in the back of the wagon, leaving very little room for anything else. Only two were able to sleep in the wagon, as long as they were willing to lie rather close to each other. They were on the road again at two, the road dark since there was no moon. Jorgen drove the wagon, not needing a lantern to see where he was going, while Ninette had been woken to begin levelling up.

Mallory remained at Ninette's side, casting magelight. They headed towards Emica and Brodie who'd found herbs for Ninette to pick.

Emica started to move away when Ninette bent to pick the herbs, turning back to face Brodie. "Did my father send a message yet?"

Brodie took the duplication paper out of his satchel. "He did." Brodie grinned. "This is so cool."

"What did he say?" Emica asked.

"That he's safe and you aren't to tell him exactly where you're going since the spy hasn't been identified and he plans to talk to the shipping company in the morning. They've had further problems." Brodie frowned. "I thought he was going to let us complete the quest."

"We've got plenty of other quests to do," Mallory assured him. "And we'll find other ones too." She turned to Ninette. "We better keep gathering herbs and veggies if we're going to get you levelled up before we reach the demonic dungeon."

Callum had figured out it'd take them approximately two and a half hours to reach Seacoast, an hour and a half to Jenlea from there, nearly two hours on to Wrentville and approximately two and a half hours from there to where they turned off the road to reach the demonic dungeon. They would have plenty of time to rest while they waited for any shops that were in Seacoast to open.

The journey to Seacoast was uneventful. Once again Mallory didn't know if that was because the area was quiet or if the magelight deterred bandits and creatures that preferred the cover of darkness to attack. It allowed Ninette, Brodie and Ryan to gain some levels during the journey. Brodie and Ryan were now halfway through character level two and Ninette was three CAS points into character level one. She would have gained more experience points if they'd been able to find resources during the last half an hour of the journey. But they couldn't find a single herb or vegetable. Nor any berries.

As they drove into Seacoast, heading towards the beach, Mallory didn't recast magelight, preferring not to draw attention to their arrival. "I wonder if someone in the area has been busy levelling up their stats too."

"It seems likely." Jorgen pulled up along the shore, on the outskirts of Seacoast. The closest cottage was about fifty metres from them, only visible due to the flickering firelight that could be seen through a window. "I'll get a campfire started and we can spread the bedrolls out by it so some of us can have a sleep while we wait for morning." He jumped down off the wagon.

"I hope the sea isn't as empty as the rest of the area around Seacoast. I want to catch some fish for Smudge." Callum lit a lantern, keeping it turned down low.

Smudge, who was curled up in Callum's lap, raised his head to make soft sounds.

Mallory laughed. "I think he's hoping the same."

"I'll help Jorgen," Emica said. "Ninette looks like she's ready to pass out."

"I can help too." Deneg joined Emica where she was removing a bedroll from Bobbi, the donkey.

Ninette, who sat leaned against the large cane basket that was overfilled with herbs, said, "I can barely keep my eyes open. I didn't realise how exhausting picking herbs and vegetables was. Taking care of sheep is easier."

Chapter Nine

"You've still got hours more of gathering resources," Mallory warned Ninette. "Quite a few hours."

Ninette groaned. "Maybe the rest of you should level up more than you have been. Not just focus on me doing most of the gathering."

Ryan chuckled. "Nice try."

"What are you putting your character level in?" Brodie asked. "And your attribute points."

"Warrior," Ninette said. "I want to focus on warrior, not multiple classes." She paused a moment. "I put two attribute points in strength and three in constitution. That gives me thirty health and fifty stamina and I now have a revive."

"What about your CAS points? You must have a heap by now," Brodie said. "What are you going to do with them?"

"I'm keeping them for character level four when I'll

be able to use a longsword," Ninette said. "By then I'll be able to reach maximum level for my longsword and the other ten I'll have earned by character level four I'll put in smithing when I eventually manage to unlock it."

Callum turned to Brodie. "We need to see if they have any crafting books while we're here. Did you check with the trader at Delten?"

"Of course I did," Brodie said. "I even asked if they'd heard of coffee."

"Thanks." Callum set Smudge beside him, barely enough space to do so. "I'll get started on fishing. I can have a sleep on the way to Jenlea." He clambered out of the wagon, Smudge following him, holding out his paws to be helped down off the wagon.

Brodie followed Callum, Fang jumping out of the wagon ahead of him. "If you catch enough, we could have grilled fish for breakfast. Would putting points into fishing help you catch them quicker? And what about that bait? Are you going to try it?"

They moved too far away for Mallory to hear Callum's answers, if he made any. She turned to Ryan. "I don't know where we're going to fit more herbs and vegetables if we can't sell them here."

He shrugged. "We might have to leave them

where we find them. Not that I like that idea. It seems like a waste."

"You could always drop them off at a farm to be turned into compost," Danae suggested.

"We could do that?" Mallory asked.

"They'd appreciate it," Danae said.

Ryan gestured to the back of the wagon. "We should probably grab a bedroll and have a sleep while we can. There isn't much space in the wagon between the herbs and Deneg's coffin."

Nodding, Mallory hopped out of the wagon and grabbed one of the bedrolls. She laid it out not far from the fire, smiling at Ryan when he rolled his out next to hers. "We need to make sure we get enough sleep before we head into the dungeon." The last thing they needed was going into a demonic dungeon while they were tired.

"We can make time to rest before we go in if we need to." Ryan stretched out on the bedroll. "Just because we reach the dungeon, doesn't mean we have to go straight in. We can rest and eat first if we're tired or hungry. Make sure we're ready to face the tougher creatures that are likely to be in a demonic dungeon."

Mallory glanced at her brother who sat beside Callum, both of them fishing. "Not everyone will be happy with that plan." Her gaze was drawn from Brodie to Deneg who stood off to one side, looking out to sea. Not that she'd blame Deneg if he were impatient to enter the dungeon. But that wouldn't help them have the best chance of success.

Ryan leaned up on an elbow. "Get some sleep. We'll sort it out."

"Yeah." She hoped so. Lying down beside Ryan, she stared up at the stars above them, none of them looking familiar. "I have to agree with Brodie. I don't want to go home." In particular, she didn't want to go to her father's place on the weekend.

Ryan took hold of Mallory's hand. "I never miss home when we're here, but I do miss Inadon when we go back."

She lightly squeezed his hand. "Me too." She didn't recall drifting off to sleep. It seemed like one minute she was staring up at the stars, her blinks becoming slower, and the next Brodie was shaking her shoulder and she opened her eyes to find the sky was filled with the vibrant colours of sunrise. "What time is it?"

"I've got a couple of patients for you. And I managed to sell a few hundred herbs and all the veggies we gathered. Other than enough potatoes to cook in the coals to have with our grilled fish." Brodie remained crouched beside Mallory.

Yawning, she covered her mouth with her hand. "What are you doing up so early?"

"I haven't been to sleep yet. Did you know some fisherman go out in their boats at night and come in at dawn?" Brodie rose to his feet. "Come on, it's time to get up. I've sold everything I could and even bought two crafting ability books. Potter and sculptor."

She sat up when her brother started to walk away. "Wait. What do you mean by patients?"

Brodie faced her with a grin. "They need to see an apothecary. I told them to come back in ten minutes. So you better hurry up and get ready. You probably only have five minutes left."

She glared at her brother's back as he tended to the fire, the mouth-watering smells making her stomach grumble. She would have to find the time to tell him not to expect to hire her out at every town or village they visited. Stumbling to her feet, she tried not to yawn. She could have done with a few more hours sleep.

The patients arrived when the first lot of fish was ready to be served, the campfire not having been large enough to cook fish for everyone at once. Fang and Smudge were curled up together on the bedroll that was closest to the fire, eating their share of the fish. Mallory's patients, when they arrived, came as a group. She treated them one at a time, frequently glancing at the next lot of fish that was being cooked.

Her final patient also glanced in the direction of the campfire, her son half hidden behind her. "We can wait until you've eaten."

Mallory shook her head. "I don't think it's ready yet." And even if it had been, she wouldn't have made her last patient wait that long to be seen. "How can I help you?"

The woman stepped to the side, pushing her son forward, he staggered, the woman catching him before he could fall. "He can't walk right. He had a bad break when he was younger and there was no one around to make sure it healed properly."

Mallory looked the boy up and down. He appeared to be about ten-years-old. She had no idea how she could help him, but she smiled reassuringly anyway. "Let me have a look." She knelt in front of him, placing a hand on his leg. She knew instantly what to do. She used her ability to set bones. There was a snap as the bone broke and went into place, the boy screaming as his health dropped significantly.

The woman went to her knees, throwing her arms around her son. "Is he all right? What happened?"

"I'm sorry." Mallory hadn't realised it would work

like that. After doing average rapid mend on him, she healed his health back to normal, relieved the enchanted necklace she wore allowed her to heal for twice the amount of her spell. "You need to stay off your leg. Let it heal again. But this time, it will set right and you'll be able to walk properly." She met the boy's gaze, trying not to feel guilty about the pain she'd caused him, but she did. The tears pooling in his eyes made her feel worse.

The boy nodded. "It feels better already."

Jorgen came forward. "I'll help you get him home. He can go on one of the horses and I'll lead him for you."

Rising to her feet, Mallory smiled at Jorgen. "Thank you. He really does need to stay off his leg so it'll heal properly." She turned to the woman as Jorgen walked away. "What he needs, is crutches."

"He has some at home. For the times he found it too painful to put weight on his leg." Keeping an arm around her son, the woman rose to her feet. "You can't imagine how grateful we are. How grateful I am."

"Uhm." Unable to think of a reply, Mallory was relieved when Jorgen came back with the riding horse they hadn't named.

While Jorgen put the boy on the horse, the woman

pressed a ring into Mallory's hand. "I know your companion said there'd be no cost when I asked if it was possible for us to barter something in exchange for healing my son, but it doesn't seem right after what you've done for him. It's not much, but it's all I can afford since I have two younger children who need to be taken care of and my husband was lost at sea last year. You might be able to get a few coins for it."

Chapter Ten

Mallory looked at the ring. "This is your wedding ring?"

The woman nodded. "I have no need of it anymore. After how long he's been gone, I can only assume he's dead. It would have been nice to know for certain though."

Mallory held the ring out to the woman, ignoring the journal notification in the corner of her vision. She assumed that since her brother made no comment that it wasn't a quest. "I can't take this. Nor can I accept payment for what I did."

"Are you sure?" The woman looked from Mallory to the ring. "Isn't there anything you need?"

Mallory shook her head. "We're good, thanks." She pressed the ring into the woman's hand, trying not to feel so uncomfortable about the many thanks. As soon as the woman was gone, she turned to her brother. "Is breakfast ready now?"

"How are we meant to do that quest?" Brodie demanded.

"Quest?" She pulled up her journal, surprised to find that the notification had been for a quest. *Widow Needs Closure: A widow in Seacoast wishes she knew the fate of her husband who was lost at sea the previous year.*

Danae joined them by the campfire. "Sometimes it's impossible to complete a quest."

"But how will her and her kids find out what happened to him?" Brodie asked.

"There are ways to track people down using things such as a lock of their hair, but we have none of those methods," Danae said.

"How?" Brodie asked.

"Mostly spells and enchantments." Danae smiled at Brodie. "It was sweet of you not to make them pay."

Brodie shrugged, glancing away as he muttered, "It wasn't like we needed anything she had to offer."

Mallory grinned at her brother's discomfort. "Better be careful, Brodie. People will start thinking you're nice."

"Between selling some of the herbs and all the spare vegetables and what your other patients paid, we didn't need it. We made twenty-two gold, thirty-six silver and eighteen copper pieces. I put the money in the chest with the rest of it. I wasn't able to sell all the herbs, or at least not the ones we gathered from around here. Apparently someone else sold a heap of herbs in the village only a few days ago."

"I guess that's why the area has been stripped bare," Mallory said. "I hope it isn't like that all the way to Jenlea."

Brodie crouched by the fire, checking the cooking fish. "If it is, we can go further off the road to look for resources." He looked up at Mallory. "Breakfast is ready if you want some."

"I wanted some the moment I woke up." She took the two empty plates her brother held out to her, holding onto them while he served the food.

It didn't take long for the rest of them to eat breakfast and they were done by the time Jorgen returned. It was only then that Mallory realised she hadn't seen Deneg since she'd woken. Keeping her voice low, she leaned in close to Ryan, who she sat next to. "Is Deneg in his coffin?"

"Yeah." Ryan took Mallory's empty plate from her. "He was in it before the sun was rising."

"How are we meant to find exactly where we're going?" Mallory asked.

"He gave Callum directions before he went to

bed." Brodie took the plates from Ryan. "I'll clean up here while you two get ready to go. I want to see if we can sell more of the herbs in Jenlea. And Ninette should focus on gathering veggies whenever possible. People have to eat. They're a lot easier to sell."

They all set about preparing to leave, their camp cleaned up and the wagon packed in no time. Mallory checked the pocket watch as they drove away from the village. It was nine o'clock. She returned the pocket watch to Ryan before turning to Esben. "Time for rapid mend."

Esben moved closer to her, smiling once she'd used her ability. "It feels nearly completely healed."

"Twice more. So be careful. You don't want to set your progress back," Mallory warned.

Esben laughed. "I'm not about to do that when I'm so close to being healed." He nodded towards the driver's seat where Danae and Brodie sat. "I might see if they need help." He clambered forward, stepping over the seat while keeping his head low.

Mallory watched him go, making sure he was careful of his injured arm. Stifling a yawn, she checked her stats, seeing that not only was she nearly a quarter of the way through her current CAS level, but they also had two reputation in Seacoast. Being an apothecary was certainly helping with their reputation. Her eyes closed after she looked over her stats, trying to decide if she should continue to put CAS points into apothecary when she earned more or focus on another crafting ability. The movement of the wagon rocked her to sleep, her shoulder being shaken jarring her from sleep. Blinking, she tried to focus.

Ryan grinned down at her. "We're in Jenlea."

Brushing loose strands of hair back from her face, Mallory sat up. "Already?"

Ryan chuckled. "You slept the entire way."

Mallory looked out past the canvas. "Did anything happen? No one was hurt?" They were parked under three shady trees along the banks of a river, the village not far from them.

"We saw a couple of bandits, but they didn't come anywhere near us. The moment they spotted us, they headed in the opposite direction." Ryan grinned. "Having so many with us is useful."

"What time is it?" She felt disorientated.

"Just after eleven. Brodie has been visiting the local shops."

"And everyone is okay?" Mallory asked.

Ryan studied her. "Are you okay?"

"Yeah, I-" She broke off as shreds of her dream came to her. So much for not having bad dreams.

A wry smile formed. "Yeah. Broken sleep obviously doesn't agree with me. We need to plan better in the future."

"Brodie being shot in the knee put everything out. We'll sort things out again. We're still getting the hang of travelling between two worlds. It'll be easier when we have our place set up in Brisbane," Ryan said.

"I guess."

He gestured towards the village. "There's an outhouse behind the tavern if you want to use it while we're here. Brodie sent Ninette back a few minutes ago to say he was nearly done and that they have an apothecary so you aren't needed."

Mallory couldn't help laughing. "Guess I should have known he'd try and sell my services. I wonder how annoyed he was to find they already had one." She clambered out of the wagon.

Ninette looked over from where she was rummaging in one of Bobbi's panniers. "Not very disappointed when the apothecary said he was in need of herbs and bought a heap of them from us."

"Yeah, that'd do it." Mallory headed towards the tavern, glancing around the village that seemed busier than the previous one. A young woman carrying a covered basket gave her a nod and a smile and Mallory returned the greeting.

By the time she returned from the outhouse, Brodie and Fang were back, Brodie handing over a crafting ability book to Ninette. "You might want to read this one. I doubt Callum will mind waiting."

Ninette stared at the book for a moment before clutching it to her chest. "Thank you. Thank you so much."

Brodie glanced away, taking a step back when Ninette continued to beam at him. "Callum wants them. Not like we weren't going to buy it anyway."

"What is it?" Esben asked from where he sat under a nearby tree.

"Smithing." Ninette showed him the book.

"That's useful." Esben rose to his feet. "We going now?"

"I'm done. I've sold everything I could," Brodie said.

"I'll go get everyone." Ninette ran along the river, still clutching the book.

"Where is everyone?" Mallory asked.

"Fishing. Or having a wash in the river," Ryan said.

Chapter Eleven

Mallory looked longingly at the river. "A wash sounds nice." She glanced in the direction Ninette had taken. "Were there any herbs or vegetables to gather between here and Seacoast?"

Brodie nodded. "Once we were about half an hour out of Seacoast. We focused mainly on vegetables and I was able to sell them easily. I also sold the coral puffballs, both the large demonic spider fangs, both bear canines and both the mage robes. All the vegetables gathered between here and Seacoast easily sold and all the herbs as well as a hundred of the ones we'd picked earlier."

"We're slowly selling everything?" Mallory asked.

Brodie nodded. "Emica said we should do better in Wrentville. It's an actual town. And it has a bank. I put all the money I made in the chest with the rest of it. I've just finished taking the mage robes to the trader. Including the forty gold pieces I sold the mage robes for, we made five hundred and forty-nine gold, eight silver and eight copper pieces."

"We made how much?" Mallory asked.

Brodie grinned. "We sold the two large demonic spider fangs for five hundred gold. We need to get more demonic resources. We'd make a killing."

"We need to get to a bank as soon as possible." Mallory glanced at the wagon where the chest they stored the bulk of their money was kept. If they lost a fight to bandits, they'd lose everything and have to start over again. She pushed that worry from her, not wanting to think about it. "How did Ninette do? Did she manage to level up?"

"She only needs three more CAS points to reach level two," Ryan said. "And Callum gained a CAS point gathering resources when she took a break."

Brodie handed over the forty gold pieces from the mage robes. "Ninette should be at least level two before we reach Wrentville, even if there isn't much to gather." He looked past Mallory. "Hell yeah. We're having fish for dinner." He stepped around Mallory.

She turned to watch him hurry forward and take one of the baskets of fish from their returning friends. They'd caught seven decent sized fish. Large enough to feed all of them for dinner, including the companion animals. She climbed into the wagon to put the coins in the chest, stumbling backwards when movement startled her. She laughed, a wry smile left behind as she shook her head at the cat that had come out of hiding from behind a sack of herbs. "I thought you were still under the seat."

The cat miaowed.

Making her way to the chest, Mallory glanced at the cat. "I have no idea what you want."

Brodie came to the back of the wagon, holding out a small fish. "Probably this. Smudge caught one for each of them."

The cat walked leisurely towards the back of the wagon, rubbing himself on Mallory as he passed her. He'd started to fill out, his ribs were no longer visible, and his short black fur wasn't as patchy anymore, the missing fur not so noticeable now he had put on some weight.

She gave him a pat before putting the coins in the chest. She stared at the closed lid, the cat purring contentedly at the other end of the wagon behind her. They had eight hundred and fifty gold, two hundred and thirty-seven silver and three hundred and one copper pieces. She slowly shook her head. It seemed impossible that they'd earned so much in such a short time. And they still had more demonic resources to sell along with around three thousand herbs, two poppets and other alchemy ingredients. A smile slowly formed. They were getting somewhere. Both here and in their world. At this rate, by the time they travelled to Merrow, they'd be able to afford a house. Maybe only a small one, but they'd have somewhere to set up a base. Somewhere to store any of the things they might want to keep like Callum's books.

"Are we leaving now?" Emica asked from behind Mallory.

Thinking the kitsune was talking to her, Mallory turned to face her only to learn she was talking to Brodie.

"We should have lunch first," Brodie said.

"It's less than two hours to Wrentville. You can wait until then," Ryan said.

"Nearly two hours," Brodie exclaimed. "That's ages."

"Have some jerky." Ryan strode over to where Bug and Augusta were grazing, glancing over his shoulder when he reached them. "I want to reach our destination before dark so we can find a good campsite."

Mallory helped wrap the fish in the canvas they used for wrapping up meat, noticing someone had washed the yellow shirt and hung it to dry on the side of the wagon. They were back on the road in minutes and heading towards Wrentville.

Ninette gathered herbs first, only Danae and Esben remaining with the wagon, Danae driving this time. When Ninette took a break, planning to read the book on smithing, Callum took out the rest of the crafting ability books and told her to read the ones she didn't know, suggesting everyone do the same. Brodie took a turn at gathering resources while Ninette rested. Brodie also gathered resources the second time Ninette took a break. He gained a CAS point just before he finished gathering resources the second time. Ninette had reached character level two and was one CAS point into the level. She put ten CAS points in smithing and her character level in warrior, adding her attribute points to strength and constitution again. Two in strength and three in constitution. She now had thirty-nine health, sixty-five stamina and a total of two revives.

Mallory felt a little better about the idea of leaving Ninette behind to guard the wagon, but not much. She still worried that Ninette wasn't a high enough level to stay on guard duty.

Before Ninette could gather resources again, Danae slowed the wagon and called out to them.

Brodie reached Danae first, arriving at the front of the wagon as it came to a stop. "What's that for?"

Mallory stepped to the side of Brodie, staring at the two large tree trunks blocking the road. Each end was cut, not snapped, and many of the branches had been removed. "Someone put them there."

Emica joined her. "It's a trap."

Ryan moved in front of them, stopping a couple of metres away from the tree trunks. "How does the trap work?"

Jorgen pointed to a narrow track going around the side of the trunks. "They'll have set something up along there to make it easier for them to deal with us."

"They use things like pits or nets," Emica said. "People always think they can outsmart the bandits. But they can't because the bandits usually run in large groups, don't stay in an area for long and always come up with different ways of using their various methods to trap people."

"How are we meant to get through?" Brodie asked.

"Invisibility." Jorgen turned to Mallory. "Can you make us invisible so we can search the area and discover what sort of trap has been set?"

"Make me invisible too," Brodie said.

"I only have enough mana to cast it twice and I

don't generate enough mana each minute to keep casting it when it wears off," Mallory said.

"You need to level it up," Brodie said.

Mallory gave her brother a look of exasperation. "With what CAS points? They all went in apothecary."

"We have five invisibility potions," Ryan suggested.

"I was keeping them for dangerous situations," Mallory said.

"You don't think this is dangerous?" Esben made a sweeping gesture towards the trap. "We don't know how many bandits are hiding and what sort of trap they have."

"I was thinking of dark forces types of dangerous situations." Mallory studied the tree trunks. There was no way they could easily get rid of them. "A pity I don't have a shrink spell."

"You need better spells," Brodie said.

Chapter Twelve

"I need more mana. Or faster regen." Mallory's gaze was momentarily drawn to the plain, silver bracelet she wore. The extra one mana regen it gave her every fifteen seconds wasn't enough. Nor the extra one mana regen every ten seconds that the ring gave her.

"What are we going to do?" Ninette asked.

Emica glanced around the area. "We're in a forest. Foxes aren't out of place here." She'd barely finished speaking when she changed forms, dashing off through the undergrowth beside the narrow path.

Mallory stared in the direction Emica had taken. "Should we go after her?"

"I can go after her." Jorgen shifted into his crystalline wolf form.

Before Jorgen could follow Emica, Esben stepped in front of him. "No you don't. We aren't common around here. If it was snowy country, then it'd make sense to see one of us. But you'd stand out too much."

Jorgen growled at Esben, advancing on him.

Esben held his ground. "You know I'm right."

Emica came out of the undergrowth, becoming human as she reached them, only her ears keeping their fox shape. "Both pit and net traps with stakes in the bottom of the pit."

Jorgen also became human. "How many bandits?"

"Sixteen. A mix of archers and warriors from what I could tell," Emica said. "A couple of the warriors had dual swords so they'd have to be at least level two and there is at least one level three archer because she has a longbow. There's also a mage. He's at least level six because he has dual wands."

"He can cast two spells at once?" Brodie asked.

Emica nodded. "If he has enough mana for both spells."

"How are we meant to take the bandits on?" Brodie demanded. "We're outnumbered and the mage is a higher level than all of us."

"Jorgen is character level six," Esben said.

"We don't know the mage's exact level," Danae said.

"We need to capture the mage," Jorgen said. "From

the look of how those tree trunks were placed, he probably knows spells to shrink and unshrink things."

"How are we meant to capture a level six mage?" Brodie demanded.

"Stealth," Jorgen suggested.

"We need to get closer so we can use the spyglass to see what the health of the bandits are," Callum said.

"Mal should go," Brodie said. "She's the one who can use an invisibility spell."

"I can cast it five times." She turned to Emica. "Would that be enough time?"

Emica shrugged. "Depends on how slow you are. But there is a spot that's fairly well hidden. As long as you reach it, you can take your time and check all their health. I can show you where it is."

"It'd be better than going in blind," Ryan said. "We could then target those with low health first. It'd make it easier if we could take some out quickly."

Mallory slowly nodded. "And help us figure out if we can take them on."

"How will we get past if we don't?" Esben asked.

"We could travel back to Jenlea and go west and eventually north to the Eastern Mine. From there we can curve around to the east and towards Longmeadow," Emica suggested.

Ryan took out the map. "That's well out of our

way. I doubt we'd make it to the dungeon today if we did that."

Mallory dreaded the thought of having to backtrack. They'd done enough going backwards lately with all the money they'd had to spend on healing Brodie's knee. "I'll see how much health they have." She held out her hand to Callum, taking the brass spyglass when he held it out.

"Want me to show you the way?" Emica asked.

Mallory nodded.

"I'll stop in front of you when it's time for you to go invisible." Emica shapeshifted the moment she finished speaking.

Before Mallory could follow her, Ryan tugged her towards him, wrapping his arms around her waist. "I'll be okay," she assured him.

His arms momentarily tightened around her. "If you're gone too long, we're coming after you." His lips briefly met hers before he let her go.

Continuing to meet his gaze, she smiled, taking a step back from him. "That won't be necessary, but thanks anyway." When he grinned at her, her own smile widened before she turned and followed Emica who waited at the edge of the undergrowth for her.

Emica kept to the road edge for about ten metres before she followed a nearly overgrown animal track.

They were partway along it when she stopped in front of Mallory, looking up at her.

Remembering Emica's directions, she left her wand in the canvas loop and wrapped her hand around the timber. She held the wand long enough to cast vanish I on herself before once again following Emica who remained in her fox form.

Emica led the way between two trees that were reasonably close together and headed deep inside a shrub at the base of one of them. She poked her head back out when Mallory didn't follow.

Mallory remained pressed up against one of the trees, eyeing the shrub as she recast vanish I, again leaving the wand in the canvas loop. Surely there wasn't enough space for a human to hide behind the overlapping leaves. When Emica drew back behind the leaves and put her head out again several times, the last time remaining hidden, Mallory crouched down low and pushed her way past the leaves of the shrub. Leaf litter crunched beneath her hand and knees, the process made awkward by the spyglass she continued to hold in one hand.

Within the shrub it was mostly hollow and, finding a good position, she put the spyglass to her eye. The bandits weren't even trying to hide and she was able to count fifteen of them. She frowned, certain Emica had told her there was sixteen.

Emica moved close to Mallory before she became human. "How much health do they have?"

"I can only count fifteen, are you sure there are sixteen?"

Emica nodded. "There's one on guard duty to watch for victims coming along the track. That's why you had to turn invisible."

Mallory looked at all the bandits again. There were several carts set well back from the track, nearly completely hidden, horses grazing nearby and a campfire burning low. Four archers were towards the back near the carts with the lowest health being eighteen and the highest twenty-four and the single mage had thirty-six health. It was the warriors that made her worry. There were nine of them scattered about the area with the majority of their health ranging from thirty-two to thirty-nine with one warrior who had ninety health. She stared at him. He had a longsword at his side and walked amongst the bandits, briefly stopping to chat or nod in answer before continuing his rounds.

"Is something wrong?" Emica asked.

Mallory lowered the spyglass. "That depends." She held the spyglass out to Emica. "What are our chances of taking on a warrior with ninety health and surviving the encounter?"

Emica looked through the spyglass. "Not good if it's a face-to-face battle. But we have two rogues, you can cast vanish I and we have five invisibility potions. If we take out the archers first, we should be able to deal with some of the warriors before they can reach us. After that, the odds should be more even."

Chapter Thirteen

Mallory started to argue Emica's suggestion. She didn't want better odds, she wanted a guarantee that none of the group would lose a revive. It was a pity she'd needed to use the poison mist potion on Rass. She started to say that to Emica, closing her mouth instead of speaking. Her lips slowly curved into a smile as her hand rested on her satchel.

"You've thought of something?" Emica asked.

"We have sleeping mist balls. All we have to figure out is a way to get as many of them as possible into the one area and we can take them out once they're unconscious." She tried to ignore the twinge of guilt she felt at that prospect. Obviously they were willing to harm innocent travellers and didn't deserve any pity for what happened to them.

"We have to keep the mage alive and awake," Emica reminded her.

Mallory nodded. "We'll figure it out, but right now, we need to get back to the wagon before anyone comes looking for us." She didn't want any of them caught in a trap. Before she could move, the sound of two men talking came close. She peered through the leaves of the shrub, needing to shift a couple of them. Two warriors were close enough that they'd see the movement of the leaves if she tried to go while they were there.

Emica leaned close so she could whisper in Mallory's ear. "I'll distract them while you head back to the wagon."

Mallory grabbed Emica's arm when she started to pull away. "What if they attack you?"

Emica grinned, shaking her head before again leaning close. "Not about to happen. I'm too quick for them. Now if it was the mage or one of the archers, I might have a problem." She drew out of Mallory's light grip and returned the spyglass before shapeshifting and darting out past the two warriors.

There was a startled cry and an archer bandit joined the two warrior bandits, reaching for his bow that was slung on his back.

Mallory slipped the spyglass into her satchel as she reached for her wand, not sure what to do. What if the archer shot Emica? They were meant to be keeping her safe. What would they tell her father? Hisoki didn't seem like the sort of person you wanted to upset.

Casting vanish I on herself, Mallory slipped out past the leaves and hurried towards the bandits. Once she was close enough, she cast flame on some twigs near the firepit, grinning when a shout went up and the three bandits chasing after Emica turned to find out what was happening. Spotting Emica disappearing into the undergrowth, Mallory turned her back on the bandits and returned the way Emica had brought her. She had no idea where the guard was and could only hope her mana lasted long enough to get her out of his sight before she became visible. She'd only needed to cast it twice on the way to the bandit camp. Surely what she'd done hadn't taken that much time.

Keeping an eye on the time counting down in her journal under 'Buffs and Negative Stats', Mallory cast the spell each time it was down to three seconds, not wanting to risk becoming visible. While keeping an eye on the time, she also scanned the area, looking for the bandit. He was nowhere to be seen. Had he moved to another location? What if it was further away from the trap and she didn't have time to get past him?

When Mallory cast vanish I for the fifth time, she

wanted to walk faster, but that'd risk making too much noise and she still didn't know where the bandit was. A rush of movement came out of the undergrowth and Mallory lowered her hand away from her wand when she realised it was Emica.

The kitsune came alongside Mallory, nudging her further across, leading the way when Mallory had moved across far enough. She didn't change back to her human form until they reached the wagon, grinning at Mallory when she did. "Guess even the archer wasn't able to catch me."

Mallory was tempted to point out that he might have if she hadn't created a diversion.

"What is their health like?" Brodie demanded.

Mallory returned the spyglass to Callum, telling them what they'd learned and her thoughts on dealing with the bandits.

Brodie stared at his sister. "Ninety health."

Mallory nodded.

"Are you sure?" Brodie asked.

"Of course she's sure," Emica said. "Besides, it's consistent with a level eight warrior."

"How will we be able to distract them?" Ninette asked.

"By kidnapping their mage." Ryan grinned when

everyone turned to look at him. "With the help of rogue stealth and invisibility potions and spells."

"They're not about to move close together if the mage vanishes," Callum said. "They'd probably search the area."

"Not if Mallory casts beacon on the ground where he was," Ryan said. "And if two drops are used to speed up the activation of the sleeping mist."

Callum slowly nodded. "That might work. Thirty seconds should be enough for Jorgen to activate the sleeping mist, capture the mage and get out of the area with him so they can be four metres away from the sleeping mist when it sends everyone to sleep. We don't need to take out anyone who ends up unconscious. They'll remain asleep long enough for us to get out of the area."

"I can manage to do that," Jorgen said.

"What's to stop the mage from trying to escape?" Danae asked.

"Can we use the sleeping mist balls directly on the mage?" Ryan asked.

"No," Jorgen said. "But I'll have the element of surprise. We can empty one of the larger hessian bags and I can throw it over his head to make it difficult for him to do anything. Holding a knife on him should also help him cooperate."

Mallory looked at each of them. "We're doing this?" With all the questions everyone had voiced, she was beginning to wonder if it was a good idea after all.

"I'm not going back to the beginning of this trip," Brodie said.

"It wouldn't be the beginning," Callum said.

Brodie shrugged. "Might as well be. I vote yes."

Mallory again looked at each of them, surprised when everyone nodded or said yes. "Okay. We need to finish making plans."

By the time they were ready, it was half past one and Brodie was complaining that lunch was ages away. When everyone outvoted him when he suggested cooking the eggs, he ate some of the rabbit jerky. They all headed off through the forest towards the trap, leaving Ninette and Esben behind.

Mallory looked over her shoulder several times, wishing they didn't have to leave the two of them to fend for themselves. Ninette wasn't that high a level and Esben's broken arm wouldn't be healed until tomorrow. What if the bandits ran and stumbled on the two of them? She drew in a deep breath. They'd have to make sure none of the bandits escaped.

Coming in close to the bandit keeping watch, Mallory cast vanish I on Jorgen. She watched the bandit, waiting for Jorgen to grab him and make sure he couldn't call for help when they attacked him. Jorgen reappeared a moment before he grabbed hold of the bandit from behind, clamping a hand over his mouth.

Mallory cast fireball at the bandit at the same time as he was impaled by three arrows and two throwing knives. She was about to cast the spell a second time when Jorgen dragged the bandit to a nearby shrub and dropped him on the ground beside it before rolling him beneath the low hanging leaves after removing the arrows and knives from his body. She scanned the area. No one seemed to have noticed their attack. Her heart raced and she was tensed to fight, but nothing came for them. She tried to relax. It was impossible. There was too much that could go wrong.

Once Jorgen returned the arrows and knives, Emica went ahead of them, leading the way to the trap, skirting around it so they remained hidden by trees and shrubs. She stopped, signalling them to be careful.

Mallory crept closer, moving over to Jorgen so she'd be able to cast vanish I on him. She needed to level it up. Or buy a more powerful invisibility spell. She held back her sigh. There were so many things they wanted and needed. Hopefully, after the demonic dungeon they'd be able to afford better gear. When they reached the edge of the cover, she turned to Jorgen.

He gave her a single nod.

Chapter Fourteen

Mallory cast the spell on Jorgen, making sure the essence crystals in her satchel were easy to access in case she needed more mana. The mage was too far from her for her to be able to cast vanish I on him. She waited half a minute before she cast it on herself and hurried forward, being as silent as possible. She was just in range when the mage was jerked backwards. She cast vanish I on the mage, rapidly followed by beacon on the ground where he'd stood, having drawn mana from one of the crystals. She was partway back to where her party was hidden when she needed to recast vanish on herself, relieved Jorgen had two invisibility potions and wouldn't need her help since she had to draw the rest of the mana from one crystal and over half the mana of another small essence crystal.

Reaching cover, Mallory turned to face the bandits.

Her mouth dropped open when she saw the bodies scattered around her beacon. Five warriors and three archers. The rest of the bandits who'd been headed towards the beacon were now running for cover.

An archer was taken out by arrows and throwing knives before he could reach cover, a warrior taken out next. There were three low level warriors and a single high level warrior left.

Checking her mana, Mallory was relieved to see it had started to regenerate enough that she could cast fireball at each of the low level warriors. Before she could cast it at the high level warrior, one of the low level ones reached her, attacking with his sword. She stumbled backwards, drawing her sword to block his next attack.

The bandit drove her backwards, stumbling when two arrows struck him.

Mallory used the opportunity to attack with both her sword and a fireball.

Emica joined her, attacking the bandit with her sword, once again in human form. Except for her ears. They remained those of a fox.

Mallory barely managed to take out the warrior, with Emica's help, when the high level warrior, wearing chain armour, attacked her. She wanted to check where everyone was, or call out for help when one of his swords cut her arm. But she didn't have the time to check or call with how the high level warrior attacked. She did manage to heal herself and somehow blocked the next attack. But that was all she could do. Defend. It reminded her of fighting Rass.

Emica shapeshifted, darting back and forth, biting at the warrior as she did.

Mallory stumbled over the body of the low level warrior, barely staying on her feet. She threw a fireball at the high level warrior, relief rushing through her when several arrows pierced his body. She wished she had the spyglass so she could see what sort of damage they were doing against him. A glance over her shoulder showed that Ryan, Callum and Danae had joined her. She couldn't see Brodie or Jorgen anywhere. But since Fang was also nowhere in sight, she assumed the wolf cub was with her brother and they were both okay. Especially since a quick check in her journal showed that their health was fine.

The warrior pressed forward, focusing on Mallory. "This is our area. Get your own to farm."

"We don't plan to farm it." Mallory blocked his attack, checking everyone's stats while she had her journal open. Ryan and Danae had both lost seven health. Nothing to worry about. Yet.

"Then you don't need to be here." The arrows that struck the warrior barely seemed to bother him and he continued to focus on Mallory.

Her arms tired as she blocked his attacks. A quick check of her stamina showed it was rapidly dropping as she blocked each of his attacks with her sword. If this kept up, she'd be out of stamina and unable to move let alone attack. Maybe they shouldn't have sold the stamina potion. She flung two fireballs at him. Neither of them seemed to make any difference. He kept attacking, the force behind his attacks causing her to continue retreating.

Ryan came in close, drawing his sword, his hunting bow slung on his back. "We're not about to leave you here to prey on innocent travellers."

The warrior focused on Ryan. "No one is truly innocent."

"No one deserves to walk into a trap." Mallory cast lightning this time.

The warrior staggered, then turned to focus his attacks on Mallory.

Ryan stepped between Mallory and the warrior, blocking his next attack.

"Use that attack again, Mallory," Callum called out.

Mallory glanced over her shoulder to find Callum lowering the spyglass. She gave him a nod before she cast lightning. A grin escaped when the warrior stumbled. She cast lightning once more, wishing her mana regened quicker so she could spam the spell at him.

Arrows struck the warrior, but they didn't seem to bother him anywhere near as much as the spell. He focused all his attention on Mallory, renewing his efforts.

She staggered under the onslaught, unable to cast a spell while she was trying to avoid being struck by his sword. She finally managed to cast lightning again. The warrior vanished and she stared at where he'd been. "I hate it when they do that." All she could hope was that they hadn't gained another enemy. Rass was more than enough of an enemy to deal with.

Ryan came to stand by her. "We should see if Jorgen and Brodie need help with the mage."

Emica became human, standing on the other side of Mallory. "What about seeing what they have here?"

"While you three search the area, Danni and I can see if Brodie and Jorgen need help," Callum suggested. "They headed back towards the wagon."

Smudge joined them, leaning against Callum's leg and making soft sounds as he stretched his paws towards Callum.

Smiling down at Smudge, Callum scooped him up and put him in his makeshift sling before turning to Danae. "Is that okay with you?"

Danae nodded, still holding her bow. "After I look for arrows. I'm down to half the amount I had."

"I'll help you," Callum said. "I used up quite a few arrows too. Hopefully we can find some arrows on the archers because I know I broke some of mine attacking the high level warrior. If chain mail can wreck so many of my arrows, I hate to think about how many I'd lose when attacking someone wearing plate armour."

Mallory helped them, healing Danae before she started on Ryan and herself. As she did, she also checked her journal. Danae needed another twenty-two experience points to gain a CAS point. She was the only one close to gaining one, that Mallory knew of, since she didn't know Emica, Jorgen, Esben and Ninette's stats.

When Callum and Danae headed back towards the wagon, having found enough arrows to replace the ones they'd used, the rest of them searched the area and looted the bodies that remained behind. Ryan called them over to where four carts were grouped together, two riding horses and four draught horses with them.

Mallory reached him first, staring at the four people who were gagged and tied to the wheels of the carts. Three men and one woman. She took a step back from them, half expecting a trap. But they'd killed most of the bandits. There were only the ones that were unconscious and the mage. Surely it'd be safe to set the captives free.

Emica joined them. "I bet they kept them for a ransom." She took out her sword, cautiously approaching the woman. "The bandits are either unconscious, dead or have respawned elsewhere." She pulled the gag down before she cut the ropes binding the woman.

The woman rubbed her wrists. "They planned to ask outlandish amounts for us. None of us are wealthy enough for the amount they were asking. I know it's a lot to ask, considering you saved our lives, but could you escort us to safety? The roads seem to be getting worse these days."

Chapter Fifteen

Mallory took out her dagger and cut the ropes on one of the men, opening her journal when a notification appeared in the corner of her vision. "We're on our way to Wrentville if that is of any use to you." She stepped back from the man as she read the quest. *Seeking Safety: Four people are in need of being escorted to safety after they were attacked by bandits.*

Emica finished setting one of the men free at the same time as Ryan set the last one free. She gestured towards the carts and horses. "Does any of this belong to the four of you?"

"I own a riding horse," one of the men said.

"As do I," another man said.

The woman gestured towards herself, one of the men, a cart and a draught horse. "They belong to us. They cooked and ate all the vegetables we were taking home to Wrentville."

Ryan glanced at each of those who'd been held captive. "Are you all from Wrentville?"

Two of the men shook their heads, one of them stepping forward. "I'm from Longmeadow, but Wrentville will be fine. I will hopefully find someone there who'll escort me home for a fee."

"We're going to Longmeadow after a couple of stops along the way," Ryan said.

"I don't suppose those stops might include calling into a few farms," the woman said. "We have a business that creates and sells dried food mixtures for adventurers. Without more stock, we won't be able to fill our current orders."

"Depending on what you're looking for, we might have the vegetables you need. We've gathered a lot of them, along with herbs, during our journey." Mallory glanced in the direction of where they'd left the wagon. "If you're interested, you should talk to my brother. He isn't far from here."

The woman inclined her head. "That sounds interesting."

Ryan scanned the area. "Is there anyone else that they kidnapped?"

"They didn't think anyone else was worth keeping alive," one of the men said.

Mallory faced the carts, noticing several barrels

amongst them. "What about all the things the bandits stole? Who gets the gear?"

"You do since you took out the bandits," the woman said. "But we wouldn't complain if you were willing to let us have our own gear and livestock."

"That sounds fair enough to me." Ryan grinned. "Even if others might complain."

Mallory laughed, certain he was talking about her brother. She glanced skywards, worried about how little time they had left if they wanted the chance to sell things at the local shops. "We better see what we can find then get back on the road."

By the time they were ready to return to the wagon, they had two of the carts loaded with barrels and hessian bags containing stolen goods. The two men mounted their horses while the man and woman hitched their draught horse to the cart. The whole time they'd searched and loaded up the gear, Mallory had kept checking on Brodie, Callum and Danae's stats, relieved they didn't change. She had no idea what they were doing, but she assumed they were safe.

When they did arrive back at the wagon, at three according to Ryan, Brodie came to meet them. "What's with the quest? Where do they want to go?"

"They need a lift to Wrentville. Or at least two of

them do and the other two will be happy with that destination," Mallory said.

"That's not so bad then." Brodie gestured towards the gear. "This is all ours?"

Mallory shook her head. "Only some of it." She left Emica explaining everything to Brodie, along with insulting his mercenary tendencies, while she joined Jorgen and Callum who were negotiating with the mage to shrink the logs that were blocking the road.

Ryan followed her, his gaze momentarily resting on the mage's bound hands. "I don't think you're in any position to make demands. Not after all you've done."

"I didn't do anything," the mage protested. "I'm as much a victim as everyone else. They caught me and used me to help set better traps than what they'd been using. It's not like I have any revives left. And I've got no one who'd come looking for me and use a revive potion or item on me."

Mallory glanced skywards. There was only a few hours left till dark and she wanted to be much closer to their destination before then. She faced the mage. "What do you want in exchange for your help?"

The mage looked from Jorgen to Mallory. "Who's the boss?" He nodded towards Jorgen. "I thought he was."

Ryan grinned. "Nope. That'd be Mallory."

She was half tempted to point out that even though she was the party leader, none of them would blindly follow her. Nor would she want them to. "We're running out of daylight. So what are your demands?"

"My horse and cart back and enough of the goods that they stole to cover what I lost." He glanced in the direction of the carts they'd brought back with them.

Brodie joined them in time to hear the mage's demands. "Now who is being a bandit? Why not take it all from us? And where can we get shrink and unshrink spells?"

The mage's gaze momentarily rested on Mallory's wand. "I bought my shrink and shrink reversal in the capital. In Shadhurst. But I've since ended up with a copy of shrink I. It's in my house in Longmeadow. If you can take me there instead of to Wrentville, it's yours. That's if you're willing to agree to the rest of the conditions."

"How much is a spell like that worth?" Brodie asked.

Emica interrupted the mage when he started to speak. "It's not much use without the other spell. I think he'll end up with the better deal with that trade."

"I could easily sell that spell for five hundred gold pieces," the mage protested.

Emica shrugged. "You might be able to, but that isn't going to help you get home." She looked him up and down. "You're not looking like you're doing too well. What were you doing on the road if you're not capable of looking out for yourself?"

"I wasn't alone. I was with a group of people. The bandits took us unaware," the mage said.

Emica turned to Brodie. "I bet he's got other spells he'd be willing to part with."

"Three spells, which includes shrink I," Brodie stated.

The mage gestured towards Mallory. "I thought you said she's the boss." He faced Ryan. "Are you stringing me along?"

Before any of them could reply, one of the men they'd rescued joined them. He glared at Mallory. "You didn't tell me you have travellers and a vampire in your group."

"What has that to do with anything?" Mallory demanded, not liking the tone of his voice.

"How can you expect us to trust you to get us to safety when you keep that kind of company?" the man asked.

"You don't have to come with us," Brodie said.

"You seriously can't expect me to travel with him." The man gestured towards Jorgen.

Before Mallory could come to Jorgen's defence, Ryan stepped between him and the man. "You heard Brodie. If you've got a problem with our friends, you're not welcome to travel with us."

"Travellers are some of the worst thieves on Inadon. Surely you can't expect law-abiding people to travel with them," the man protested.

Emica rested a hand on the hilt of her sword. "Say another word about my friend and you will regret ever having spoken." The smile she gave the man dared him to speak.

The man took a step back, remaining silent.

"If you're finished interrupting, we're busy here," Ryan said.

The man looked at each of them. "You'll see me safely to Wrentville?"

Emica's hand remained on her sword. "Only if you keep your mouth shut and stop annoying us."

The man looked at each of them once more before he gave a curt nod and retreated.

Ryan stepped to the side, momentarily resting his hand on Jorgen's shoulder before he returned his attention to the mage. "What do you say? You happy with those terms?"

The mage looked between Jorgen and the man who'd insulted him before he spoke. "Shrink I and two other spells."

Brodie held out his hand to the mage. "Done."

The mage hesitated. "Along with my other requests?"

Brodie continued to hold out his hand. "Yeah."

The mage shook his hand. "Should we sort out my cart now?"

Brodie nodded. "I'll help you with that while everyone else finishes getting ready to leave."

Chapter Sixteen

Mallory waited until the mage was out of hearing before she turned to Jorgen, ignoring the journal notification that she assumed was a quest for the mage. "Are you okay?"

"It's not the first time I've encountered that kind of attitude," Jorgen said. "I appreciate your words of defence."

Ryan slung an arm around Jorgen's shoulders. "It's what mates do. Come on, we better make sure Brodie doesn't rip the mage off. The sight of all that stuff to sell might be too much for him to resist."

Emica glared in the direction of the man who'd insulted Jorgen. "We should have left him behind. On principle."

Mallory was half tempted to agree. "We better get organised to go if we want to have any chance of reaching the area before midnight. Which isn't unrealistic with all the hold-ups we've had."

Emica laughed. "We won't be that late. It's less than four hours' travel. And whatever amount of time it takes us to sell everything in Wrentville."

They shared out the rest of the rabbit jerky before they started out to Wrentville, Brodie complaining that they should have cooked something for lunch. They stirred up the dust of the road, a procession of carts, horses and the wagon, hopefully too large a group for anything to bother them. Mallory, Brodie, Emica and Deneg were the only ones in the back of the wagon since everyone else was helping Ninette, or in Esben's case driving one of the carts since he'd insisted it was simple enough to do one handed. The woman's partner drove the other spare cart for them.

Brodie, who sat beside Mallory, demanded, "How did you all get so much XP?"

Emica, who was sitting across from Mallory on Deneg's coffin, grinned. "That high level warrior was worth ten XP."

"Ten?" Brodie stared at her. "We need more like that."

"Oh no we don't." Mallory doubted they could have managed taking on several of that level all at once. "You weren't there to take him on. You don't know how hard he was to fight."

"I should have stayed," Brodie muttered.

"It was good that you went with Jorgen in case he needed help," Mallory said.

Brodie met her gaze. "Dad would have thought it a stupid move."

Mallory shrugged. "I've never agreed with the way he sees things."

"I don't think much of your father, from the little I've heard." Emica made her way to the back of the wagon. "I'll give Ninette a hand." She jumped out of the moving wagon, stepping to the side to avoid the horse drawn cart that followed the wagon.

Brodie watched Emica stride away, lowering his voice when he spoke. "Do you think she heard us when we were speaking about Dad?"

Mallory shrugged. "Does it matter?"

"How good can she hear with fox ears?"

Again Mallory shrugged. "Don't worry about it, Brodie. We've got other things to focus on."

"Yeah. Like all the veggies the two we rescued want to buy off us. I said I'd go talk to the woman during the trip. We should also see what's in those hessian bags and barrels. See if there's anything worth keeping."

"You talk to the woman and I'll check the contents in the carts," Mallory said.

"Okay." Brodie hopped out of the wagon and waited for the cart that followed so he could clamber up onto it as it drove past him.

Mallory was about to jump out of the back of the wagon when Danae, who drove the wagon, spoke.

"Does your father ever hurt you?"

Mallory turned to face Danae, who frequently glanced over her shoulder. "Not physically."

"There are other ways to hurt people," Danae said.

"Yeah." She paused a moment, trying to think of a way to explain. "He doesn't deliberately hurt either of us. He's not like that." Or at least she didn't think he was. "He just wants us to do well and can only see one way of achieving that. And neither of us seem capable of living up to his expectations."

This time, when Danae looked over her shoulder, she held Mallory's gaze for a moment before facing forward again. "I'm sorry."

"Yeah, me too." Mallory jumped out of the wagon when Danae didn't say anything else. She was sorry her brother still cared what their father thought of him. Sorry that he'd probably never have the approval he clearly needed. Reaching the cart Esben drove, she gave him a nod in greeting before clambering into the back and checking through all the contents. There was a mixture of items, some of them obviously from travelling merchants or wagoners transporting goods. She couldn't help wondering if they'd travelled without guards or if they hadn't had enough guards to survive the attack.

Deciding there wasn't anything they needed out of that cart's contents, she jumped out and waited for the next one to come alongside her. Again it was mostly trade goods. The only thing different was a belt pouch containing a ring and a letter. She examined the ring, a simple gold band with a dark red stone set in a star shaped setting flush with the band. A woman's ring. Opening the letter, she scanned the contents, sorrow washing over her. It was dated a month ago and written by Remora, from Longmeadow, letting Milos know that he didn't need to search for the ring that had been stolen from her family a generation ago, that he didn't need to prove himself in her eyes. It was only her father who demanded proof of his abilities. That she would leave her family behind rather than have him risk himself to marry her.

Returning the letter to the belt pouch, she again examined the ring. Had he died? Or did he have a revive? She slipped the ring into the belt pouch. The rest of the items could be sold. The ring needed to be returned to Remora. She put the belt pouch into her satchel before jumping out of the wagon and heading back to the one where Ryan was putting vegetables in a hessian bag.

He looked up to smile at her. "About twenty minutes until we reach Wrentville."

She clambered into the wagon to sit beside him. "That went quick." It had obviously taken her a lot longer than she'd thought to search through everything. She opened her journal, the notification still in the corner of her vision, having meant to read over the quest a lot sooner than this. While she read it, she took the belt pouch from her satchel and handed it over to Ryan. *Another Victim: A mage is in need of an escort to Longmeadow, having been an unwilling accomplice to bandits. He has offered three spells in payment with one of them being shrink I.*

Ryan looked up from the letter. "We need to find Remora and Milos."

"Yeah, we do." She closed her journal. "That was my thought too." She reached for Ryan's hand once he'd returned the contents to the belt pouch. "And it's not up for a vote."

Ryan chuckled. "Others might argue, but it never even occurred to me to do anything else."

"Brodie won't argue." She was certain of it. "Do you think Milos is alive?"

Ryan lightly squeezed her hand. "I don't know. But we'll try and figure it out."

"Some fathers really suck."

"You worried about the weekend?" Ryan asked.

Chapter Seventeen

Mallory shrugged in answer to Ryan's question. She was more worried about the weekend on her brother's behalf. "We could stay home. We don't need a babysitter."

Ryan shifted closer to her. "Then why don't you tell your mum that?"

Mallory sighed. "I can't." There were so many complications. "It isn't that simple." She remained silent when everyone headed back towards the wagon, opening her journal to check Ryan's stats since it had been his turn to gather when Ninette had a break. He'd gained a CAS point and had thirty-eight of the next one hundred and twenty-four experience points he needed for his next CAS point.

Ninette sat across from Mallory, once she'd found a spot for the resources she'd brought back to the wagon. "We're getting close to Wrentville and it looks like someone has picked the area clean. We're about ten minutes away."

Danae glanced over her shoulder. "How did you go?"

"I gained two CAS points and only need another eight XP for my next one," Ninette said.

"Hopefully there'll be more resources for you to gather on the way to the turnoff," Mallory said.

"I hope so," Ninette said. "But at least I'll gain my level when we reach Wrentville when I earn XP for a new location."

Brodie hurried alongside the wagon, clambering up to sit beside Danae on the driver's seat. "They gave me directions to their place. They want all the veggies and some of the herbs." He looked over his shoulder, a wide smile briefly appearing. "And they'll let a trustworthy merchant know that we have goods for sale."

Mallory glanced around the back of the wagon. "It'll be good to sell some of the herbs and veggies."

"It'd be good to sell all of them," Brodie said.

"I also want to bank most of our money," Mallory said. "Is it possible to have a joint bank account?"

Jorgen nodded. "They require a hand print of all those who can access the account."

"That sounds easy enough." Mallory looked out

the rear of the wagon as they slowed. The town was surprisingly busy after the many villages they'd visited. Not as busy as back home in Brisbane, but it was more people than she was accustomed to seeing while on Inadon.

The trip through the cobblestone streets, to the home of the couple they'd rescued, was slow. There were other riders and wagons on the streets, along with people walking along the side of the road and occasionally crossing it. As they drew to a stop, the cat came out from under the driver's seat and jumped down to the ground before darting off down the side of a neighbouring house.

Brodie glanced at Ryan before he nodded in the direction the cat had taken before jumping out the back of the wagon, Fang jumping out after him. "A good thing you didn't get attached."

Callum put Smudge in the makeshift sling. "Maybe Kitty was just waiting for the right place to make his home before he left us."

"Probably bailed rather than be stuck with that name." Brodie strode towards the couple who were at the front door of their house.

Mallory eyed the contents in the back of the wagon, trying not to sigh. "I suppose we better sort through everything and see what we can sell."

Before they could sort anything, the two men came over to them and thanked them for escorting them to Wrentville. Seconds later, Brodie joined them along with the couple who also thanked them for escorting them home. Mallory didn't have time to add anyone else to their party so they could gain experience points for completing a quest.

"It was no trouble," Ryan said.

Mallory nodded in agreement with Ryan when the couple looked in her direction. "We were coming here anyway." She checked the journal notification, surprised to find it was actually two. One finished and the other still active.

Seeking Safety: You escorted everyone safely to Wrentville. You earned twenty experience points each.

Trouble At Thornlight Shipping Company: After the recent information they received, the shipping company is in need of someone to look into their current problem.

Before she closed her journal, Mallory checked everyone's stats. Only Danae had gained a CAS point. Everyone else was a long way off gaining one. She closed her journal as the two men left, one of them giving the travellers a look of disgust. Turning back to the wagon, she began sorting out what they wanted to sell. It took them a bit over an hour to sell as much as they could. Between the couple they rescued, and the merchants they were introduced to, they managed to sell all the herbs and vegetables except the handful of vegetables Brodie kept for dinner, eight small demonic spider eyes, the two dresses, two black trousers, brown trousers and a beige shirt from the chest Rodina had given them, six bone dust of the undead, twenty knuckle bones of the undead, both the poppets to a mage which Jorgen declined half the money for since he'd only needed it to pay his passage home, the yellow tunic that had been washed and the two carts and horses drawing them. Brodie had wanted to keep the horses, but the sale wouldn't have gone through without them. He'd also sold the cloth bag of jewellery. The merchant able to tell him which handful of jewellery had enchantments on them and what they did. They kept only a gold ring, the simple band engraved with demonic runes for the word 'regen', that would regen one mana every ten seconds. They also learned the silver armband increased stamina regen and sold it too.

After visiting the various merchants and traders, they made one thousand one hundred and thirty-two gold pieces as well as being offered a hundred gold pieces worth of goods in exchange for some of their resources at one of the shops. The trade had seemed preferrable to hanging onto the resources and there were things they needed to buy. Mallory slipped on the mana ring before looking through the available spells. Most were too expensive to buy and some were well above her level. She tossed up between buying ice shard and water blast, both being twenty-five gold pieces and both having the same attack stats as fireball and lightning strike. The difference was that they had bonus damage against demonic creatures. Which should come in handy in a demonic dungeon.

Brodie held up two small, gold hoop earrings. "Callum and I could each wear one of these."

Ryan grinned. "Did you and my brother have something you wanted to tell me?"

Brodie glared at Ryan. "For the traveller's bead."

Callum laughed, taking one of the earrings from Brodie. "I'm afraid you're not my type, Brodie. But I will have the earring." He turned to Mallory. "That's if we can afford the twenty gold pieces for them."

She thought of all the money they now had. It seemed like a lot, but she had no idea how much it was going to cost to set up a base when they reached Merrow. "Get the earrings." It was probably a better idea than her brother trying to grow his hair too quickly and ending up causing all sorts of questions back home.

"What else are we spending the gold on?" Brodie stopped in front of some potion bottles. "What about XP potions for-"

Ryan interrupted him. "No."

"But Fang-"

Again Ryan interrupted Brodie. "She'll level up with you. There are other things we should get first." He glanced at the earrings. "You've probably wasted enough money today on things that aren't completely necessary."

"What else do we need?" Brodie asked.

"This." Callum held up a black, hooded jacket.

"What do we need that for?" Brodie demanded.

"It's mage cloth armour. It reduces damage by one and increases mana regen by one every five seconds," Callum said. "With this, it'll bring your mana regen up to thirty-four mana a minute. Enough to cast vanish each time it wears off and still have a bit of mana to spare for something else."

Mallory hurried across the shop to look at the garment, taking it from him. The cloth was soft, feeling as comfortable as her wand felt to hold. "How much is it?" She spotted the price before Callum could speak. "Oh. We can't afford it." It was eighty gold pieces. She dreaded to think how much it would have cost if it hadn't been secondhand. Yet being able to cast vanish I more frequently would be useful.

Ryan joined her, checking the price. "I think we can't afford not to get it. You need all the mana you can get."

"Yes, but–"

Ryan interrupted Mallory's protests, taking the jacket from her. "We need to increase your mana regen. This will do it." He looked past Mallory to the merchant. "Do you have anything else that increases mana?"

"A spell. Siphon."

Mallory had noticed it when she'd looked through the spells and it was well and truly out of their budget. "The jacket will be enough for now." She made her way to the counter where Brodie was trying to talk the merchant down. Smiling, when her brother gained them a discount, she handed over the twenty gold pieces before heading outside, clutching the mage jacket against her chest. She finally had armour.

Chapter Eighteen

Taking out ice shard, Mallory read over the spell, the parchment vanishing in vapour once she was done. Her steps slowed when she saw Deneg leaned against the side of the wagon, watching them approach. She glanced to the side, following Deneg's gaze. He watched Callum. At Callum's expression, she wanted to remind him that Deneg had already walked out once. She kept the words to herself. It wasn't like Callum didn't already know and he certainly had a good memory.

Stepping away from the wagon, Deneg waited for them to reach him, light from a nearby lantern highlighting his features. "I thought you would have arrived at the location by now."

Ryan shrugged. "There were a few problems along the way."

"You are still planning on going to the dungeon," Deneg said.

"Of course we are," Brodie said. "After we go to the bank and have dinner." He strode to the driver's seat of the wagon and clambered up. "Where's the bank?"

Deneg leapt onto the wagon to sit beside Brodie. "I can take you there." He took the reins from Brodie, waiting until everyone was in the wagon before he got the horses moving.

It didn't take them long to reach the bank, a stone building with the words 'Inadon International Bank'. Below the words were runes which Danae told them said the same. Mallory shoved the coins into a couple of the bags that had been used for herbs, giving one to Ryan and another to Callum while keeping a bag for herself. Of the group funds, she left only ten gold, seven silver and twenty-one copper pieces in the belt pouch along with the silver piece from Eswen.

Danae remained in the wagon. "I'll wait here for you."

Jorgen, Emica, Esben and Ninette all made similar comments.

Mallory led the way inside, Ryan at her side, Brodie and Callum following with their companion animals. She stopped several metres in from the door, scanning the interior. She frowned. Was it larger inside than it had appeared from the outside?

The demon behind the counter wore a short, sleeveless black tunic that was several shades darker than his glossy skin, the demonic rune tattoos barely visible on his arms. He looked them up and down. "Can I help you?" His voice was polite, but distant.

Mallory stepped up to the counter and put her bag of coins on it. "We'd like to open an account we can all access."

The demon took a thin, black stone from under the counter and placed it in front of Mallory. Runes had been carved around the outside. "Palm against the tile."

Each of them did as requested, answering the questions the demon asked of them regarding their names and who they were. He looked them up and down when they said they were trying to become guardians. The demon frowned, muttering under his breath as he linked a joint account to their handprints.

"What happens if someone loses their hand?" Brodie asked. "Like if it's chopped off or something."

"It's more than just your handprint. It reads your essence." The demon returned the tile to the space beneath the counter, nodding towards the bags of coins everyone had placed on the counter. "What do you wish done with this money? Individual accounts were automatically created when a joint account was formed."

"Put it in our joint account," Ryan said.

They all nodded, watching as the demon counted out the coins. Finished, he swept them all into a tray he took from under the counter and returned it under there. Like the tile, it had been made of the same thin, black stone with runes carved around the edges. He met Mallory's gaze. "You have one thousand nine hundred and seventy-seven gold and eight silver pieces in your account. Is there anything else I can help you with today?"

Mallory stared at him, amazed their funds had grown so much in the past few days. A smile slowly formed. "No. Thank you."

He inclined his head, remaining silent as they strode outside.

Danae stood outside the door. "I forgot I needed to sort out the account from the Guardians." A wry smile made a brief appearance. "I won't be long."

"Want me to go with you?" Brodie flushed. "I mean in the bank."

Danae smiled up at him. "I'm fine. But thank you for offering."

Ryan clapped Brodie on the shoulder once Danae

had entered the bank. "Just get it over and done with and invite her on a date or something."

Brodie muttered under his breath, the words too low for anyone to hear as he headed to the wagon.

Mallory watched her brother go, wishing she could tell him the same. But he didn't need both of them telling him to hurry and ask. A grin escaped. Maybe she should remind Danae that she might be the one that would have to do the asking.

Ryan slipped an arm around Mallory's waist. "What are you up to?"

Laughter bubbled up and she tried to contain it. The task was impossible and her grin remained in place when her brother shot her a look and glared at her. "I'm not up to anything." She turned to face him, meeting his gaze. "Yet."

Ryan grinned. "Yet."

"Yeah." Her lips met his when he lowered his head and she drew away when a noise startled her.

Danae let the door of the bank close behind her. "I'm ready to go now." She smiled. "Did you see that we have one rep for here? We've gained rep in nearly every place we've visited."

Before anyone could comment, Kitty ran across in front of Danae and leapt up onto the wagon to dive under the seat.

Danae laughed softly. "I guess he wants to stay with us after all."

Deneg took them to a place outside Wrentville where they could have a campfire, Brodie insisting they have dinner before they travelled on.

It was nearly half past eight by the time they'd cooked the fish and the rest of the vegetables. During the meal, Mallory told everyone about Remora's ring and handed it around when a couple of them asked to look at it. The mage remained by his cart, having bought food from the tavern while they'd been busy at the bank. Mallory considered inviting him to join them at the fire, but decided against it just in case he was another one from this area who didn't like travellers or vampires.

Once they were back on the road, Mallory took out her leather bound notebook and wrote a few lines about the day, smiling as she thought back over it. They were certainly making progress with the money they now had in the bank. It was well and truly past time.

"What are you grinning about?" Brodie demanded, having remained in the wagon since he was planning to have a nap.

"The money we have."

"Think it'll be enough to buy a house in Merrow?" Brodie asked.

Danae, who was driving the wagon, glanced over her shoulder. "You could afford a simple two room wooden house with a thatch roof and have change. It probably won't be all that spacious and may be in a less desirable area."

"We need to earn more money." Brodie finished getting comfortable, stretching out beside Fang, his hand resting on her back. "Good thing we're doing the dungeon." He closed his eyes.

Chapter Nineteen

Mallory put her notebook away and did rapid mend on Esben before she went to see if Ninette needed any help. Such as more light than the lanterns gave off. She cast magelight as she walked towards the young warrior.

Ninette turned to face Mallory. "I'm just about to have a break. Did you want a turn?"

Mallory shook her head. "Everyone else needs a chance to catch up."

"It's my turn," Callum said. "I've got ten minutes, I don't think you'll need that long to gain a CAS point with how close you are. Probably five minutes at the most."

Mallory checked her journal. She only needed forty experience points. She really wanted to say yes. "I should let-"

Ryan interrupted her. "Better start gathering

resources before you waste all the time standing around protesting."

She started to argue his comment, shaking her head a couple of times when she saw the expression on his and Callum's faces. "Okay." She picked the carrots Jorgen pointed out before hurrying over to where Emica stood near some herbs. With everyone's help, it took her just under five minutes to gain the experience points she needed. She turned to Callum. "Your turn now." She was halfway through character level five and now had a spare CAS point. It made her feel better to know she had a spare one if she should need it.

The evening passed quickly and they ran into no trouble along the way. The mage followed behind them in his horse drawn cart, keeping pace with them. Deneg regularly disappeared, returning to let them know the way ahead of them remained clear. Ninette did most of the gathering during the journey, which was a bit over two and a half hours. Ryan gathered during her next break and then Brodie, who was woken to have a turn. He then took over driving the wagon so Danae could gather resources.

Deneg led the way when they turned off the road, showing them to a clearing a few minutes from the turnoff. "We can't take the wagon through the Valley

Of Wandering Souls. There isn't always space between the trees."

Before clambering out of the wagon, Mallory grabbed a small essence crystal out of the chest and put it in her satchel that contained a nearly empty one. She tried to make sense of Deneg's words. "That makes it sound like there is space sometimes."

Danae laughed softly. "That's because there is. The wandering souls are the trees."

Mallory was half tempted to recast magelight. But she could clearly see Danae and the half-elf appeared to be serious. "How does that work? How do trees move around?"

"They walk." Deneg gestured into the darkness ahead of them. "It would be nice if we can return to the wagon before daylight so I'm not stuck in the dungeon all day waiting for dark."

Mallory turned to Ninette. "Are you okay to set up camp here or do you need us to stay and help the three of you?" She glanced at Jorgen and Esben, not bothering to count the mage in her calculations since he seemed to prefer keeping to himself.

Ninette nodded. "We can manage. I can use some of the vegetables we gathered on the way here along with the last of the dried venison to make up a stew for when you return from the dungeon."

"Hell yeah," Brodie said. "XP, treasure and a meal at the end of it."

Ryan chuckled. "Then how about we get started." He grabbed the leather backpack that was almost empty.

Mallory cast magelight. "Is everyone ready?"

Deneg took a leather bound notebook from inside his coffin, tucking it into his satchel he wore so that the strap went across his chest from shoulder to hip. "We need to go through the Valley Of Wandering Souls. The entrance to the dungeon is on the far side of it."

Mallory followed Deneg, glancing at Ryan who walked beside her, his sword drawn. Around her was Brodie, Callum, their companion animals, Danae and Emica. For a moment she worried that the seven of them wouldn't be enough. Or nine if she counted the companion animals.

They strode through a forest of broad limbed trees, their thick trunks ending in roots that snaked across the ground before sinking into it. They were about five minutes into the forest when one of the trees drew its roots up out of the ground and lumbered forward to a clear spot before settling in and sinking its roots back into the ground.

Mallory, who'd come to a stop at the sight, stared

at the tree that towered over all of them. "Are they dangerous?"

"Depends on if you upset them," Deneg said. "They don't make a good enemy since they tend to stay in large groups."

"They prefer to avoid the rest of the sentient races," Emica said. "We're too reckless and don't give matters enough thought before leaping into a situation. They like to ponder a matter for months, or even years, before making any decision."

"They have a lifespan that allows them to do that," Danae said. "Like a tree, they can live for hundreds of years."

Deneg took a step in the direction they'd been heading. "In case you've forgotten, I'd like to have this done before sunrise."

They continued through the forest, Mallory needing to recast her magelight before they reached their destination. She stood in front of the narrow crack between two boulders, her light showing a path that angled down sharply. It would be tight for Ryan with his broad shoulders and if they needed to bring anything large out. She supposed they could always return to the camp and ask the mage for help. Shrinking and unshrinking spells would come in very handy.

"Are we going in there?" Emica gestured towards the entrance. "Or standing here admiring it?"

Deneg, who'd been looking at one of the pages in his notebook, returned it to his satchel. "Going in. The dungeon is off this cave system. When we reach the end of this entrance tunnel, we turn right."

Mallory continued to peer inside. "How long is the tunnel?"

"About sixteen metres long." Deneg moved closer to Mallory. "Did you want me to go first?"

She stepped back out of the way to allow him to enter first. That was not an offer she was about to turn down. Who knew what was in the cave. Look what they'd encountered last time they went into a cave. Although, admittedly, it had been attached to a mine.

Brodie stepped past Mallory, following Deneg. "Where is the treasure?" Fang remained at his heel, whining as she followed.

Deneg glanced over his shoulder. "It's not as simple as that. We have to collect all the keys that will allow us to access the final room that contains a treasure."

Mallory sighed heavily. Of course it wasn't simple. She nearly told Deneg that he should have told them that little detail. Not that it would have mattered to Brodie. She hurried after them, the rest of her party following. Their footsteps sounded loud as they followed the cave tunnel downwards. She checked her journal notification. She'd gained fifteen experience points for a new location. A quick glance at everyone's stats showed that both Callum and Danae had gained a CAS point. Closing her journal, she glanced up.

The tunnel ceiling was low enough that her fingertips would have brushed against it if she'd stretched out her arm. But at least it looked like it wasn't about to collapse in on them. A glance at the wall showed they seemed equally stable. The tunnel also wasn't as narrow as the entrance, with enough space that even a warrior in full plate armour would have been able to stride along the tunnel with no problems and possibly have a companion at their side. All they needed to worry about was what might live down here. A shudder ran through her when she remembered the spider eyes they'd gathered after taking on the demonic spider. She really hoped there was nothing like that in here.

Ryan came alongside her. "Are you okay?"

"Yeah. Just remembering the last time we were in a cave."

Ryan chuckled. "Spider fangs and eyes?"

She shuddered again. "I hadn't been thinking about the fangs until now."

Ryan chuckled again. "But you were thinking of the eyes."

Brodie spoke before Mallory could say anything else. "What's to the left?"

Mallory stepped out of the tunnel and into a spacious cave, looking in the direction Brodie faced. "We're in here looking for a treasure, not exploring every part of the cave."

Brodie walked towards the tunnel that was headed in the opposite direction to the one they needed to take. "What if there's something good? What if-" His words were interrupted by strands of a web flying towards him, ensnaring him and dragging him into the dark tunnel.

Chapter Twenty

It took Mallory a few seconds to register what had happened. She broke into a run, drawing out her wand, Ryan at her side, Fang and Deneg in the lead. "Brodie!" She called out his name over the sound of Fang barking. Fear raced through her when he didn't answer. "Brodie!" Again the only sound was Fang. She slowed her pace as she came to the end of the short tunnel that had led off the cave they'd been in.

Ryan stepped between Mallory and the three large spiders that were in the cave they entered. "I can't see him."

Mallory's gaze was drawn to the cobweb cocooned bodies, some of them looking human, scattered across the ground amongst what looked like large egg sacs. "What if he's one of them?" She nodded towards the cobwebbed body lying not far from them.

Callum came to a stop on the other side of Mallory,

Smudge in the makeshift sling occasionally making his warning cry while Fang barked at the spiders. "This looks like the perfect situation for you to use flame."

"Kill it with fire sounds like a good plan to me," Ryan said.

Mallory looked at each of the spiders that remained where they were. "Why haven't they attacked? Why are they standing there staring at us?"

"They shouldn't be." Emica glanced around the cave, before tilting her head back. "You might want to look up."

Mallory raised her gaze, her mouth dropping open and her heart feeling like it might have stopped for a second. Six large spiders made their way over the cobweb-crossed ceiling towards them. "Nine. How are we meant to take out nine spiders?"

"Until this battle is ended, Brodie won't respawn," Danae said.

Callum took out the spyglass. "They've only got twenty-five health each. It should be simple."

Emica sheathed her sword. "As long as we avoid being caught in a web." She shapeshifted the moment she'd finished speaking, attacking the nearest spider.

Mallory threw flame at the other two spiders,

stumbling back when those above began to drop down to attack.

Fang barked, trying to attack one of the spiders, and Ryan ordered her back, getting between her and the spider.

Mallory drew her sword, slashing at the cobwebs that came towards her, trying to cast fireballs at the oncoming spiders. Half her attacks missed as she stumbled and struggled to avoid spiders and cobwebs. "Why didn't the demonic spiders throw webs at us?"

Danae blocked a cobweb with her bow, stumbling to the side as she tried to avoid another one. "Different variety of spider. These ones don't carry their young around."

The moment one of the spiders was killed, Mallory used reanimate on it, relieved her mana didn't take as long to return with the jewellery and mage armour she wore. But she still had to be careful. It wasn't limitless. Or even able to regen as quickly as it had when she'd used all the jewellery while they'd been in Velkden. As soon as another spider was taken out, she reanimated it. The battle went more smoothly with two spiders to help them and she began to stop worrying about the fight. It finally looked like they'd survive the attack.

One of the spiders managed to hit Callum with

a web and he was knocked to the ground when the spider leapt on him, trying to cocoon him in its web. Smudge screeched a warning cry, trapped in the makeshift sling.

Ryan ran towards the spider, slashing at it in an effort to drive it off his brother.

Mallory threw fireballs at the spider, changing over to ice shard to get in the habit before they reached the demonic dungeon. The ice shattered as it hit the spider, becoming vapour and vanishing. A sound behind her had her spinning in time to see a spider leap towards her. She cast ice shard at it as she threw herself to the side, colliding with Danae, the two of them ending up on the ground.

Danae rolled out of the way of the spider that leapt towards her, taking her bow with her, some of the arrows spilling from her quiver.

Mallory cast ice shard at the spider when it turned towards her, tensing when it continued to come for her.

An arrow pierced the spider and it dropped to the ground. Danae grabbed one of the arrows off the ground beside her, only half risen from where she'd sprawled.

Mallory rose to her feet, reanimating the spider as she did, her heart racing. A glance around the cave showed only a couple of spiders were left. They were quickly taken out and she stood where she was, scanning the area in the hope she'd see her brother. He didn't appear.

Danae came to stand beside Mallory. "He should be back soon."

Hearing the worry in the half-elf's voice, Mallory turned to her. "Then why don't you sound convinced?"

Danae smiled briefly. "I guess I'm a little worried we'll have to clear out all the cave before he can respawn. We shouldn't have to, but it's always a possibility."

Callum held out some arrows to Danae. "We lost a few, but I've taken five from the spares so we all have twenty arrows in our quivers."

When Ryan crouched by one of the spiders, his skinning knife in hand, Deneg said, "You don't need to worry about gathering resources from everything you come across. The treasure will be more than enough for everyone. Stopping to search every creature will take too long."

Ryan checked his pocket watch. "It's only just gone midnight now. We've got more than enough time."

Mallory stared at Ryan, surprised the fight had taken so little time. It had felt much longer. Before she could comment, Brodie appeared not far from her, a ghostly figure that gradually became solid. She hurried forward. Before she could hug him, he stepped back out of the way.

Danae hurried over to Brodie. "You're back." She threw her arms around him.

Brodie stood stunned for a moment before he awkwardly returned her embrace.

Mallory grinned, half tempted to point out that when she'd hugged him last time he'd died, he'd told her not to maul him. "Are you okay?"

Brodie nodded, letting Danae go a second after she drew away from him. "Yeah, I–" He broke off. "Aw, come on. Look at all the XP everyone gained. I'm going to end up way behind again. It's not fair. And now I'm down a revive."

Callum stood up from where he'd crouched beside a spider to see what he could harvest. "You were willing to lose a revive for Fang."

"That's different." Brodie patted Fang who'd come over to lean against him, her tail wagging as Brodie patted her on the head. "She'd be worth losing a revive for."

Ryan slipped his backpack off. "That's all the spiders checked." He put in six fangs and fourteen spider eyes, wrapping the eyes that he, Callum and

Emica had gathered, in a piece of canvas. "We need to keep going." He glanced at Deneg by the tunnel entrance. "We're on a time limit."

Deneg returned along the tunnel they'd taken to the spiders' lair.

Mallory hurried after him, unable to resist giving her brother a look over. He seemed the same as ever. But she knew how unsettling it was to die and respawn.

Reaching the first cave they'd entered, they continued straight ahead to the tunnel leading off it. This tunnel was only two metres long and they entered another cave where eight goblins sat around a campfire, several of them squabbling over a half cooked meaty bone. The goblin closest to the campfire grabbed hold of a club and hit the fighting goblins over the head, stopping in mid-swing when he noticed them.

Chapter Twenty-One

Mallory automatically threw a fireball at the nearest goblin. Casting ice shard when she attacked him a second time. Before she could attack another goblin, they were all down, their bodies scattered around the still burning campfire. She remained tense, ready to fight for a moment. Nothing moved.

"Hell yeah." Brodie victory punched the air. "Goblins are so easy for gaining XP."

Mallory grinned when she checked his stats. "Did you attack all of them?"

Brodie returned her grin. "Nearly." He peered in a wooden cup beside the fire, sniffing it before he downed the contents.

"Brodie!" Danae dashed to his side.

Brodie made a face. "It doesn't taste anything like the smell."

Danae took the cup from him, cautiously smelling it. "Goblin ale."

"It tastes like crap," Brodie said. "Not like any ale I've ever had before."

Deneg came forward to look Brodie up and down. "We have about an hour before it starts to effect him. Six at the most before he's unconscious."

Mallory stared at her brother. "It's poisonous?"

Emica shook her head. "Goblin ale and food made by goblins cause goblin blight. He shouldn't die from it, but just in case, I hope he has another revive."

Mallory frowned. "How odd. When you said goblin blight, I knew the symptoms. They start with nausea, progresses to dizziness, blurred vision, trembling, weak limbs, shortness of breath and then unconsciousness."

"We better keep moving then." Ryan searched one of the goblins. "What is the shortest amount of time we have?"

"Four hours," Mallory said automatically. She briefly smiled. "Apothecary is more useful than I thought."

Ryan rose to his feet. "Let's get these goblins searched so we can return to the wagon before Brodie passes out. I'd rather not have to carry him."

"Are you sure it won't kill me?" Brodie's gaze was fixed on the cup Danae held.

Danae placed the cup on the ground beside the fire. "No, but you'll get very sick and if you were somewhere dangerous by yourself, you'd be vulnerable to whatever attacked you."

"It's not fair," Brodie muttered. "I'm going to get even more behind with my XP."

"Then stop eating and drinking random things you discover," Mallory said.

"I didn't think it'd be a problem," Brodie protested. "The goblins were obviously drinking it. So I didn't think it'd be poisonous or anything. And I was able to eat the jerky we found on them last time."

"That's different," Emica said. "They don't make jerky. You can only get goblin blight from things they've made."

Ryan put the items they found into his backpack. Two pairs of goblin boots and a chisel. "We need to keep moving." He turned to Deneg. "Where to now?"

Mallory turned to look in the direction Deneg pointed in, surprised to see a large, timber door with a wide stone door frame made from individual stones that had demonic runes carved into them, only the keystone blank. She supposed she had been focused on the goblins and then worried about her brother.

Brodie strode towards the timber door. Before he could reach it, Deneg stepped in front of him. "You might not want to rush ahead. Unless you have a limitless supply of revives."

Danae reached Brodie's side. "If the correct word isn't used to unlock the door, trying to open it will unleash a curse on you."

"What sort of curse?" Callum asked.

"It could be anything. The demon who locked it would have chosen a suitable curse to attack any who tried to enter without his permission," Danae said.

"A fire attack. Fifty health an attack and it strikes every five seconds." Deneg nodded towards the door. "Two of us need to press the stones to spell out the word 'scorch'. It was the name of the demon's favourite horse."

Callum moved closer to the door. "It's the alphabet, on either side of the door, isn't it?"

Deneg stood on the opposite side of the door. "Do you wish to do this with me?" He gestured towards the runes.

Callum nodded. "Which ones do I push? I only know a few of them."

Deneg pointed out each of the runes. "You ready?

We can't take more than a few seconds between each letter and we have to push them at the exact same time."

Callum's hand hovered over the first rune he needed to press. "Should we go on the count of three?"

Deneg held his hand in front of the same rune on the opposite side of the door. "That would be too long. On two. For each one."

Callum nodded, smiling when Smudge peeked over the edge of the makeshift sling and held his paw out towards the runes. "Not this time, Smudge."

The river otter made a sound of disappointment, lowering his paw, but remaining peering over the edge of the makeshift sling.

"Ready?" Deneg asked.

Mallory didn't know if she should move back in case something happened or ready her wand to heal them if they were struck by a fireball. Not that she could heal enough to keep either of them alive if that did happen.

"Ready," Callum said.

Deneg inclined his head. "One, two."

They both pressed matching runes, the stones sinking in slightly, rising again before they managed to press the next stone. The moment they pressed the last runes to spell out the word 'scorch', the door swung open. A lantern hanging from the ceiling inside the dungeon sprang to life. The flame rose high before settling down in the ornate, iron-framed lantern.

Callum entered the dungeon first, his bow in hand. "It's empty with only a single door leading off the room."

Mallory was last into the room, peering around Ryan's broad shoulders after checking that the notification was only for finding another location. The door leading out of the room was similar to the one they'd used to enter the dungeon. The only difference was that it didn't have any runes carved into the stone doorframe.

Brodie reached for the door handle. "We need to find more dungeons. Twenty XP for entering a location is good. I mean, we don't even have to clear it out or anything."

"Should you-" Mallory broke off when her brother swung the door open. Her grip tightened on her wand. Nothing attacked. The corridor was empty, a single lit lantern casting a pool of light on the marble tiles halfway along it. "Why aren't there any creatures? I thought it'd be filled with them."

"There'll be creatures," Deneg said. "And puzzles to get through."

"Puzzles." Brodie turned to face Deneg. "What sort of puzzles?"

"Various types. More complicated than the entrance lock," Deneg said.

Emica strode along the corridor. "Aren't we on a time limit?" She glanced at Brodie. "Although he doesn't seem to be bothered by the ale. Maybe he's part goblin. They eat all types of random food without getting sick."

Mallory hurried after Emica. "We're both human."

Ryan glanced at Brodie with a grin. "Debatable."

"Who are you calling–" Brodie broke off when a large dog leapt out of a side corridor and knocked him to the floor.

Mallory backed away when it was followed by another two dogs, all of them chest height. They had dark red leathery skin, their eyes were black pools and their mouths were open wide to show sharp teeth, saliva dripping onto the marble tiles. She cast a fireball at the dog in the lead, mentally berating herself for not remembering to use ice shard against the demonic dogs.

Deneg leapt onto the back of one of the dogs, sinking fangs into the throat of it before it rolled and dislodged him. The second dog spun to attack Deneg who'd landed on his back.

Mallory cast ice shard at each of the dogs, arrows sinking into them. They snapped and snarled, neither slowing.

Ryan attacked the dog that landed on Deneg, Emica going for the second one, having shapeshifted into her fox form.

Seeing Deneg had plenty of help, Mallory headed for her brother, only Callum fighting the dog that attacked Brodie. She cast ice shard at the dog as she hurried forward, also casting health I on Brodie to heal some of the health he'd lost in the attack. He only had a single revive left to lose. He couldn't afford to die again.

The dog attacking Brodie collapsed on him and he struggled to rise. "Someone get it off me."

Callum dragged the corpse off Brodie before he turned to help with the other two.

Chapter Twenty-Two

Mallory healed her brother twice more before she faced the fight. The two dogs were down before she could help and she checked everyone's health, trying to ignore the fear that flared when she saw how low Ryan's health was. The first creatures to attack them had nearly taken out two of them. "Can we wait before we go on so I can heal everyone?"

Ryan searched one of the dogs. "Might be the only way we'll survive the dungeon."

"You're on a time limit." Deneg nodded towards Brodie.

"I feel okay," Brodie said. "There's nothing wrong with me."

Ryan rose to his feet. "We ended up with four canines." He looked between Brodie and the direction they'd been heading. "We better keep moving. Another twenty minutes and it'll have been an hour since Brodie had the ale."

"There's nothing wrong with me," Brodie protested.

"Then let's get this done while that remains the case." Ryan slung the backpack into place, having put the four large, demonic dog canines in it.

Brodie followed Ryan. "Why won't any of you listen to me? I'm all good."

Mallory grinned, scanning the area as she followed the two of them, the rest of their party behind her. "Mum always says Brodie has a cast iron stomach. Maybe he will be okay." She checked everyone's stats. Only Ryan had gained a CAS point. She also finished healing everyone who'd lost health points.

Brodie glanced over his shoulder. "See. Even Mal thinks I'm going to be good."

"It was goblin ale," Danae said. "Unless you're a goblin, you will end up with goblin blight."

Deneg went ahead of them. "We need to enter this door that leads into the next room and from there onto the first puzzle room."

Deneg opened the door at the end of the corridor, slipping inside and to the side. "Clear."

Mallory followed when he entered the room. She stopped not far into the room. The ceiling arched far above, several lit lanterns hanging from chains that gleamed in the light. Her gaze slowly travelled across the room. It was empty. "Should it be so quiet in here?"

Deneg shrugged. "It might be quiet for now, but I'd be surprised if it stayed like that." He crossed the marble floor, heading for the door in the far right corner. "We're not near the room with the first key."

Mallory looked over her shoulder at the door they'd used to enter the room. Were they up to dealing with a demonic dungeon? Maybe there was an easier treasure to go after. She checked her journal, glancing through the quests they hadn't done. The only one that might provide enough money to rescue Deneg's brother was probably just as dangerous as the dungeon. Actually, going after a staff that was in a sunken ship with undines had to be worse. They'd been powerless against the creature and she dreaded to think what would have happened to them without Smudge's help.

"You coming?" Ryan stopped beside Mallory.

After a glance around to see that everyone was heading for the next corridor, she met his gaze. "Do you think we can manage this?"

Ryan grinned. "I guess we'll soon see."

"Ryan–"

He interrupted her. "We've got revives. As long as we do, we can take a few risks."

She took a deep breath, slowly letting it out. "Okay."

"Ready?" He glanced towards the doorway everyone else had walked through.

"Yeah." She walked beside him, hurrying along a corridor that took a sharp turn to the left, a closed door ahead of them with another door at the end of a short corridor that headed to the right.

Deneg opened the door, waving them back when they would have entered. "There are supposed to be four stone statues by the door that need to be placed on pillars to activate the puzzle."

Mallory peered past him. There was a metre wide stone ledge going the width of the room in front of the door and another one going the width of the room on the far side. Between them was nothing. No marble floor, only blackness. Wall lamps hung on the far side of the room on either side of an ornate timber chest and more hung on either side of the open door she peered through. But there was nothing else. "Can't we use something other than the statues?"

Deneg pointed to two marble tiles on either side of the door. "Ryan and Brodie might be heavy enough to lower those tiles, but I doubt the rest of you would be."

"What if the rest of us stand together?" Danae asked.

"We need two people to cross the pillars that will rise up out of the pit," Deneg said.

Mallory's gaze was drawn to the impenetrable darkness. "How deep is the pit?"

Deneg shrugged. "The notebook didn't say."

"If you give me the backpack, and I hold Smudge, I should be close to Brodie's weight," Emica said.

"I'm heavier than I look," Callum said. "What happens if we stand on the tiles and we don't weigh enough?"

"Nothing." Deneg glanced towards the pit. "Not a single thing. And unless something does happen, we can't get across the room to the first key."

"What happened to the statues?" Callum asked.

Again Deneg shrugged. "They should have been here."

Callum stepped into the room, going to the second marble tile on the right. The moment he stepped onto it, the tile lowered with a grinding sound, sinking five centimetres below the height of the floor. He stared at his boots. "Is that it? Is it meant to go any lower than that?"

"That is it," Deneg said.

Ryan gave the backpack to Danae before he entered the room and went to the left, standing on the far marble tile. Like the first one, it lowered with a grinding sound.

Brodie stood on the other tile to the left and Emica went to the right. Even with her holding Smudge, the tile didn't lower.

Danae approached Emica. "There should be enough space for me to stand on the tile with you. If you don't mind."

Emica nodded, grabbing hold of Danae's arms when the half-elf stood close to her, causing the tile to lower. "I hope this won't take long. I'm not sure how long we can stay like this without losing our balance. There's less space than it appeared now the tile has lowered."

Numerous grinding sounds had Mallory looking into the pit. Her mouth dropped open when she saw stone pillars rise out of the darkness. They were evenly spaced and sized, a variety of runes carved on them. She backed away from the edge, running into the wall. "No. Absolutely not. You can't expect me to jump from pillar to pillar. I'll swap with Danni or Emica."

Deneg rushed forward, holding up a hand when

Danae started to move. "Stop. If you step off the tile the pillars will lower and it'll take hours for them to reset so they can be activated again."

Mallory slowly shook her head. "I can't do it." She wasn't athletic and there had to be more than half a metre between each of the pillars that were about twenty centimetres square. "I'll fall."

Deneg pointed to a pillar three from the left. "You jump on that one first. We need to spell out the horse's name again. We also have to make sure we jump at the same time or the pillars will drop, taking us with them."

Mallory stared at the rune carved into the top of the pillar. Her gaze was drawn to the pillars spread out before her, each of them carved with a rune. She couldn't do this. There were eight rows of pillars across the width of the room, and five rows across the length of it. "We need to come up with another plan."

"Come on, Mal," Brodie said. "Do you know how hard it is to stand in the one place for so long?"

Chapter Twenty-Three

Mallory studied her brother. "Are you okay? Do you feel nauseated? Or dizzy?"

"Will you stop asking?" Brodie demanded. "There's nothing wrong with me. Maybe it was normal ale."

Danae shook her head. "It was definitely goblin ale. Nothing else smells like that."

Deneg gestured towards the pillars. "Are you going to help me with this or should I seek out other adventurers?"

"Mal!" Brodie exclaimed. "Come on, Mal."

"Mallory." Ryan waited until her gaze met his before he continued speaking. "If you can't do it, we'll figure something else out."

His earlier words came back to her. She had more than enough revives. It wasn't like she'd die permanently. A shiver ran through her. But even though it wouldn't be a permanent death, the sensation was far from pleasant. She took a deep breath before she came away from the wall and took the couple of steps between her and the pillar. "Okay. I'm ready." Or at least as ready as she was ever likely to be.

Deneg stood in front of a pillar three in from the right. "We don't have to rush this puzzle. What is important is to make sure we both jump at the same time. We have maybe a couple of seconds to land before the pillars drop into the pit."

She tried to swallow. It was difficult. "Okay." It surprised her to hear how normal her voice sounded. She was about to go from pillar to pillar over a pit that appeared to have no bottom. Or at least none that was visible.

"I'll say 'one, two, jump' each time," Deneg said. "Although it really is only a very large step forward."

"Maybe for you. It's nearly a jump for me," Mallory said.

"Hurry up already," Brodie said.

"I hate to agree with him," Emica said. "But we're struggling to stay on this tile."

Mallory stared at the pillar. The rune was a straight line with one angling upwards from the bottom left and down from the top right, reminding her of an angular 's'. "I'm ready."

"'One, two, jump.'"

Mallory took a large step forward as he said the word, wobbling as she tried to gain her balance. She held out her arms, heart racing as she steadied. Relief rushed through her and she turned her head to look at Deneg. "That wasn't so bad."

"Be more careful. You looked like you nearly fell."

She shrugged in answer to Deneg's comment. It wasn't like she could argue it. He wasn't wrong.

"If either of us falls, we won't be able to respawn until the puzzle has been completed. Just like you can't respawn until a fight has ended."

"What?" Mallory began to turn towards the ledge she'd left.

Deneg held up a hand. "You can't go back. Only forward. Going back will trigger other problems."

"Why didn't you tell me?" Mallory demanded.

"I didn't think I'd need to until I saw how unsteady you were."

She took another deep breath, staring at the pillars ahead of her. She spotted the rune for 's' twice more. On two pillars one row back from the far end of the room. "Okay. Let's get this over and done with."

"We need to go forward one, then left, forward one then right two."

Her gaze travelled across the pillars as he

mentioned them, memorising the path. The next rune reminded her of an angular, back to front 'j'. "I'm ready to continue."

"How about you call them then?" Deneg suggested.

Mallory nodded. Before she called the first one, she took another deep breath, letting it out slowly as she focused on the pillar, trying to ignore the bottomless pit. "One, two, jump." She took a large step as she said the last word, trying to regain her balance. When she swayed forward, she blurted out, "One, two, jump." She landed on the 'o', gaining her balance and trying to slow her breathing. Deep breaths didn't help. All that would help was reaching the other side of the room.

"Are you okay?" Ryan asked.

She nodded rather than speak the lie. Focusing on the next pillar, she said, "One, two, jump." Again she wobbled and hurriedly called out the next pillar. It didn't help. Swaying, she stretched out her arms, wishing she didn't need to have her feet so close together.

Deneg held out a hand to her, his fingertips grazing hers. "One, two, jump."

She moved as he spoke the last word. The pillar she

landed on was one next to him. She clung to his hand. "Now where?"

"Forward one."

She looked at the pillars that were one from the far end. "Can't we just jump from them to the other ledge?"

"If we don't jump on the correct pillars, they'll drop back into the pit and we'll be stranded there," Deneg said.

"Don't tell me we have to jump all the way back."

"No. If we activate all the correct pillars then a ledge will be created along the sides, the gaps between the pillars filled so we can walk across them back to the door." Deneg nodded to the pillar in front of them. "Are you ready?"

She nodded, moving when he gave the command, wistfully looking at the ledge that was tantalisingly close. "Now where?"

"Left three, forward one then right one."

"Okay. She clung to his hand a moment longer before letting go. "One, two, jump." She called out the next two rapidly, reaching the pillar that was against the left wall. Leaning against the wall, she tried not to think about how close she'd been to falling over the edge. "Where is your notebook?" She turned so she could see Deneg all the way across the other side of the room.

"In my satchel."

"How can this maze be completed if we fall?"

"Don't fall." Deneg gestured towards the chest. "Ready to continue?"

She wanted to tell him how little she thought of his plans. He should have left the notebook with Ryan. "Ready." The word was clipped. She hadn't bothered keeping her annoyance from her tone. "One, two, jump." She headed forward, glad to remain by the wall. "One, two, jump." This time she had to move away from the wall and she swayed where she stood. Before she could call out the order again, bats rushed up from the pit, flying towards her and Deneg.

They surrounded them, making it impossible to see the next pillar. She tried to knock them away, grabbing her wand as she struggled to keep her feet. Arrows pierced some of the nearby bats and they dropped back into the pit, taking the arrows with them. Mallory crouched on the pillar, randomly casting ice shard in the hope she hit some. Her fingers wrapped around the edge of the pillar and she remained crouched, hitting out at the bats with her wand, unable to always cast a spell with how they flew around her.

"You ready?" Deneg called out.

"No." How did he expect her to do anything with how the bats flew around them?

"We only have to reach the ledge," Deneg said. "Then they'll go. So call it."

A bat scratched her cheek with razor-sharp claws and she breathed in sharply at the pain. "Okay." She tensed, ready to jump for the ledge. And this time it would be a jump. "One, two, jump." She threw herself forward, shielding her face with her empty hand, colliding with the far wall. She leaned against it, the sound of screeching bats fading. She didn't look, staying pressed against the wall as she tried not to think about the pit she'd crossed. A grinding sound had her spinning to face the room. Pillars rose along the edges of the room to fill the gaps between those along the left and right walls.

Deneg opened the chest in the middle of the ledge.

"That's it? We did it?" Mallory came away from the wall. "We have the first key?"

Deneg held up a large, wrought iron key. "We have the first key."

"Does that mean we can move," Brodie asked.

Deneg put the key in his pocket. "The notebook didn't say."

"We can wait a few more minutes," Ryan said.

Mallory peered inside the chest. It was empty. "That was a large chest for a single key."

"The treasure is in the final room." Deneg headed for the ledge running along the right side of the room.

Mallory hurried along the ledge to the left. "So unless we get all four keys there won't be any treasure for us?"

"No." Deneg reached the far ledge, turning to face Mallory when she joined him. "Or at least nothing of extreme value."

Chapter Twenty-Four

Mallory started to tell Deneg he should have shared all the details with them, but decided it didn't really matter because they'd have helped Deneg raise the money to rescue his brother anyway. She turned to Ryan. "What's the time?"

"One thirty." Ryan returned the pocket watch to his belt pouch.

"Are you sure?" It had felt far longer than twenty minutes to her.

Ryan grinned. "Yeah, I'm sure." He turned to Deneg. "Can we get off the tiles now?"

Deneg nodded, heading out of the room to wait for them in the corridor.

Mallory was the last one out and she gave the room one more look over her shoulder before she stepped out and closed the door. They had another three rooms to face. She tried not to sigh.

Ryan slipped his hand in hers, stepping close. "You okay?"

She nodded. "Yeah, but the next pit someone else can cross."

Ryan chuckled. "Deal."

"Aww, that's unfair," Brodie exclaimed.

"What is unfair?" Deneg stopped in front of the door at the end of the short corridor that had been on the left as they came out of the pit and pillar room.

Ryan chuckled. "I'm going to assume he's talking about the XP Callum, Danni and I earned from shooting bats."

"I would have lost my throwing knives if I'd attacked them," Brodie said. "I don't have a heap of spares like you do with the arrows."

"We don't have many spare now." Callum handed arrows to Ryan and Danae to replace the ones they'd lost, slipping several into his own quiver. "We now only have eight spare. We used up eight of them in that last room. I hope we'll be able to collect what arrows we use in the next room."

"You should be able to do that," Deneg said. "But before you go in this room, I need to explain what has to be done since there won't be time for explanations once we're in there."

"I hope is not another pit," Mallory said.

"It's a lesser demon," Deneg said.

"That doesn't sound too bad," Brodie said. "Lesser has to be better, right?"

Danae laughed softly. "If only it worked like that. Lesser means they're more beast than sentient."

"What does that mean in terms of attack and health?" Callum asked.

"The notebook doesn't say how powerful the creature is," Deneg said. "It only tells how to fight it."

Brodie's expression brightened. "We'll gain XP from a fight?"

"Sounds like it's going to be a boss fight," Ryan said.

Mallory studied Deneg, but nothing about his expression gave away what they had to face. "How do we fight the lesser demon?"

"To the right of the door is a tile you need to stand on to activate the opening to a pool of weapon poison specifically designed to take down this particular lesser demon. Once your weapons are dipped in the poison, two people will need to go to the middle of the room where there are two pillars, one on the left and one on the right. Standing on these two pillars deactivates the spell preventing the lesser demon from taking damage. Each time it loses twenty-five percent of its health, it summons minions to protect it. If you take too long taking out the minions, they begin to heal the lesser demon," Deneg said.

"That doesn't sound too bad," Ryan said. "Callum can keep the pool of poison open, Mallory and Emica can stand on the pillars while Danni, Brodie and I stay near the poison and attack with ranged weapons. Then when the minions spawn, Callum can continue to attack the boss while the rest of us work on getting rid of the minions."

Brodie reached for the door handle. "So we can do this room now?"

Deneg shifted to prevent Brodie from opening the door. "It's a wonder you're still alive with the way you always want to rush ahead."

"I thought you were in a hurry," Brodie said.

Worried about her brother, Mallory took several steps towards him as she glanced around the group. "Is everyone ready?" When they agreed, she faced Deneg. "We're ready. You can step out of the way."

Deneg met her gaze. "Your spells will have no effect against the lesser demon. Only attacks from weapons dipped in the poison will damage it."

"But my spells will work on the minions, won't they?" Mallory asked.

"Yes." Deneg held her gaze a moment longer

before he turned and opened the door, entering the room and stepping out of the doorway.

Mallory took a second to scan the room before she ran to the pillar on the left, scrambling up on it. The pillar was approximately waist high and sank at least ten centimetres into the floor as she put her weight on it. Across the room from her, Emica did the same. A seven foot tall demon with broad shoulders, dark leathery wings and oxen like horns on his head was between them, a glowing red runic circle on the tiles below him. The moment Emica was on the second pillar, the light of the runic circle faded and went out.

Three arrows and two throwing knives struck the demon and he roared, chains around his ankles and attached to iron rings in the floor preventing him from reaching any of them. Molten rocks formed in his hands and he launched them at Danae who threw herself to the side.

Mallory spotted Deneg near the doorway, staying well back from the fight. "If you're not planning to attack, you could stand on the pillar so I can use my sword."

Deneg raced across the room, stepping up onto the pillar as Mallory jumped off. "If he throws that molten rock at me, I won't be standing here waiting for it."

She had no idea what to reply. Could only hope

that the demon focused on those who attacked. Drawing her sword, she dipped it in the pool of poison, her blade looking no different.

Callum returned his spyglass to its holster. "This could take us a while. He had a hundred and forty health when we came in and we've only managed to get him down to a hundred and nineteen health after one attack."

Mallory ran towards the demon as everyone attacked again. Before she could reach him, he was surrounded by eight skeletal figures, leathery skin sunken in around bones. They whirled slings around, flinging iron slingshot at them. One hit her and she breathed in sharply as it took four health from her.

"Focus on the minions," Ryan called out.

Mallory was already working on the minion closest to her, having drawn her wand. She needed to attack it four times with fireball to take it out. The next one she attacked with ice shard, only needing to attack it twice with the spell's bonus against demonic creatures. The rest were sprawled across the floor before she had a chance to attack them. Hoping there was enough weapon poison on her sword, she slipped her wand back in the loop on her belt and ran towards the lesser demon. She had no idea if her attack made any difference. Not having any way to tell, she spun and raced back to the pool of weapon poison. Before she reached it, twelve minions spawned. They were the same skeletal figures as before.

This time, Mallory used ice shard against the first one she attacked, able to take out another one and help with a third and fourth. The rest were down before she could attack them.

"This fight better not last too much longer," Brodie said. "I've only got sixteen throwing knives left and I'm not about to collect them while we're in a fight."

"We'll be out of arrows if it goes on too long." Ryan dipped an arrow in the weapon poison before firing it at the lesser demon that roared and struggled to escape his chains, regularly throwing molten rock at them.

"I've helped out with a couple of the minions," Callum said. "In between attacking the boss. That should help with the arrow situation a bit."

Chapter Twenty-Five

Mallory dipped her sword in the weapon poison and managed to attack the lesser demon before a third lot of minions spawned. She breathed in sharply when she was struck by two lots of slingshot, stumbling as she avoided another hit. It took a moment for her to count up how many minions had spawned. Sixteen. They were well and truly outnumbered.

Brodie went down under an attack from four of the minions, Fang barking frantically.

Fear raced through Mallory. They had two more keys to find after this one. Brodie couldn't afford to lose all his lives. She used up her mana to reanimate three of the corpses. A quick check on everyone's health showed they would be fine. Especially since the minions only did four damage at a time. They all should have enough health to survive the rest of the battle. She'd no sooner finished thinking that when

Ryan's health dropped by ten, the lesser demon managing to hit him with one of his attacks.

"Focus on the lesser demon," Deneg called out. "His attacks are becoming more frenzied."

Mallory was surrounded. There was no way she could reach the weapon poison. "Someone else will have to attack him."

"I can help Callum," Danae said.

Mallory cast ice shard at one of the minions Brodie fought. She couldn't help thinking about the essence crystals in her satchel. Should she use one? Yet they hadn't even made it halfway. How could they manage the rest of the dungeon if she needed to use one so soon? Before she could voice her concerns, the lesser demon vanished in a burst of flames, leaving behind a large, wrought iron key and a mask, the last couple of minions vanishing with him.

"Hell yeah." Brodie, who'd been closest, picked up the key and mask, slipping the key into his belt pouch before raising the mask to his face with a grin. "How cool is this?"

Mallory started to check her journal since there was a notification in the corner of her vision.

Danae took a step towards Brodie, hand half raised. "Brodie-" She broke off when the mask made contact with his face. It changed state, becoming semi solid as it slid across most of his face to create a deep red, leathery cover.

Mallory stared at her brother, the notification remaining unchecked. "Will that be a problem?" She dreaded to think what sort of trouble he'd discovered this time.

Brodie tentatively touched the mask, only his jaw, mouth and eyes visible. "How do I get it off?"

"It's demonic," Deneg said. "There'll be a word to say that will deactivate it."

"How do I figure out what the word is?" Brodie asked.

"It's usually on the inside of the mask written in demonic runes," Danae said.

Brodie tugged at the edge of the mask. "It's stuck?"

"I'm going to assume this will be a problem," Ryan said dryly.

"Yeah, unless you can find a demon who can deactivate it." Emica laughed. "Maybe you'll think twice about touching things if you don't know what they are."

"I doubt it," Ryan said.

Mallory took several steps towards her brother. "There's no way you can go home wearing that."

Brodie lowered his hands, a grin slowly forming. "You're right. We're stuck here."

"We can keep looking until we find a demon who'll help you remove it," Danae said.

Brodie shook his head. "I like it. Do you think it'll do anything?"

"It should have some level of defence," Emica said.

Deneg gestured towards the bodies scattered around the area. "Did you want to gather resources from the demonic revenants before we move on?" He nodded towards a door at the far end of the room.

Ryan crouched by one of the skeletal figures. "There's a glow at the chest."

Danae took a step back from him. "Shrivelled hearts might be worth a lot, but you have the chance of getting a putrid heart from demonic revenants."

Callum joined them. "Is that as bad as it sounds?"

"Worse," Emica said. "You get that stench on you and you're stuck with it for days."

"What are the percentages?" Callum asked.

"Maybe five percent," Danae said.

"How much do they sell for?" Brodie asked.

"Two hundred gold," Danae said. "Or thereabouts."

Brodie's mouth momentarily dropped open. "Two hundred?" When Danae nodded, he spoke again. "What are the chances of getting shrivelled hearts?"

"Approximately fifty percent," Danae said.

Mallory backed away. "Don't even think about me helping. Not for twice that gold."

"If there is a putrid heart, does that mean it will get on you?" Callum asked.

Danae shook her head. "If you're careful, and don't cut into it, it won't get on you."

"Can you see the difference between a shrivelled and a putrid one?" Ryan asked.

"The shrivelled ones are shrivelled," Emica said. "The putrid ones look diseased."

Brodie crouched by the demonic revenant Ryan remained beside. "Let me get my throwing knife out of it first." He drew the knife, looking down at his body that was being encased by a material the same as the mask. "Whoa. How cool is this?" He rose to his feet, stretching and moving about. "I have armour." He grinned, miming throwing his knife.

"It's given you a buff," Callum said. "Twenty percent less damage from fire based attacks. And a debuff. Minus five charisma."

Mallory studied her brother. His armour looked very much like what she'd expect for a rogue. "Would it be a set style of armour or does it conform to the wearer's class?"

"It could be either," Danae said.

Deneg gestured towards the demonic revenant

Ryan remained crouched beside. "Are you planning to gather resources or shall we continue to the next room?"

Ryan cut open the chest cavity and removed a shrivelled heart. "It looks mummified."

"At least it's better than the spider eyes," Mallory said. "No goo for starters."

Ryan chuckled. "There is that."

While Ryan and Callum gathered resources, Danae and Brodie collected ammunition and Mallory finally managed to check her journal notification. It was a CAS point. She healed herself as she went over everyone's stats. Brodie, Callum and Danae had all gained a CAS point. She also began healing them once she'd finished healing herself.

By the time Ryan and Callum had finished gathering resources, they had sixteen shrivelled hearts, had managed to avoid cutting into three putrid ones, had six slings and five bags of slingshot. Brodie was down to iron throwing knives, having replaced some of the steel ones he'd lost with the spare ones that had been in his satchel. He was two short to fill the slots in his vambraces. Ryan, Callum and Danae only had sixteen arrows left each.

Ryan finished putting the items in his backpack. "Maybe I should share my arrows out between the two of you." He looked from Callum to Danae. "I can use my sword."

"You might as well wait and see," Emica suggested. "Other than this room, we haven't had that many fights."

"We've lost a lot of arrows considering how few fights we've been in," Ryan said.

"If it comes to it, Callum and I can use slings," Danae said.

Ryan started to reach for his backpack. "Did you want one now?"

Danae shook her head. "I'll wait and see what's next. I should have enough arrows to get me through at least one more fight."

Deneg stood by the door on the far side of the room. "Does that mean we can solve the puzzle in the next room now?"

Brodie strode towards Deneg. "I hope there's something to fight. I want to see what my new armour does."

Chapter Twenty-Six

Mallory hurried after her brother. "You can't keep the mask on forever."

"It's not like I know the word to take it off." Brodie grinned fleetingly. "I guess that means we have to stay here. Or at least I do."

"There is no way I can go home without you. How would I explain that to Mum?" Mallory followed her brother through the doorway, Deneg having opened the door.

"That I ran away from home? Or I'm not going to Dad's."

Mallory stayed behind her brother, the corridor only wide enough to walk single file. They turned left into the next corridor, another door in front of them. "Once we finish here, we're going to find a way to remove your mask."

Brodie glared at his sister, but didn't comment.

Deneg, who'd been looking through his leather bound notebook, looked up from it. "This is the easiest room. A wall runs down the middle, not quite reaching the ceiling, and there are drawers set in the walls of the room on either side of it. You need to compare the runes on all the drawers opposite each other and only open the ones that match."

Brodie tried to reach for the doorhandle. "That does sound easy."

Deneg brushed Brodie's hand away. "Not so fast. If you open the wrong drawers, you'll be attacked by a fireball. And if you don't find all the matching drawers quickly enough, the puzzle resets. Same happens when you open the wrong drawer."

"How much health does a fireball hit for?" Mallory asked.

"Five," Deneg said. "But it does strike both people trying to open the drawers."

"Now can we go in there?" Brodie asked.

Deneg swung the door open, stepping inside and out of the way so everyone else could enter. "Do not touch the drawers until we're ready to start."

Mallory eyed the wall that ran down the centre of the room, starting a metre and a half from the entrance. On either side of it, she could see rows of drawers running down the length of the room. "How long do we have to open the matching ones?" She went further into the room, counting up the amount of rows and columns. Eight across and six down.

Ryan took out the pocket watch. "I can time it."

"Who will help me open them?" Deneg asked.

"Me," Brodie said. "This looks pretty cool. Will there be anything in the drawers? Like treasure or something?"

Deneg shrugged, heading towards the left hand side of the room. "Let me know when you're in position. The time won't start until we open one of the drawers."

"Okay, I'm in front of the first row." Brodie looked the drawers up and down. "My first one is a hook."

"What is the name of the letter?" Deneg asked.

Mallory joined her brother. "It's the letter C."

"Tell me all the letters going down the first column," Deneg said.

Mallory started to protest that she didn't know all the demonic runes. She smiled instead. "The demon really loved his horse."

Ryan chuckled. "He used the same letters again?"

"Yep." She read out the six letters in the first column.

"The second one and the bottom one match," Deneg said.

"Should I open them now?" Mallory asked.

"Read out the second column first," Deneg said. "That way we can figure out the first two columns without having to worry about the time."

Mallory automatically nodded, briefly smiling as she reminded herself of the wall running down the centre of the room. "Okay." She read out the second column.

"Third from the top," Deneg said. "Now we need to make sure we open these three drawers exactly the same time as each other. You call it."

"Same as before?" Mallory asked.

"Same as before," Deneg said.

"One, two, open." Mallory opened the first drawer, hoping Deneg did the same. She paused for a second, half expecting to be struck by a fireball. Nothing happened. She counted for the next two drawers.

"Read out the next column," Deneg said.

Mallory did as he said, opening the two drawers that he named, after counting first. They had two rows left when the drawers they'd opened began to close. She stepped back from the wall of drawers. "Did we do something wrong?"

"We ran out of time. We need to do it faster," Deneg said. "We'll read out the first three columns before we start opening drawers."

"What if we mess it up? I really don't want to be hit by a fireball." Mallory looked along the rows of drawers. "Is there a way to get more time?"

Ryan put the pocket watch back in his belt pouch. "You had five minutes."

Again Mallory looked along the length of the wall. "Another two minutes. At the most."

Callum gestured towards the wall. "What if Danni and I go to the other end and figure out the last two columns?"

"I could help," Brodie said. "I think I've got them figured now."

"Maybe you better sit this one out," Ryan suggested. "I recognise this handful of letters. Emica and I could do the first two columns." He faced Mallory. "That would only leave four columns for you and Deneg to sort out."

Mallory slowly nodded. "That sounds a lot easier." She faced the centre wall, even though she couldn't see Deneg through it. "Does it matter what order the drawers are opened in?"

"The notebook didn't say."

"Sounds like that notebook doesn't say much at all," Brodie muttered.

Mallory took a deep breath. The last thing she wanted was to be struck by a fireball, but it looked like it was a risk she'd have to take. "You've all got enough health to cope with losing five and I can heal us before we leave the room. We should give it a try."

Emica stood in front of the column closest to the door. "I'm ready."

There was a chorus of similar comments around the room and Deneg telling Danae to go first. Once the other two teams were sorted, he and Mallory figured out their first two columns.

Mallory rested a hand on the drawer she needed to open. "I'm ready."

"Call it," Deneg said.

She did, turning to Ryan once she'd finished calling her first two columns. "Your turn." She moved along to the third column while Ryan counted for his and Emica's drawers. As soon as he'd finished, she listed the runes on the column in front of her, opening them once they figured out which ones matched. After she'd done the next column, Danae counted down for the drawers her and Callum needed to open.

A grinding sound filled the room and they all turned to face the wall in the centre. It slowly lowered, revealing a niche in the far wall.

Danae, who was closest, took out the key along with two potion vials. She dropped the key into her belt pouch and held the vials out to Mallory. "You are going to want these."

Taking the potion bottles, Mallory read the handwritten labels. A smile slowly formed. "Eight weeks. Eight weeks each."

"Eight weeks of what?" Brodie demanded.

Mallory's smile became a grin as she held up the potion vials. "Timeless potions."

Brodie victory punched the air. "Hell yeah. That's better than XP."

Ryan chuckled. "You sure?"

Brodie nodded. "Yeah. We're going to need more of them since we're not going home."

Chapter Twenty-Seven

Mallory carefully put the vials in her satchel. "We are going home. We'll find someone to help us with that mask."

Emica stepped in front of Brodie. "Do this." She placed her fingertips across her cheekbones and her thumbs along the edge of her jaw. She waited for him to copy her before she spoke. "Now just keep saying random words until you find the right one."

Brodie quickly lowered his hands. "That will work?"

Mallory pointed a finger at her brother. "If it does, you better start working your way through a dictionary."

Brodie took a step back from his sister. "Aww, come on, Mal. That'd take me forever."

"Probably because he's never opened one before," Ryan said.

"I don't need them. The computer tells me when I spell something wrong," Brodie said. "And tells me how to spell it."

"I've read one," Callum said.

"You can buy them in Shadhurst," Emica said.

"I don't want to wait that long to sort this out," Mallory said.

Deneg gestured towards the door they'd entered the room by. "We've got one more room left."

Brodie hurried towards the door. "I hope there's creatures to kill. I still want to try out my new armour." He absently patted Fang's head when she whined at him. "Something that uses fire based attacks."

Following her brother, Mallory slowly shook her head. "The point is to avoid being hit."

"Then how will I know if it works?" Brodie asked.

"It's armour," Emica said. "Of course it works."

"It could be broken," Brodie said.

"Then it wouldn't activate. Besides, it's demonic. They last decades, if not centuries before being completely broken," Emica said.

"How was I meant to know that?" Brodie demanded.

Deneg slipped past Brodie and Emica, leading the

way along the corridor and taking the first left. The short corridor led to another closed door.

"What do we have this time?" Callum asked.

"Demonic fleetfoot goblins," Deneg said.

"Goblins," Brodie exclaimed. "Hell yeah. Easy XP."

"Why have I got the feeling that demonic ones are tougher than normal and fleetfoot will add to the problem?" Ryan asked.

Emica grinned. "They're fast. About twice as tough as a normal goblin and really fast."

"We have to kill them and put together the tiles they're carrying to create a picture. Once all that is in place, we'll have the last key," Deneg said.

"How hard can they be?" Brodie asked. "Kill them, take the tile, make the picture and then we're done."

Callum eyed Deneg up and down. "What's the catch?"

"They respawn. Quicker the longer we take," Deneg said.

"What if we just keep them from the tiles once we kill all of them?" Mallory asked.

"They respawn under the tiles and cart one away as they rise from the floor," Deneg said.

Mallory stared at him, wanting to ask him if she'd heard correctly. But he looked serious. "I'm beginning to think the pit trap was easier than this one will be."

Deneg inclined his head. "Is everyone ready?"

"Will they attack?" Callum asked.

"The notebook didn't say," Deneg said.

Mallory took a deep breath, glancing around the group. When everyone nodded, or exclaimed enthusiastically in her brother's case, she faced Deneg. "We're ready." Yet she didn't feel like she was. Fleetfoot. How fast were they? Too fast for them to attack?

Deneg opened the door, hurrying inside. "Attack whichever ones you can. And shut the door behind you so none of them can escape.

Ryan, who was the last one in, closed the door as he drew his sword. "Okay, they're a lot faster than I expected. Especially considering they're carrying marble tiles."

Mallory held her wand, her gaze drawn to each of the goblins, their skin a red dark enough it was almost black. "They're too fast." She tried to count them, but they were even too fast for that.

"How many of them are there?" Brodie demanded. "And how are we meant to attack them?"

"Sixteen. One for each of the tiles." Deneg dashed across the room and attacked one of the goblins, snatching the tile from midair when the goblin vanished.

Mallory stared at him open-mouthed for a moment. "We don't have to grab the tile off them when they vanish, do we?"

Deneg placed the tile in the empty square in the middle of the room. "I don't know."

"Of course not," Brodie muttered. "That notebook only has half the information."

Mallory cast ice shard at one of the goblins, completely missing. "This is impossible."

Emica grinned. "Someone grab the tile when I take one out. Just in case the tiles can break." She shapeshifted, streaking across the room to attack one of the goblins. Ryan hurried after her, grabbing the tile when the goblin vanished.

Mallory tried to attack another one. Again she missed. Deneg took out another goblin and she wished they'd leave bodies behind so she could reanimate them. Maybe one of their own would have been able to catch them.

Callum lowered his bow. "We aren't fast enough. What about making us invisible so they don't see us coming?"

Mallory studied the goblins. "They're too unpredictable. Who would know which direction they were going in?" She slowly shook her head when two goblins almost collided with each other. "Actually, I don't think they know which direction they're going in."

Callum returned the spyglass to its holster. "We only need to get a couple of decent attacks in to take one out. They have fourteen health."

Mallory spotted one of the tiles, that Deneg and Ryan had put in the centre, rising. She cast ice shard at the goblin, quickly sending a second attack against it. The goblin vanished, the tile settling back into place.

Callum nodded towards the four tiles randomly placed in the centre area. "Looks like that might be the way to go. The majority of us keep them from respawning while Deneg and Emica take out the rest of them." He'd barely finished speaking when a goblin respawned underneath a tile. He fired an arrow at it, hitting it a few seconds before Mallory cast ice shard at it.

"What happens when most of them have been taken out and we can't keep up with them respawning?" Danae asked. "How are we meant to keep them from carrying the tiles away before we can finish the picture?"

Brodie darted forward and picked up the tile that

had been carried by a goblin Emica had taken out. "What I want to know is what the picture is." He stood in front of where the picture would go, holding the tile.

"It's the horse," Callum said. "One of the goblins is carrying around a tile that has a horse's leg on it."

"He must have really loved that horse." Brodie placed the tile in the space in the centre of the room.

Mallory attacked a goblin that respawned under a tile, two arrows also piercing it. "This is taking too long. There's no way we can complete this at the rate we're taking them out."

Ryan collected a tile dropped by a goblin Deneg had killed. "We're not fast enough to catch them. Maybe if I could do traps, it'd make a difference. I'd put more points in hunting, but we don't have anything here to make the traps from."

Mallory stared at Ryan, a smile slowly forming. "A trap."

Ryan nodded. "But I don't have the resources to make any even if I did add more points into hunting."

"Lightning trap. I could put some of them down." She glanced from Emica to Deneg. "Once I add everyone to our party so they don't trigger them."

Deneg dashed across the room to hold out his hand. "How much does your trap hit for?"

"Thirteen." She added Deneg to the party, surprised to find Emica at her side when she let go of his hand. She rested her hand on the kitsune's head, adding her too.

"You might have to use the essence crystals to put enough traps down," Callum said.

Mallory shook her head. She didn't want to use the crystals unless she absolutely had to. "I can put six down. My mana isn't as slow to regen these days." Not that she was completely happy yet with the rate it regened. She still wanted to increase it.

Callum drew Mallory back when she took a step away from the centre area. "I've been watching them. There's a bit of a pattern to their movements. There are points they regularly cross. It's not much of a pattern since their movements are mostly random, but it should help you trap some of them."

Chapter Twenty-Eight

Mallory watched the goblins, nodding when she saw what Callum meant. Before she'd placed all six of her traps, two of them were triggered. The first one that was triggered, Danae shot the goblin to finish him off and the second time Callum shot the goblin. Before Mallory could place her sixth trap, a goblin respawned and she attacked it instead.

Another one of Mallory's traps was triggered and she attacked the goblin that was momentarily still. He vanished. "This is working." She turned to Callum. "Thanks for pointing out there was a bit of a pattern."

Callum started to speak, needing to attack a respawning goblin instead. Once the goblin had vanished, he turned to Mallory. "Someone needs to start arranging the tiles so they display the picture."

"Brodie has the lowest attack stats," Ryan said.

Mallory laughed. "I'd rather not be here all

morning. Have you ever seen Brodie try and do a jigsaw puzzle? Even a simple one." She cast another two traps since she'd regained enough mana.

"Everyone else is doing more than attacking everything possible so they can gain extra XP," Ryan said.

"I can do the puzzle," Callum said. "I can put my bow on the floor beside me. It won't be that hard to pick it up and help attack any goblins that respawn."

Mallory attacked another goblin that respawned beneath a tile, lifting it off the floor as it rose upwards. "Do what you can, Callum. We've got this under control for now. Hopefully it'll stay that way until you get the chance to finish the picture." Another goblin rose beneath a tile and she attacked it. Before it was down, another one respawned. Both times Brodie and Danae helped her take them out.

"You might want to move quicker than that." Ryan drew back an arrow, aiming it at a goblin. "They seem to be respawning faster."

Callum shifted one of the tiles. "I can't go any faster than I'm already going. The picture seems to have a lot of greenery in it so I don't know if each of them have their own location or can go anywhere."

Mallory glanced at the tile Callum held, needing to attack another goblin before she could say anything.

She didn't get the chance to speak. Danae beat her to it.

"There's a small amount of black on the edge of that one." Danae pointed to the tile. "It might be part of the horse."

Mallory tried not to focus on how little mana she had left. "Leave them till last if you have to. Just keep putting the picture together before all the goblins respawn." Another two respawned as she spoke.

Brodie threw knives at each goblin. "At least it's good XP. And I need all the XP I can get."

Ryan ran forward to attack a goblin that respawned. "Move quicker, Callum."

Emica joined them, in human form, carrying a tile. "How is the picture coming along?"

Deneg came over with the last tile, dropping it into place before he attacked a goblin as it respawned. "They'll start to respawn quicker now we've taken all the tiles from them."

Mallory cast ice shard at one of the goblins as it respawned. "Hurry, Callum." Another respawned and she cast ice shard at it too before she placed two lightning traps down. "I'm going to run out of mana at this rate."

"I'm running low on arrows," Danae said.

"You can have mine," Ryan offered. "My sword does more damage than my hunting bow."

"I'll help with the picture." Emica shifted one of the tiles.

"Why don't we all help with the picture and then it'll be done quicker?" Brodie asked.

"What about the ones that respawn?" Mallory attacked another goblin, instantly needing to attack yet one more the moment that one had vanished. Once again both Brodie and Danae helped her with the goblins. "We can barely keep up with them."

"Nearly finished sorting it out," Callum said. "And it's definitely a horse. A demonic horse."

Emica shifted one of the tiles. "There–" She broke off when she noticed that two goblins had respawned. "We're never going to get this done."

Mallory took out a goblin, with Callum's help. A glance across the picture showed that another goblin had already respawned. "There has to be a way to stop them respawning."

"All we need is a few extra seconds without another one respawning." Callum fired at yet another goblin, Danae helping him with it. Once again, another goblin respawned before they'd taken out the first one.

Mallory opened her journal and checked through

all her spells. Nothing would help. She needed more spells. A lot more spells.

Callum held out his hand to Ryan. "Give me the pocket watch."

Ryan handed it over before attacking a goblin.

"Leave the next one," Callum said.

"What if it runs away with the tile?" Brodie demanded.

"Keep it in place." Callum looked between the tiles and the pocket watch.

"How do we keep it in place?" Emica asked. "They want to run the moment they respawn."

"I need some sort of spell to freeze things into place," Mallory said.

"I wonder if the mage back at camp has a spell like that." Ryan dived onto the tile, the goblin staggering and remaining in place. He grinned. "Looks like we've found a way to keep them from running around the room."

Brodie dived onto the next tile held by a goblin. "Not sure how long this will hold them in place."

Callum continued to look between the tiles and the pocket watch. "One more and then we take the three of them out at once. Mallory, you and Danni can take out the first one that respawned, Emica can help me with the second one and Deneg can take out the third one. Do it the-" He broke off, barely pausing a second. "Now." He shoved the pocket watch in his belt pouch and grabbed the bow.

Mallory cast ice shard at the first goblin, the creature vanishing before she could attack it again, an arrow having gone straight through it and across the room. "Now what?"

"We take out the next thirteen that respawn and then we should have enough time for the tiles to fall into place before any others respawn," Callum said.

Ryan grinned. "Nice plan."

"What if the increased respawn rate prevents that from working?" Deneg asked.

"That's why I did three." Callum took out the pocket watch again. "We just need to keep taking them out each time they respawn."

Mallory attacked one of the two goblins that had respawned, the tile falling back into place. Two more were taken out before she had a chance to attack them, but the forth she managed to get a hit in on it. "I keep feeling like I might lose count."

"Don't worry," Callum said. "I'm keeping track."

Chapter Twenty-Nine

Mallory started to attack another goblin, lowering her wand when two arrows took it out.

One of the arrows landed beneath the tile, preventing it from sitting flat, and Ryan lifted the corner of the tile so he could take the arrow. Stepping back, he held it out to Danae, waiting until she took it before he spun and attacked a goblin with his sword.

Mallory lost track of how many goblins they'd taken out. It was hard when she was focused on fighting them rather than keeping count. She was about to ask Callum how much longer, when he spoke.

"Four more to take out before we reach the gap we created by holding off on taking out the three." Callum put the pocket watch in his belt pouch and readied his bow.

Mallory cast ice shard at the one that respawned

while Callum spoke. She went to attack one of the other three that had respawned when Danae took one out. Her arrow kept the tile from falling into place and Mallory threw herself forward, pulling the arrow out from under the tile. It settled into place as the last two goblins vanished, the picture momentarily glowing. She lay on the floor where she'd landed, staring at the key in the middle of the tiles. "We did it?" Coming up into a crouch, she scooped up the key and slipped it inside her belt pouch, grinning as she rose to her feet. "We did it." The relief that washed over her made her stand still for a moment. She'd begun to think it an impossible task.

She stared at the tiles. It was a horse. He had flames in his eyes and more flames rose up around his hooves, smoke curling from his nostrils. Instead of the typical coat of a horse, his skin was black and leathery with dark red flame-like socks and a red blaze. He stood in a forest clearing, his head up and his ears pricked. "I can't believe we did it."

"It took forever," Brodie muttered.

Callum glanced at the pocket watch before he handed it back to Ryan. "Half an hour."

"See," Brodie said. "Forever." He headed for the door. "Now where is the treasure room? We've collected our ammo, I've managed to level up again and we have the four keys."

"I levelled up too," Emica said.

Mallory hurried after her brother. "Wait up. How do you feel?"

"What do you mean?" Brodie glanced over his shoulder as he stepped into the corridor.

She managed to grab hold of his hand, frowning when she found no illness. "You're well."

Brodie dragged his hand out of her grip. "Of course I am. Why wouldn't I be?"

"The goblin ale," Danae said.

"I keep telling all of you that I'm okay," Brodie said.

"Maybe it'll take longer," Emica suggested.

Mallory shook her head. "No. If he had goblin blight, I'd be able to detect it, even if he wasn't showing symptoms yet. He's perfectly healthy."

Emica looked Brodie up and down, stopping in the corridor in front of him as she did, blocking his way. "Are you sure you're not part goblin?"

Brodie glared at her. "I'm more human than you."

Emica laughed. "I wouldn't want to be human."

Brodie's cheeks flushed slightly. "That's not what I meant." He glanced past Emica. "Are we going to see what the treasure is?"

Emica stepped to the side, waving him ahead of her. "Lead the way, Goblin Boy."

With another glare for Emica, Brodie turned left when Deneg called out the direction.

Mallory removed the extras from the party as she waited for Danae, glancing over her shoulder. "Are you sure all people end up with goblin blight from drinking goblin ale?"

"I've never heard of anyone who hasn't," Danae said. "Some races have a natural immunity, but not humans. Are you sure there isn't anyone in your family who was something other than human?"

Mallory studied her brother's back as she headed along the corridor well behind him. Surely she would have known if one of her ancestors had been something other than human. "Positive. I guess it's like Mum has always said. Brodie has a cast iron stomach and can eat anything without getting sick."

Brodie glanced over his shoulder before he turned right at the end of the corridor. "I heard that."

Mallory grinned at her brother, hurrying after him to see he'd picked up his pace as he headed towards a closed door. A shiver of excitement raced through her. No other corridors branched off from this one. The only direction they could go was through that door. They were about to find out what a demon's treasure looked like.

Brodie eyed the lock. "How do we know which key to use in these two locks? And where do we use the other two keys?"

Deneg glanced at his satchel, not taking the notebook out. "It doesn't say. Only that we need to use two keys on two separate doors to reach the treasure room."

"Of course it doesn't say," Brodie muttered.

Callum shifted Brodie to the side, examining the two locks. "Either there's a single scratch at the bottom of this lock and two at the bottom of the other one, or they mean something." He held out his hand to Brodie. "Let me see your key."

Brodie took out his key, examining it. "I think there are three marks on the part that sticks out."

"The bit," Callum corrected.

Brodie shrugged, letting Callum take the key.

Callum examined the key. "What do the other ones have on them?"

Mallory had been taking her key out of her belt pouch before Callum had asked. "Two marks on the bit."

"I have the first one," Deneg said.

"I've got the fourth one." Danae held it out to Callum.

Callum put it, along with the third one, in his belt pouch.

Deneg stepped close to Callum, putting the key in the lock, turning it before moving closer to Callum as he made space for Mallory in front of the door.

She inserted the key, turning it before trying the handle. Nothing happened. She turned the key in the other direction. Again nothing. She tried turning the key Deneg had inserted. The door remained locked. "What am I doing wrong?"

"It might be like all the rest of the puzzles," Callum suggested.

Deneg stared at the door for a moment before taking out the key he'd inserted. "I should have thought about it being another shadow game."

"Shadow game?" Callum asked.

Deneg gestured towards the door. "The puzzles demons like to use. Ones where you have to shadow another person for them to work." He turned to Mallory. "Take your key and we'll insert and turn them together."

"Okay." She removed the key, looking to Deneg. "Want me to count?"

Deneg held the key in front of the lock. "When you're ready."

"What if it's booby trapped?" Callum asked.

"The notebook didn't mention any," Deneg said.

Mallory held her key in front of the lock. "We have to try something. We can't stand here all morning." Taking a deep breath, she glanced at Deneg before returning her attention to the door. "One, two, insert." She pushed the key in, turning it as soon as it was in place. The click of a lock filled the silence. She reached for the handle.

Before Mallory could open the door, Deneg grabbed hold of her hand. "You're as bad as your brother."

She drew her hand from his light grip. "You said it wasn't booby trapped."

"I said the door wasn't booby trapped." Deneg gestured towards the door. "Inside is another matter."

Brodie groaned. "What now? When do we get our treasure?"

"Only step on the tiles that spell out the name of the horse. They aren't in any order. Just don't step on a tile if it has a rune that's not in 'Scorch' or it will activate a trap," Deneg said.

"What sort of trap?" Brodie asked.

Deneg shrugged. "The notebook didn't say."

"So we can go in there now?" Brodie asked.

Deneg swung the door open. "I'll meet you on the other side of the room." He raced lightly across the tiles, reaching the door on the other side of the room in seconds.

Brodie blocked the doorway. "How are we meant to cross this?"

Chapter Thirty

Standing on the tip of her toes, Mallory peered over her brother's shoulders. "A pity you don't have more points to put into dexterity." She stared at the tiles. Someone was sure to set off the trap. The tiles were fifteen centimetres square. Her gaze was drawn to her brother's boots. Enough space if he managed to stand directly on each tile and tip toe his way across the room.

"What about Fang?" Danae asked. "She'll have to stay out here."

Brodie stepped back from the doorway and picked up the wolf cub, nearly tripping over his sister in the process. "I'm not about to leave her behind."

Mallory eyed Fang, who'd gained well over a kilogram since they'd found her. "Maybe you should let someone else carry her."

"Why?" Brodie asked.

Mallory looked from the tiles to her brother's feet. "There's not much space to stand."

"Want me to carry her?" Danae asked.

Brodie shook his head. "I can manage. I've got points in dexterity these days."

Mallory wanted to order her brother to let someone else carry Fang. Anyone else. But she could see by his expression that he wasn't about to let anyone carry her. "Who's going next?"

"I will." Emica stepped lightly on a tile, making her way across the floor, weaving from side to side as she chose where to stand. Reaching the other side of the room, she faced them, standing beside Deneg as she beckoned them over.

"Did you want to go next?" Mallory asked her brother.

He shook his head. "Someone else can go."

Callum went next, followed by Danae and then Brodie. Mallory watched as her brother crossed the room, holding her breath when he wobbled at one stage. Her breath escaped in a rush as he reached the other side.

"You want to go next?" Ryan asked.

Mallory nodded, glancing across the tiles to figure out the best path to take. Several times the distance between suitable tiles was nearly too far and she found herself wobbling, worried each time that she'd be the one to set off the trap. Reaching the far side, she faced Ryan, smiling at him.

"We should open the door while we wait," Brodie said. "That way we can see what the treasure is the moment he gets over here."

Callum took out the two keys. "Who wants to shadow me?"

Deneg took the key, meeting Callum's gaze. "I would love to."

Mallory wanted to warn Callum away from Deneg. She didn't want to see him hurt again. Instead, she lowered her gaze, not wanting to see the look in his eyes at Deneg's words.

"Let me know when you're ready," Callum said.

"I'm ready when you are," Deneg said softly.

"One, two, insert," Callum said.

At the sound of the lock clicking, Mallory's gaze was drawn to the keys. The door swung open and a rumbling sound started up behind her. She spun to face Ryan.

He ran towards her, jumping from tile to tile, many of the tiles falling away. "The moment you opened the door, the floor started to fall away."

Callum tried to drag Mallory into the next room with him. "Hurry. Before all the floor goes."

She drew out of his grip, trying to ignore the tiles to the left and right of her that were slowly disappearing. "What about Ryan?"

"Get out of the doorway so he can get through it," Callum said.

She stepped back through the doorway, ignoring the journal notification in the corner of her vision. Everyone else had already passed through into the treasure room. She barely spared them a glance, her attention focused on Ryan, her hands clasped tightly together. She wanted to call out to him and beg him to hurry. She remained silent, not wanting to distract him.

Ryan stumbled as a tile gave way beneath him. He went down, pushing himself up with a hand as he gained his footing. He threw himself the last bit of the way, colliding with Mallory, his arms wrapping around her. "Are you okay?"

Her arms tightened around him. "I'm the one who should be asking that. I thought you were going to fall."

"You and me both. I guess no one was meant to have been out on the tiles when the door was opened." Ryan looked over Mallory's shoulder. "I bet your notebook didn't tell you that."

Mallory looked towards Deneg in time to see him

shake his head. Her attention was caught by the treasure room. It was five metres wide and three metres long with a door in the far left corner. None of that held her attention, other than to make her hope the door was another exit since the one behind her was now a bottomless pit. "What is this place?" Her gaze was drawn between the open chests, an ornate bed in the right hand corner, a table set with gold crockery and cutlery and a solid gold statue on a stone plinth that was embedded with jewels that reflected the light from the ornate lanterns hanging on either side of it. The statue was about thirty centimetres tall and was of a slim, willowy woman holding a sword.

"A demon's treasure," Deneg said.

Mallory kept one arm around Ryan, gesturing towards the bed with the other hand. "Then why is there a bed in here?"

"It's made from demonic timber," Deneg said. "And from the runes carved into it, I'd say it has protective spells to keep those who sleep in it safe."

Brodie picked up one of the gold goblets. "How are we meant to get everything out of here?"

"The bed should come apart." Danae pointed to large timber pegs slotted into each of the corner posts of the bed. "Knock those out and it should come apart into easily transported sections."

"Good thing you sold the table and chairs," Emica said.

Ryan chuckled. "Not that we'll be able to fit these ones on for certain."

"We need to bring the wagon closer," Brodie said.

"We need to find a way out of here." Emica indicated the way they'd entered the treasure room. "It's not like we can go back out that way."

Deneg picked up the statue, taking a cloth sack out of his satchel. "The door in the far corner leads out of here, but once we go through the next door, there's no way to open it from the other side once it's closed." He slipped the statue into the sack, putting it into his satchel, the sack covered top of it visible above the opening.

Mallory checked the journal notification that had appeared when she'd entered the treasure room. "I gained XP for a location?" She checked the stats of the rest of her party. They'd all gained experience points and Ryan had gained a CAS point. He was now one CAS point off character level three.

"A demonic treasure room is a unique location," Danae said.

"Who cares about the XP," Brodie said. "Look at all this treasure. We need to figure out how to get it out of here."

"I can stay here and keep the door open," Emica offered.

Chapter Thirty-One

"What if there are still creatures in the area?" Mallory asked Emica.

"I could stay too," Danae said.

"I can stay," Brodie hurriedly offered.

Emica grinned, glancing between Danae and Brodie before she turned to Mallory. "If it's all cleaned out, nothing should respawn in the time it takes you to bring the wagon back. Or the donkey and panniers if there's no space to get the wagon through. Not that I know how you're going to get everything out of the cave opening. There wasn't much space."

"I'm not leaving the table behind," Brodie protested.

"You plan to carry it out of here on your own?" Ryan asked.

Brodie turned to Callum. "You'd help me, wouldn't you?"

Callum laughed. "For someone who was never interested in RPGs, you've certainly got into the hoarding aspect of them."

Brodie glared at those who laughed, Danae and Emica looking confused. "I bet it's worth a fortune. It's demonic treasure."

"It might just be the items on it," Danae said. "The table may only be here for display purposes."

"How do I find out?" Brodie asked.

"You need to be a higher level in bartering," Danae said. "You can start assessing the value of things at level fifty-six."

"We need to earn CAS points faster." Brodie sighed heavily. "Okay. I'm putting three points in cooking. The only one that made a difference is level ten. You now have the ability to preserve food with salt." He paused a moment. "That should come in handy." Again he paused a moment. "The other thirteen points I'm putting in bartering. It didn't change things much. At level five I gained a ten percent chance of increasing the price received when selling multiple items. At level ten I gained a ten percent chance of receiving a discount when purchasing multiple items. They should help and I'll keep putting points into it."

"Did you want me to stay here?" Emica asked. "Alone. I don't need help."

Mallory glanced around the group, nodding when the majority nodded. She turned to Emica. "Thanks. That would be good."

"Why don't we carry it all to the cave so we don't have as far to cart it when we get back?" Brodie asked.

"In here it's protected in case someone tries to come along and steal it," Callum said. "Emica can close the door and be safe until we return."

"Should we pack everything before we leave?" Danae asked. "In case we need to leave here in a hurry when we return."

Ryan glanced around the room. "It shouldn't take too long." He picked up a gold plate.

"I hope not." Deneg helped pack up the treasure.

Ryan checked the time before he started helping. "We've got time to deal with this before sunrise and get you back to your coffin."

It took them longer than expected, Brodie insisting the furniture be pulled apart, including the table when they realised it could be dismantled. Deneg strode towards the exit. "I'll barely have enough time to return to my coffin."

Mallory followed him along a short corridor, a sharp right turn at the end. "Did you want to run ahead of us so you can be in the coffin before the sun rises?"

Deneg opened the door at the other end of the corridor. "I–" He broke off when four demonic dogs faced them, snarling.

Mallory grabbed her wand she'd put away while they'd packed up the treasure room. "Go. Leave them to us."

"They'll follow." Deneg threw himself at one of the dogs, attacking with a stiletto.

An arrow flew past Mallory and she cast ice shard at one of the dogs before entering the room.

"Emica, stay in the corridor. No matter what happens." Ryan glanced over his shoulder as he spoke, sword drawn as he followed Mallory into the long, narrow room.

Mallory cast ice shard at each of the dogs, stumbling out of the way as one of them ran towards her. An arrow distracted it and it faced Danae, snarling. Mallory cast ice shard again, backing away when the dog again fixed its attention on her.

Danae shot it. The dog growled, continuing to stalk towards Mallory. "I'd begun to think we could keep it undecided as to who to attack."

Before Mallory could cast ice shard again, Deneg tackled the creature to the floor, sinking fangs into its throat as he sank the stiletto into its chest. She looked away at the gush of blood, relieved to find the rest of the demonic dogs were dead. She lowered her hand, glancing over her shoulder at a sound.

Emica gave her a nod and a smile before closing the door to the corridor.

Mallory took a second look at the wall. "If I didn't know it was there, I'd have never known that door existed."

"I need to go." Deneg wiped the back of his sleeve across his mouth, removing most of the blood.

Brodie gestured towards the demonic dogs. "Aren't we going to search them?"

"They'll still be here for us to search when we return," Danae said.

"Then we'll do it once Deneg reaches safety." Callum opened the door leading from the room, peering through it. "We're at the start again. The room we entered after taking out the first lot of demonic dogs is ahead of us."

Deneg slipped past Callum. "I know the way."

Mallory hurried after the two of them, the rest of the party following her. "You really should run ahead." She cast magelight when she stepped out of the demonic dungeon and into the cave where they'd taken out the goblins.

"I think it's already too late." Deneg led the way to the entrance. He shrank back from the edge of the cave. "I can't go out there. The sun is about to rise over the horizon."

Mallory started to ask if there was something they could do, frowning instead. The narrow entrance had been broken open, rocks scattered across the ground, a clear pathway between them. And that wasn't the only difference. "I'm sure that tree wasn't so close to the cave when we came in." She eyed the distance between the damaged cave entrance and the tree.

Callum studied the tree. "I'm pretty sure it wasn't. But more importantly than that, what happened to the cave entrance? Should we be worried about a cave in?"

The tree raised limb like roots from the ground and moved ponderously forward. It lowered its head as it came near, eyes barely visible between the ridges of the bark. It slowly blinked. "Come, adventurers."

"We don't have time for this." Deneg made a sweeping motion towards the tree. "I need to find a way to return to my coffin." He glanced over his shoulder. "And you need to take your items somewhere safe. I have what I need to save my brother's life."

"Adventurers, we have need of you."

"We can't turn our backs on a wandering soul," Danae said. "They're a gentle race and would harm none. Unless of course they were threatened or someone harmed them."

The wandering soul gestured behind itself. "Help us, adventurers. My people die."

"What can kill a tree?" Brodie asked.

"Fire," Callum said. "Or at least I assume it'd kill one. I suppose things could always work differently here when it comes to how to kill sentient trees."

Deneg remained well back from the damaged exit. "I smell no smoke in the area."

"Fire kills trees, and wandering souls," Danae said. "But there are other things too. Like poison."

"Adventurers, please." The wandering soul stretched one of its lower limbs towards them. "Save us, adventurers."

Chapter Thirty-Two

Mallory looked from Deneg to the tree then back again. She wasn't sure how to help either of them. But the wandering soul sounded desperate and surely Deneg could wait until night to leave the cave. "What if you wait with Emica while we see what the wandering soul needs?"

"How long do you expect me to wait?" Deneg demanded. "My brother has already waited long enough. I don't even know if he still lives. Or, if he does live, for how much longer he'll be able to survive."

Again Mallory looked between Deneg and the wandering soul. She had no idea what to do. Why did everything have to be so urgent?

"We could split into two groups," Danae suggested. "Some of us can see what the wandering souls want and some of us can go after the wagon.

Or bring Bobbi back if there's no way to bring the wagon this close."

Brodie faced Danae. "Which do you want to do?"

Danae shrugged. "I don't mind."

Mallory eyed the trees in the direction they'd left the wagon. "I don't know if there is enough room for the wagon." She was pretty certain many of the trees had shifted, making it more unlikely that they'd be able to bring the wagon through to the cave entrance. "We might all have to help bring everything out of the dungeon."

The wandering soul lowered its head even further so it was eye to eye with Mallory. "We create a path, you come help, adventurers."

"That sounds like a good-" Brodie began.

Callum interrupted him. "What if it's something we can't help with? Does the path created for the wagon close up and it becomes stuck here?"

"Is that possible?" Brodie asked. "Would they do that to our wagon? What if it's something a human can't do?"

Danae stepped between Mallory and the wandering soul. "If you can make sure there's a pathway that allows us to bring our wagon to the cave entrance, and back to the road once we're finished, some of our party will go with you to see if there's a way in which we can help your people."

The wandering soul lowered its head even further, some of the leaves brushing the ground. It held it in that position for a couple of seconds before it slowly raised it. "I will tell my people." It shuffled back from the cave before sinking its roots into the ground, its eyes closing as it settled into place.

"What's it doing?" Brodie asked.

"Communicating with its people," Danae said.

Callum studied the wandering soul. "How does it do that?"

"Through the root systems of its and other plants." Danae remained in front of the wandering soul.

"What are we waiting for?" Brodie asked.

"An answer," Deneg said. "And it won't necessarily be any time soon. Its people that are dying may take years to die. It never specified."

"We have to stay here for years?" Brodie exclaimed.

Danae sighed. "I thought I'd covered everything. I should have mentioned a time frame too."

"I'll wait in the treasure room, well out of reach of the sun." Deneg retreated before anyone had a chance to comment.

There was a moment of silence before Ryan broke it. "How about some of us return to the wagon and bring Bob back so we can make a start on bringing things out of the dungeon? Even if we can bring the wagon all the way to the cave entrance, we're still going to need her to bring things out of the treasure room. There's no way we're getting a wagon inside the cave, even with the way the entrance has been widened."

"I can help you," Callum offered.

"I'll wait here for the wandering soul to finish talking to its people," Danae said.

"I'll stay here too," Brodie said.

Mallory grinned at her brother's comment, turning to Ryan. "Do you need me to help?"

Ryan crossed the distance between them, slipping his arms around her waist to tug her close. "We won't be long." His lips brushed across hers. "Anything you need me to bring back if we can only bring Bob?"

Mallory shook her head, her arms slipping around his neck. She tugged his head down for one more kiss before she let him go. "Be careful. Who knows what's in these woods." She tried not to think about the spiders that had been in the cave. Or the drop bears that had been amongst the trees set back from the beach out past Buckneth.

"Bring back some food," Brodie said. "Ninette said she was making stew for us."

"You can wait until we return to camp," Ryan said. "Unless we bring the wagon back. But I'm not carting stew around the countryside. It's not like we have a thermos or something to store it in."

"We should buy something like that," Brodie said.

Before Mallory could point out that they had more important things to buy, Callum spoke.

"You could always come back to the camp with us."

Brodie looked between Callum and Danae. "I'll wait here."

Mallory barely managed not to laugh at her brother and how disappointed he sounded, her gaze on Ryan, Callum and Smudge until they disappeared amongst the trees. She started to turn towards the cave entrance. "Someone should let Emica know what's happening."

"I'll tell her." Brodie took a step towards the cave entrance, looking from Danae to Mallory. "Don't go anywhere." He glanced at the wandering soul. "Even if the wandering soul wakes up."

"It's not sleeping," Danae called out after Brodie, who hurried into the cave.

Brodie gave a half wave over his shoulder, Fang at his side keeping pace with him.

Mallory waited until her brother was out of sight

before she glanced at the wandering soul. "Do you really think it'll take years?"

Danae shrugged. "I don't know. It's always possible, but it sounded more urgent than that with how it insisted we go with it."

"It didn't sound at all urgent to me." Mallory thought of the long, drawn out tone the wandering soul had used. "If anything, it sounded the opposite of urgent."

Danae briefly smiled. "I've talked to wandering souls before. It sounded urgent."

Mallory studied the wandering soul, still not certain Danae was right. "Okay." A sound had her spinning to face the cave entrance.

Brodie came running out of the darkness, the duplication paper held aloft. "Hisoki sent a message." He came to a stop beside Danae.

Mallory reached for the piece of paper, lowering her hand when her brother drew it out of her reach. "What did he say? Have you told Emica?"

Brodie nodded. "She was the one who asked me to check if he'd sent a message. He asked around about Rass. Him and Zorlla are in Shadhurst and Rass has been asking about us. He found out that Rass believes we're from Buckneth and has sent someone there to keep watch for our return."

"We can't go back to Buckneth?" Mallory asked.

At the same time, Danae asked, "Do we need to go to Buckneth?"

Brodie opened the piece of paper, holding it out to Danae who handed it to Mallory after a glance at it. His gaze remained on the piece of paper as his sister read over the contents. "We have to go back there. How else are we going to get directions to the nest? Whatever we earn from this dungeon we need for gear and getting to Merrow. We won't always be lucky enough to find someone who has a notebook with the puzzle answers for other dungeons."

"It's usually only demonic dungeons that have shadow puzzles," Danae said.

"And lots of treasure." Brodie returned the piece of paper to his belt pouch when Mallory handed it over.

"We'll have to tell everyone else and vote on it once we all know what's happened," Mallory said.

"I'm not about to-" Brodie broke off when the wandering soul opened its eyes and looked at Danae.

"I have spoken to my people. We will meet your terms if at least two of you come with me to see my people."

"Is this a matter that can be dealt with in a day?" Danae asked.

The wandering soul nodded, a shiver of movement

running through its leaves. "It is possible for you to settle the matter before the sun sets on this day."

"And if we don't?" Danae asked. "What if it's beyond our capabilities? Would you expect us to remain until the problem is solved or would you let us leave, knowing that we've done the best we can?"

The wandering soul once again didn't answer immediately. "If we can see you have done your best and are incapable of further help, then we will accept your obligations to us are met."

Danae turned to Mallory. "Does that sound fair to you?"

Mallory nodded. She hadn't noticed anything that might cause a problem for them. "I think so."

The wandering soul bowed low, the leaves of its upper branches once again sweeping across the ground. "I shall ask my people to clear a pathway for you while you come with me to see them."

Chapter Thirty-Three

Seeing a journal notification in the corner of her vision, Mallory opened it to discover a quest had been activated. *Wandering Souls In Danger: Wandering souls need your help and in exchange for you looking into the problem, they will create a pathway between your camp and the cave leading to a demonic dungeon to allow you to bring your wagon close.*

"You want us to go with you now?" Brodie asked.

The wandering soul dipped its head. "My people are dying."

Danae smiled at Brodie. "We don't all need to go. Only two of us."

Mallory interrupted before her brother could suggest going with Danae. He only had one revive left. "You can wait for Ryan and Callum and let them know what's happened while I go with Danni to see if we can help the wandering souls."

"What if it's dangerous?" Brodie asked.

The wandering soul deeply dipped its branches again. "If needed, I will escort you back to this location once you have either solved, or tried to solve, the problem to the best of your abilities."

Mallory dredged up a reassuring smile for her brother. "We'll be fine. Stay here so we know where to find you once we're done."

"What if two of you aren't enough?" Brodie asked.

"Then we'll come back to get the rest of you." Mallory took a step towards the wandering soul, again dredging up a reassuring smile for Brodie. "Quit worrying. We won't be long."

"You are willing to follow?" the wandering soul asked.

Mallory nodded. "Lead the way."

The wandering soul lumbered across the ground, its slow movements faster than they looked. Mallory at times struggled to keep up with him, casting glances towards Danae at her side. Neither of them spoke, silently following the wandering soul who led them to a cluster of trees that had a large area around them where no other tree stood.

"This can't be good," Danae said.

Mallory examined the trees in the tight cluster. They were different to the other trees in the area.

They had what looked like large fruits up the length of their trunks, each fruit hanging from a single point. Most of them were about the size of a tennis ball. "I'm obviously missing something. What is the problem?"

Before Danae could answer, a bark sounded behind them. Brodie, following Fang, came towards them with a grin. Ryan, Callum and Smudge followed behind him. "We sent Emica to get the wagon and left Deneg to keep the door open for us." He patted Fang's head. "Good girl."

Callum came to a stop beside Mallory. "They remind me of Jaboticaba."

"Of what?" Brodie asked.

"Grape tree," Callum said.

"That isn't fruit on the trees," Danae said. "They're tree leeches."

The branches of the wandering soul rustled. "My people are dying."

"Is that all we need to do?" Ryan asked. "Remove the tree leeches?"

The wandering soul dipped its branches. "Save my people."

Danae grabbed Ryan's arm when he reached for his sword. "It isn't that simple."

Ryan lowered his hand, stepping back from Danae

and out of her light grip. "How do you get rid of them?"

"If we disturb or touch them, they'll come after us. Once they're full from tree sap, or blood from creatures or sentient beings, they burrow into the ground where they hibernate and change into their final form. I've seen them swarm a creature and all latch onto it, leaving it drained in less than a minute," Danae said. "They prefer tree sap though and destroy forests in days, or even hours if there are enough of them. But not just any trees. They feed on demonic, magical or sentient trees."

Mallory stared at the rounded tree leeches. A few of them were nearly twice the size of tennis balls, some were only the size of golf balls. "There has to be hundreds of them."

"How do we kill them?" Callum asked.

"The easiest way is fire." Danae glanced at the wandering soul who stood beside them, his roots sunk into the ground. "But that would also kill their host."

"How long do we have before the wandering souls die?" Callum asked.

The wandering soul rustled its branches. "The sap is half gone from most of them."

"What is that in hours?" Brodie asked.

"They don't see time the same way we do." Danae faced the wandering soul. "How many times has the sun set since the tree leeches found your people?"

"None. They came in the dark," the wandering soul said.

"So in less than twelve hours, they've half killed your people." Callum patted Smudge when he made a distressed sound. "That isn't going to give us a lot of time to destroy them."

"How do they communicate with each other?" Ryan asked. "The tree leeches. If we capture them one at a time, while invisible, will they call for help?"

"They communicate through the sound of their wings. They rub them together and make various sounds from low to a high-pitched whine when they're in danger," Danae said.

"Can we squish them like bugs?" Brodie asked.

"How far does the sound of their wings travel?" Ryan asked.

Danae shrugged, her gaze going from Ryan to Brodie. "They have a rather solid shell. They wouldn't be easily squished."

"What about clearing an area and drawing them all to it and setting them alight once they're away from the wandering souls or anything else that might burn," Callum suggested.

"No fire," the wandering soul stated. "No fire." A shudder ran through it, causing its leaves to rustle.

"How else do we kill them?" Ryan asked.

"We could travel to Longmeadow and see if we can buy tree leech mist," Danae suggested.

"What if we don't have enough time for that?" Callum asked. "Without a proper time reference, we don't know how long we have to solve the problem."

"I have an idea." Ryan took out his pocket watch and held it up to the wandering soul. "See that hand that is slowly moving around?"

The wandering soul rustled its leaves.

"When it reaches the top, focus on how much time passes until it moves around the face and reaches the top again." Ryan continued to hold the pocket watch in front of the wandering soul.

Again the wandering soul rustled its leaves, remaining silent as it focused on the pocket watch. Once the secondhand had travelled around once, it spoke. "Many of them. Many, many of them. Hundreds."

"How many hundreds?" Callum asked. "How many hundreds did it take for a quarter of the sap to be taken from one of your people?"

"Possibly three hundred. Maybe three hundred and

fifty." A shiver ran through the leaves of the wandering soul. "Too many to count clearly."

"So we have at least five hours to reach Longmeadow, buy the tree leech mist and return." Callum turned to Danae. "How long does it take for the tree leech mist to work?"

"Minutes?" Danae slowly shook her head. "I don't know exactly. But it's quick."

"If you save my people, adventurers, we will reward you," the wandering soul said.

Mallory checked her journal notification and found it was an update for the quest. *Wandering Souls In Danger: If you solve their problem, the wandering souls will reward you.* A smile momentarily formed. That almost guaranteed Brodie would want to help. She'd no sooner finished thinking that, when her brother spoke.

"How long will it take us to get to Longmeadow?"

Callum, who was looking at the map of Ruby Isle, glanced up. "Give me a minute." When he looked up again, everyone was watching him. "It'll take us just under two hours to reach Longmeadow going at an average pace. So four hours a round trip, half an hour for the unexpected and we should return here in time to save the wandering souls." He glanced at the one standing with them. "Providing the calculations for the time passed are correct. Or underestimated."

"We better get started then," Ryan said. "We don't have time to waste."

"We await your return, adventurers," the wandering soul said.

Chapter Thirty-Four

Not knowing how to reply, Mallory nodded and fell into step beside Ryan who led the way back towards the cave entrance. She waited until they were far enough away from the wandering souls that she hoped they couldn't hear. "What if it isn't enough time?"

"We'll do the best we can." Ryan slipped his hand in hers, momentarily tightening his grip. "It should be enough. It shouldn't take us too long to find someone who sells tree leech mist."

Danae came alongside them. "An alchemist should sell it. Or at least know where we can purchase it."

"Is there an alchemist in Longmeadow?" Brodie asked from behind them.

Danae glanced over her shoulder. "I don't know. I've never been to Longmeadow before."

"Emica might know. She's been to a lot of towns and villages on this side of Ruby Isle," Ryan said.

"We could ask the mage. It's his village," Callum suggested.

Ryan chuckled. "Between the dungeon and the wandering souls I forgot all about him being from there."

"What are we going to do about the treasure and getting Deneg out of the cave?" Mallory asked.

"We can carry the coffin in and use it to take him to the wagon," Ryan said. "With the way strength works on Inadon, that shouldn't be a problem."

"The treasure will be in the wagon by the time we reach it," Brodie said. "Or it should be. Emica, Ninette and Jorgen offered to load it up while we were gone. Esben wanted to help, but Jorgen told him he couldn't. That it was only another couple of hours until you finished healing his broken arm."

"I won't be able to do it until we're part of the way to Longmeadow," Mallory said. "Or when we reach it. I can't use rapid mend on him again until nine."

"It'll be before we reach the village," Callum said. "I'm sure he'll be glad not to keep being told he can't do anything."

"I know exactly how he feels. It's so annoying

when you've got a broken bone. So much you can't do," Brodie said.

Mallory didn't point out that getting an arrow to the knee had probably been his fault for running straight into danger. Like the rest of them, she remained silent, no one speaking until they reached the cave entrance where the wagon was now parked, laden down with flatpack furniture and chests of treasure. She came to a stop, staring at it, barely giving the mage and his horse drawn cart a glance. "Where are we meant to fit?"

"On top of the chests?" Callum suggested.

Mallory sighed. It was going to be an uncomfortable journey. At least it'd take less than two hours. Unless they were unable to sell the treasure in Longmeadow and were stuck with it a lot longer.

Jorgen and Ninette came out of the cave, carrying a chest between them. Jorgen nodded in greeting.

Ninette smiled at the sight of them. "This is the last of it." She helped Jorgen put the chest in the wagon, needing to put it on top of another one.

"We need to take the coffin in to collect Deneg," Ryan said.

Jorgen turned to face them, leaning against the back of the wagon. "That's done. The mage helped us with moving the coffin. He has a lot of utility spells."

"So we can go?" Mallory looked between the cave entrance and the wagon.

"Esben wanted to see the treasure room," Jorgen said. "Emica will be back with him in a minute."

Ninette grinned. "He wanted the XP from the treasure room."

"Don't blame him," Brodie said. "It's so hard to earn XP with a broken bone."

Esben and Emica came out before anyone could comment and they finished getting ready to leave, Ninette dishing up the stew for them to eat along the way.

Mallory sat cross legged on a chest, having a spoonful of the stew as Jorgen drove them towards the road. "We need to find a shrink reversal spell."

Danae, who was sitting across from Mallory on Deneg's coffin, made a sweeping gesture that encompassed the contents of the wagon. "It wouldn't help with all of this. You'd have to shrink everything individually. You can't shrink a chest and its contents. What you need is a bag of holding for the smaller items. Or one of those compact dwellings with enchanted containers that will shrink the contents in them when the dwelling is shrunk."

"Bag of holding," Mallory repeated. She stared at the half-elf, certain she couldn't have heard her correctly. They were one of her favourite items in games. Being able to own one would be amazing.

Danae nodded. "They allow you to carry more than what they appear to be able to carry. Basic ones carry a hundred kilograms worth of items, but you can get ones that can carry as much as five thousand kilograms."

"Hell yeah," Brodie exclaimed. "We need some of them."

"They aren't cheap," Danae warned.

"We have a demonic treasure to sell." Brodie rummaged in one of the chests, sitting on the one at the back of the wagon. "Look what I found." He held up a gold statue of a horse in one hand and a jewelled bit and bridle in the other. "It probably fell off the horse when it was stored. I bet we'll get more for the statue with the bridle on it."

Callum took the bridle from Brodie before he could put it on the statue. "There are runes on it."

"There are also jewels," Brodie pointed out. "Do you think they're rubies? They're such a dark red."

Callum studied the bridle, frowning. "I recognise the word Scorch, but I'm not completely certain of the rest of them." He let Smudge, who was curled up in his lap, take the bridle. "I'll get out the rune book and decode it once I've finished reading this one." He picked up the leather bound book that was beside him on the coffin.

"What is that book?" Mallory stared at the plain cover. "And where did you get it from?"

"It was amongst the treasure. The demon who created the demonic dungeon wrote about making it as a place to store some of his most valuable treasures while he was in other worlds. Including his horse and the female warrior who led his army," Callum said.

"There was no horse or warrior in there," Mallory said.

"Only this one." Brodie held up the gold statue.

"I wonder who took the horse and warrrior," Ryan said.

Callum looked up from the book. "Apparently he had a falling out with his warrior and she wanted to help another demon while he was gone. He refused and she said that he couldn't stop her."

"He might have killed her instead of putting her in the dungeon," Danae said.

"How long ago was this?" Esben asked.

"What was the name of the demon?" Ninette asked at the same time.

Callum turned back to the start of the book. "Azerron. And I don't know how long ago it was." He returned to the page he'd been reading.

"Oh." Danae spoke the word softly, drawing it out slightly. "Are you sure that's the demon's name?"

Callum nodded. "Yeah. And the name of the warrior is Jenet Grayrock. He also wrote that he stored his army in a dungeon in Eridell, but so far hasn't mentioned where."

"Are you completely certain it's Azerron?" Danae asked.

Callum held out the book, open to the first page, his finger marking the place he was up to. "You can see for yourself."

Danae shook her head, not taking the book. "I've only heard of one divine demon called Azerron."

Jorgen glanced over his shoulder. "He's worshiped by many of the dark forces. A powerful demon."

Chapter Thirty-Five

Mallory looked between Jorgen and Danae. "The dungeon doesn't have to have been created by a divine demon, does it?"

"Only divine demons can create them," Esben said.

"Oh." Mallory felt her heart sink and her stomach turn. "This can't be good." Her gaze was drawn to all the treasure they'd taken from Azerron.

"How would he find out?" Brodie continued to rummage in the chest, the horse beside him.

"Let's hope he never does," Danae said.

Brodie held up a small, gold helmet. "Look what I found. It's got runes on it too. Guess he liked to decorate all his statues."

Danae looked between the bridle and the helmet several times before she held her hand out to Brodie. "Can I have a look?"

Brodie handed the helmet over. "What's wrong with them? You sound worried. Are you?"

Danae examined the helmet, handing it over to Emica. "I think it says activate Jenet Grayrock."

Emica took the helmet, looking it over before handing it back. "I think I know where Scorch and Jenet Grayrock are."

Mallory wanted to beg her not to say. She had a bad feeling she already knew.

Danae took the bridle from Smudge and the horse statue from Brodie and clambered out the back of the wagon. "We'll find out for certain in just a moment."

Mallory reluctantly followed, Brodie already standing by Danae and the rest of the group, that had been in the back of the wagon, joining her. "Should you be doing whatever it is you plan to do?"

Jorgen glanced over his shoulder. "Should I stop?"

Ryan waved him on. "Keep going. We can't afford to stop. Or at least the wandering souls can't afford for us to stop."

Danae placed the statue on the ground before she put the bridle on it. The statue rapidly grew in size, changing in colour. Danae stumbled back out of the way. "Scorch." The word was soft as the half-elf reached for her bow.

Mallory stared at the horse in front of her, stamping

a foot and snorting, smoke curling from his nostrils. It was the horse from the tiles, flames in his eyes and dark red flame-like socks and a red blaze, the rest of his leathery skin black. "Is he dangerous?" Her hand rested on her wand.

The horse reared, flames rising up around his hooves when they struck the ground, the flames dying down when there was nothing for them to catch on fire. He tossed his head, snorting again.

Ryan took several steps towards the horse. "He's magnificent."

"Can we keep him?" Brodie asked. "He's cool."

"How do we make him a statue again?" Mallory glanced at Scorch's hooves. "I really don't want to set the place on fire."

Danae took a hesitant step forward. "Easy, boy. Let me take that bridle off you." She reached for him.

The horse backed away, tossing his head.

"I don't think he wants you to do that," Brodie said. "Can't say I blame him. I wouldn't want to be stuck as a statue either."

Scorch came closer to Brodie and lowered his head, sniffing at the mask, snorting before he backed away.

Mallory laughed. "I don't think he was expecting Brodie. Maybe it's Azerron's mask."

"Draw a weapon," Esben suggested. "It might make you more familiar to him."

Brodie took out a stiletto, the armour again sliding over his skin until he was covered by it. Brodie looked down at his body. "This will never get old. I'm keeping the mask on forever."

Scorch again came up to Brodie, this time resting his head on Brodie's shoulder, snorting several times before he nudged Brodie towards his side.

"I think he wants you to ride him," Danae said.

Ryan glanced over his shoulder. "We should probably catch up with Jorgen before he gets too far ahead."

"I'll meet you back there." Brodie raced ahead on Scorch, flames left in his wake, some of them leaving behind patches of burnt grass, Fang running alongside them.

Mallory stared after her brother and Scorch. "How do you stop the horse from setting everything on fire? I don't want to burn down forests."

Danae followed the path Brodie had taken. "There'll be a word to use which will let Scorch know he isn't going into battle. And another word to let him know it's time for battle. They'll activate and deactivate the flames."

"How will we figure them out?" Mallory asked.

Emica grinned. "A dictionary?"

Danae laughed softly. "That's one possibility, but he might also tell you."

Mallory frowned, trying to make sense of Danae's words. "Who might tell us? Azerron?"

Danae shook her head. "Scorch."

"He'll be able to talk?" Callum asked.

Again Danae shook her head. "There are people who can speak with animals, or enchantments, spells and potions that can temporarily give you that ability."

Mallory tried not to sigh. It seemed like the more things they ended up with, the more things they needed. And she was pretty certain all those options were bound to be expensive.

They reached the wagon to find Brodie talking excitedly to Jorgen. The demonic horse reminded Mallory of the demonic dogs they'd fought. "We didn't end up searching the dogs in that last room of the dungeon."

Emica climbed into the back of the wagon. "I searched the bodies and found two canines. I put them in the chest with the rest of your gear."

Mallory joined her in the wagon, sitting on the same chest she'd sat on earlier. "Thank you."

Silence fell again and Mallory drifted off to be

woken by Ryan when it was time for her to heal Esben. "It's nine already?" She tried to stretch, but it was impossible with how little space there was in the wagon.

Ryan returned the pocket watch to his belt pouch. "It's nearly a quarter past nine. We're not that far from Longmeadow."

Jorgen glanced over his shoulder, still driving the wagon. "We've actually made better time than we expected." Glancing over his shoulder again, he smiled, nodding towards Brodie who continued to ride Scorch beside the wagon. "I spotted a couple of bandits, but it looked like they thought better about attacking when they saw Scorch."

Esben moved closer to Mallory. "I owe you for all you've done in healing my arm."

She rested her hands on his arm, using rapid mend to finish healing him. "You don't owe me anything. You and Jorgen are part of our group." She thought that sounded better than telling him that she wouldn't charge a friend or relative of Jorgen's. And technically he was part of their group. Or at least travelling with their group. It was just that she didn't yet know him as well as she knew Jorgen.

Esben held her gaze a moment. "Jorgen did the

right thing when he gave you a bead. You are someone one of our people can trust."

"Thank you." She felt uncomfortable with his praise considering her earlier thoughts.

Jorgen glanced over his shoulder. "Longmeadow ahead."

Chapter Thirty-Six

Relieved by the interruption, Mallory turned her attention to the village they approached. From what she could see, it seemed to be nearly as big as Wrentville. The road leading into the village was busy and the people walking alongside it and those travelling on it all sent long glances in their direction. "Should we put Scorch away?"

Emica shook her head. "People occasionally have demonic animals. Even if you came into the village on something completely common, you'd still draw attention. People like to know what's going on and who's arriving."

"How can you call this a village?" Callum asked.

Emica frowned. "Because that is what it is."

"It's almost the same size as Wrentville. Why is it a town when this one isn't?" Callum stared out the back of the wagon, studying the buildings and people they passed.

"Population," Emica said. "It's not far off being considered a town."

"The mage is indicating that we should pull over," Jorgen said.

"We'll see what he wants." Ryan jumped out of the back of the wagon and strode towards the mage.

Mallory hurried after him, Callum at her side with Smudge in the makeshift sling. She winced when she saw the flames Brodie continued to leave behind. They died out almost as soon as they formed on the cobblestones. "Should we be telling him to wait outside the village?" She gestured towards her brother.

"As long as nothing catches on fire, no one should complain," Danae said.

Callum chuckled. "You might want to buy a spell that puts out fire."

Mallory sighed. "There are a lot of spells I need to buy." She picked up her pace, reaching the mage's cart in time to catch her brother's words.

"Of course I remember your directions."

"What directions?" Mallory looked from the mage to her brother and back again.

It was Brodie who answered. "I asked him about an

alchemist. He'll meet us there. After he's collected his spare spells from home. It'll save us some time so we can get back to the wandering souls before they die."

"I'll be as quick as possible," the mage said. "It's good of you to offer to help the wandering souls."

"We couldn't exactly stand back and let them die," Mallory said.

"Some would," the mage said. "Wandering soul timber is valuable. It's used to make golems."

"What do golems do?" Brodie asked.

"They make good servants or soldiers," the mage said.

"Cool. How do we get one?" Brodie asked.

"That depends on what type of golem you want. The ones you need wandering soul timber for are made by carving a life-sized figure out of demonic timber and hollowing out a cavity for a heart made from wandering soul timber. Demonic runes are used to activate them and when that happens, the chest cavity closes over to protect the heart which is the only way to destroy them." The mage gestured to his left. "I'd best go home and fetch the spells so I don't hold you up."

Mallory took a step towards the mage, half raising her hand to stall him. "Wait. Do you have a spell that puts out fire?"

The mage shook his head. "No, but I know someone who does and I'm pretty certain they're interested in one of my spare spells. Did you want me to take the time to find out?"

Mallory glanced at Ryan, Brodie and Callum. When they nodded, or in Brodie's case shrugged, she turned back to the mage. "Yes. I'd appreciate that."

With a single nod, the mage urged his horse forward and headed down the road.

Ryan looked up at Brodie who was still on Scorch. "Which way?"

"This way." Brodie led the way through the streets, remaining on Scorch.

Mallory checked the journal notification that had appeared in the corner of her vision when they'd reached the village. She was surprised to find it wasn't just experience points for a new location. It was also an update to their quest. *Another Victim: The mage has agreed to attempt swapping one of his spells for one you are seeking.*

A couple of streets later, Brodie looked over his shoulder. "It's just ahead. I'll meet you there." He urged Scorch into a canter, leaving them behind, Fang racing at his side.

Mallory slowly shook her head, her gaze on the flames that lasted longer than they had been since reaching the cobblestone road. "We really need to figure out how to stop that horse from leaving fire behind. Otherwise, something is going to burn."

Ryan grinned. "It's Brodie. Of course something will burn."

They reached the shop as Brodie came back outside. "The alchemist will take herbs in trade. He has tree leech mist." He ran over to the wagon that was pulling up across the road from the shop, leaving Scorch at the hitching post in front of the shop. "He wanted all the herbs. And some of the veggies. He also said the trader over there would probably want the rest of the veggies." He gestured further up the road as he clambered into the wagon.

Mallory followed her brother. "Are you sure that will be enough? We've only got about fifteen hundred herbs. So approximately fifteen gold pieces. Possibly a bit more if we ended up getting some of the less common herbs."

Brodie handed a hessian bag of herbs to his sister. "He's running low on some supplies otherwise he would have charged us more." He gave one or two hessian bags to everyone else, keeping two for himself.

Mallory carried the hessian bag of herbs to the

shop, walking beside her brother. "What about the treasure? Are we going to sell that?"

"Of course we'll sell it before we leave Longmeadow." Brodie entered the shop.

Mallory followed him inside, stepping out of the way so that the rest of their party could enter. The shop was dim and an elderly man brought a tall cane basket out of the back room and placed it beside several others that were in front of a long timber counter.

"Put all the herbs in the baskets." He watched as they filled the baskets, occasionally nodding and muttering under his breath. Once all the sacks had been emptied into the baskets and the vegetables he'd wanted placed on the counter, he handed over a potion vial. "It was a pleasure doing business with you."

Brodie handed the potion vial to Mallory. "Any time." With a grin, he headed outside.

Ryan caught up with Brodie at the wagon where he was rummaging in a chest from the dungeon. "Before we go selling anything, we need to talk about the statue." He glanced at Deneg's coffin.

"What about it?" Brodie looked up from the chest. "It's Deneg's."

"If she's anything like Scorch, she's a living person. We can't let her be sold," Ryan said.

"Especially since the money gained from selling her would be used to set someone else free," Callum said.

"It's not like we can open the coffin." Brodie gestured towards the coffin as he spoke the word. "He locks it."

"Then we need to find somewhere safe that he can come out during the day so we can tell him about Jenet," Ryan said.

"We could take him back to the cave," Danae suggested. "It does seem wrong to sell her like she's some slave. Especially since whoever buys her wouldn't know she's real."

Brodie looked from the wagon to the shop he'd indicated earlier. "What about selling the treasure? Can't we do that?"

Mallory wanted nothing more than to gain back the space the chests were taking up. But Ryan was right. They couldn't let Deneg sell Jenet. "Not until we talk to Deneg about what he wants to do. He might want to sell his share of the treasure somewhere else."

Brodie sighed. "Can we at least sell the rest of the veggies and stuff like the shrivelled hearts?"

"As long as you don't take too long." Ryan checked the time. "You have fifteen minutes."

"That's not long enough. We can take longer than that. Nothing hassled us along the way," Brodie protested. "I bet the trip back will be just as quiet."

"It might be different without the mage. Having both the cart and wagon might have been the reason everything left us alone." Ryan checked the pocket watch again. "You're wasting time."

Muttering under his breath, Brodie grabbed hessian bags of vegetables. Callum, Ninette, Jorgen and Esben helped him. He headed towards the trader, muttering that there wasn't time to get anything other than the vegetables.

Chapter Thirty-Seven

Mallory started to follow Brodie, stopping when she spotted the mage coming towards them. She waited by the wagon for him, Ryan, Danae and Emica remaining with her. She couldn't wait to find out what spells he'd have for her to choose from.

He pulled up behind them, jumping down from the driver's seat of his cart. "I was able to get that spell you were interested in."

"Thank you." Mallory took the parchment he held out to her.

"And the other one we agreed upon." He handed over another parchment. "Shrink I."

"Thanks." She took the second parchment.

"I also asked the mage who I swapped spells with about a shrink reversal spell. There's a mage that lives on the road west of Longmeadow that heads north. She lives on the other side of the river and west of the road where the river flows into the lake. She might have the spell you're looking for."

Brodie returned before Mallory could say anything. "What spells did you get?"

"I have four you can choose from," the mage said. "Nightfall which causes your target's vision to go black, spellbound shield which gives the warrior you cast it on a shield for ten minutes, slow target which slows your target for two minutes and teleportation link I that can be cast at one location and as long as it is recast within an hour, it will transport you, your companion animal and the gear you're carrying or wearing back to that location."

"You can only transport one person?" Brodie asked.

"Levelling it up to fifteen will allow you to teleport two people and their belongings and level thirty allows you to transport three people," the mage said.

Mallory wanted all of them. Or at least all of them except spellbound shield which she couldn't currently see a use for. The other two would have been useful in their fights against Rass as well as in their recent boss fight.

"Come on, Mal," Brodie exclaimed. "How hard can it be to choose? If I wasn't allowed to take too long, then you can't either. Pick teleportation link. Then you can run any errands that need to be done."

"Slow target and nightfall would be useful too," Mallory said.

Ryan checked his pocket watch. "I hate to agree with Brodie, but we are running out of time."

Brodie glared at Ryan. "What's wrong with agreeing with me. None of you ever want to agree with me."

Emica grinned at him. "Do you really want the answer to that question?"

Callum interrupted Brodie before he could do more than open his mouth. "Can we buy two of the spells?"

"For market price," the mage said. "Which ones were you wanting?"

"Nightfall, slow target, teleportation link I," Mallory said without hesitation.

"Four hundred and fifty gold pieces for nightfall, five hundred gold pieces for slow target and a thousand gold pieces for teleportation link I," the mage said.

"A thousand gold," Brodie exclaimed.

"That's what you'd pay in a shop," the mage said.

"A trader wouldn't give you that price for them,"

Brodie argued. "You'd be lucky to get three quarters that value."

"They're good spells. I'd get more than that for them," the mage said.

"We don't have time for this," Ryan said. "We have to get back to the wandering souls."

As much as she wanted all three spells, Mallory wasn't about to let the wandering souls die so her brother could haggle over the price. "I'll take teleportation link I."

"What about the rest of them?" Brodie asked.

Ryan spoke before Mallory had the chance. "How about we think about it?" He turned to Mallory. "We could return after we've dealt with the wandering souls if you're still interested in them."

"Unless he sells them before we can return." Brodie gave a nod towards the mage.

"I don't have plans to sell them yet. I've kept them to sell the next time I'm in Shadville. I'll get a better price for them there," the mage said.

"When are you next going there?" Callum asked.

The mage shrugged. "Not for at least a month."

Ryan took a step towards the wagon, his gaze going between Mallory and the mage. "Then let's wrap things up so we can get back to the wandering souls."

When the mage tried to hand Mallory the final spell, she shook her head. "Wait a moment." She quickly added everyone to their party before accepting the scroll, smiling when a journal notification appeared in the corner of her vision. "Where do you live in case I do want the other two spells?"

"You can find me at the tavern at midday and again at six each evening. It's better than preparing my own meals since I have no points in cooking. I've focused on putting them into some of my spells."

With a nod, Mallory hurried to the wagon that the rest of her group were in, Scorch was tied to the back of the wagon with the riding horse and donkey. She checked her notification as she brushed past the animals and clambered into the back. *Another Victim: You were rewarded with three spells for your party. You also earned twenty experience points each.*

Emica sat beside Mallory. "Thanks for adding me to the party. That XP brought me to about halfway through this CAS point."

"That XP gave me a CAS point and now I only need one more to reach character level three," Callum said.

"I gained enough XP to reach character level three," Danae said. "I put my class point in archer and an attribute point in strength, dexterity and charisma and two points in constitution. Which means I now have thirty-three health, fifty-five stamina and still have twenty-five mana." She paused a moment. "You have reached level three archer. You can now wield longbows."

Jorgen, who was again driving, glanced over his shoulder. "Thanks for adding Esben and me too."

"You're all welcome." Mallory removed each of the extras from the party before turning to her brother. "How much did you get for the rest of the veggies?"

Brodie held out nine gold and eight silver pieces. "We also managed to get a crafting ability book. Mason." He took the book out of his satchel and held it out too.

Mallory took the coins and book. "I'm surprised they didn't have more with how large a village it is."

"They did, but it was only books we already have," Brodie said.

Mallory looked from Brodie to Scorch and back again. "You're not riding?"

"I will once we all have a chance to read the new book." Brodie gestured to the book his sister held.

Mallory tried to hand it back to him. "You can go first."

Brodie shook his head. "No, it's okay. You can."

Chapter Thirty-Eight

Mallory opened the book and read over the opening lines before handing it over. *Mason is a crafting ability that allows you to make different sizes and styles of structures from various types of stone. You will be able to make simple structures such as rock walls all the way up to castles.* "I wonder how long it'd take to build a castle."

"That would depend on your level and how many you had working with you." Danae took the book Brodie held out to her. Once she was finished, she held it out to Ryan.

He shook his head, gesturing for her to hand it to someone else. "I'm going to put some of my CAS points into hunting." He was silent a moment. "You have reached level six hunting. You now have the ability to use an enchanted skinning knife. You have reached level seven hunting. You are ten percent more likely to spot tracks. You have reached level eight hunting. You now have the ability to gain inferior quality hides and pelts. You have reached level nine hunting. You now have the ability to use an enchanted hunting bow and arrows. You have reached level ten hunting. You now have the ability to use a ground snare."

"You can set traps when we camp somewhere," Brodie said. "And what about the rest of your points? You've still got fifteen of them."

"I'm trying to decide if I use more for hunting or go with something else," Ryan said. "There are a few crafting abilities that sound interesting."

The journey back to the Valley of Wandering Souls was quiet, Brodie riding ahead on Scorch. They reached the wandering souls at a quarter to twelve, well before the time was up. Brodie came alongside the wagon. "Will this take long? It's nearly lunch time and we don't really have anything for lunch. We should have kept levelling up instead of everyone staying with the wagon."

"With what we're carrying, it's probably best we stay with the wagon," Ryan said. "We don't want to risk losing everything."

"It won't take long for the tree leech mist to work," Danae said. "It'd be best if someone could take it over to the trees while they're invisible so the tree leeches aren't disturbed and some of them fly away."

Jorgen parked the wagon well away from the dying wandering souls, leaning over the back of the seat to hold out his hand. "I'll take it. I can also use stealth so they don't hear me coming."

Mallory handed over the potion vial. "How does it work? And how is it activated?"

"Remove the stopper and leave it on the ground amongst the wandering souls. A fine mist will start to rise up after a few seconds and fill the area around it. The tree leeches will begin to fall off the wandering souls over the next few minutes," Danae said.

"Two quests in a day. Always good for XP and for being paid when we return home," Brodie said. "If we do decide to return home."

"We'll have to," Mallory clambered out of the wagon. "We can't stay here indefinitely."

Callum interrupted Brodie when he started to argue with Mallory. "Talking of XP, why didn't we earn any from entering the Valley Of Wandering Souls?"

"Because we didn't reach the heart of it," Danae said.

Callum glanced around. "Where is the heart of it?"

Danae shrugged. "It changes depending on where

the majority of the wandering souls are at the time. They are the heart of the valley."

Callum faced the group of wandering souls with the tree leeches on their limbs. "That should mean that the majority of the wandering souls in this area aren't in danger."

"That won't last unless the tree leeches are killed," Emica said. "They can quickly wipe out an area."

Mallory turned to Jorgen who stood beside her. "Are you ready to become invisible?"

Jorgen nodded.

"Actually, I should add everyone to the party first in case the quest is completed once the potion is used," Mallory said.

Esben joined them. "I could do with more XP."

Mallory waited until she'd added everyone before she made Jorgen invisible. She tried to keep track of where he was, but it was impossible. The moment she'd made him invisible, she hadn't been able to find him. Not even through sound. He was obviously using stealth like he'd suggested.

Jorgen appeared beside Mallory.

She jumped back with a start, pressing a hand against her chest. "I didn't realise you'd finished. How long does your stealth last?"

"Thirty seconds. It lasted long enough for me to leave the potion."

"Look." Brodie pointed at the wandering souls. "The tree leeches are dropping off. I hope they're dead and aren't going to burrow into the ground or attack us if we go over there."

"They are dying," Danae said. "If they were alive they'd immediately be trying to bury themselves in the ground, not lie about risking something attacking them."

"So we did it?" Brodie asked. "We completed the quest already?"

"They're still dying. We might have to wait until they're all dead to complete the quest," Mallory said.

"The wandering soul is headed our way," Ryan said.

Mallory turned to see it stride towards them, four saplings at its side, darting back and forth as they explored. "For some reason I didn't expect the young ones to be so little. I half expected them to be born fully grown."

"They remind me of Precious," Callum said softly.

"Who is Precious?" Esben asked.

"Mal killed him. He was Callum's companion," Brodie said.

"It wasn't like that," Mallory protested. "You make it sound worse than it was."

Ryan chuckled. "He was a failed experiment. Mallory had no choice other than to take it out."

The wandering souls reached them, bringing an end to the conversation. The saplings hung back while the fully grown one stopped in front of them, bowing low, its leaves brushing the dirt. "I want to thank you, adventurers."

"We're glad we could help." Mallory said.

"You were promised a reward for your services, adventurers."

"Yeah, we were," Brodie said. "But you didn't say what it was."

The wandering soul again lowered its branches, shaking them so the leaves rustled. Along with some leaves, two branches dropped to the ground. They were about eight centimetres in diameter and a metre long. "Thank you." Straightening, the wandering soul turned and headed back in the direction he'd come from.

Mallory ignored the notification in the corner of her vision, watching as the group of wandering souls lumbered away, the saplings darting around them. "I wonder if those are the offspring of some of the ones who were dying."

"One of the young wandering souls hasn't left." Callum nodded towards a thick shrub the young wandering soul peeked around.

"What does it want?" Brodie stared down at the branches the wandering soul had left behind, barely glancing at the young wandering soul.

"It's probably curious," Danae said. "They're very inquisitive at that age."

Brodie picked up the branches, examining them. "What are we meant to do with these? They don't seem like much of a reward."

"That's what's used to make timber golem hearts," Emica said. "They're extremely valuable."

"They are?" Brodie continued to examine the branches. "Cool." He shot a look towards Mallory. "Unless we're not allowed to sell these either."

Chapter Thirty-Nine

"We should return to the cave so we can see if Deneg will wake up and talk to us about Jenet Grayrock." Mallory clambered into the back of the wagon.

Brodie followed, bringing the branches with him. "We really need to sell some stuff. We're running out of space. We should have kept that cart instead of selling it." He stowed the branches in the wagon before getting back on Scorch.

Jorgen returned to the driver's seat and turned the wagon towards the cave.

Callum, who sat at the back of the wagon on the edge of Deneg's coffin, stared at where they'd been. "It's following us."

"What's following us?" Brodie glanced over his shoulder from where he rode abreast of Jorgen.

Emica leaned forward to see past Danae who sat beside her. "Who is following us?"

"The young wandering soul," Callum said.

Mallory leaned forward to see past Ryan. "Will that be a problem?"

Danae shook her head. "The young wandering souls tend to wander around and explore the world. More so than the grown ones."

"We don't have to worry about it?" Mallory continued to watch the wandering soul as it meandered back and forth, following them at a distance. After a few minutes of watching it, she checked her journal notification. *Wandering Souls In Danger: You were rewarded with wandering souls timber for your party. You also earned ten experience points each.* She'd also gained a CAS point and was now three CAS points off gaining another character level. The quest notification reminded her she still had extras in the party and she removed them since they had no quests that were about to be completed.

The young wandering soul was still following them when they pulled up in front of the cave, coming close as Jorgen, Callum, Ryan and Emica took the coffin out of the wagon. It came within metres, sinking roots into the ground when it came to a stop.

Mallory took several steps towards it, moving slow so as not to startle it. This close she could see it wasn't quite as tall as her. "What is it that you find interesting. Maybe I could answer your questions if you have any." She smiled when eyes became visible amongst the bark, barely open as the young wandering soul met her gaze.

"Box."

Even though she'd suggested the young wandering soul ask questions, hearing its voice startled her. It was a lighter tone than the fully grown wandering soul. "All the chests in the wagon?" She gestured towards the wagon.

There was a rustle of leaves and the young wandering soul made a movement that could have been it shaking its head. "Box. Earth mouth." It lowered one of its narrow branches, pointing in the direction of the cave.

"The box that was taken into the cave?" Mallory asked.

The young wandering soul lowered its branches, raising them again almost immediately. "Cave." It spoke the word slowly, as if testing it. "Box. Cave."

"The box taken into the cave is a coffin."

"Coffin?"

Callum joined them, catching the end of the conversation. "It's where the dead are laid to rest." He turned to Mallory. "We're ready to wake Deneg if you want to join us."

Mallory started to turn towards the cave, stopping when the young wandering soul spoke.

"Dead box."

"Ahh, yeah." She supposed that was close enough. She gestured towards the cave. "I'm going in there to talk to someone. The person in the coffin."

"Living in dead box?"

"Not exactly." Mallory had no idea how to explain a vampire to it.

Callum laughed. "That's one way of putting it. Vampires are referred to as the living dead."

Brodie came out of the cave, remaining at the entrance. "Are you two coming? Ryan won't let me wake Deneg until we're all there."

"We're coming." Mallory turned back to the young wandering soul. "You're welcome to stay here or come with us if you want." She started for the cave, glancing over her shoulder at a noise. The young wandering soul followed, keeping its distance. She wanted to reassure it that they wouldn't harm it, but had no idea how to convince it.

Brodie led the way to the first cave, gesturing towards the coffin everyone stood around. "Who's going to wake him?"

Callum stepped forward. "I will." He rested his hand on the lid of the coffin, glancing at those watching him before he spoke. "Deneg, can you wake up? We need to talk to you. You're somewhere safe and away from the sunlight." There was silence. "Deneg?"

Again the silence stretched out. "Callum?"

The sound of Deneg's voice startled Mallory. She'd been about to suggest they try something else to wake him.

"Yeah," Callum said. "We need to talk to you."

"Where are we?"

"Back in the cave. The one leading to the demonic dungeon." Callum paused a moment. "There's no risk of the sun reaching you in here."

A clicking sound preceded the lid of the coffin opening. Deneg sat up, his gaze on Callum. "Is something wrong?"

"In a way." Callum glanced at the statue that rested in the coffin, lying half out of the satchel, the sack no longer covering the head of it.

"This is taking forever," Brodie said. "How hard can it be to tell someone that they can't sell a statue because it'd be making someone a slave?"

Deneg glanced around the group before

clambering out of the coffin to stand beside it. "Can someone explain what is going on?"

Callum again glanced at the statue. "It's about Jenet Grayrock."

"Who?" Deneg asked.

This time, Callum glanced at Mallory, who nodded, not wanting to be the one to tell Deneg the bad news. Or at least she hoped it would be bad news for him and he wouldn't insist on selling the statue. She had no idea what to do if he didn't agree to set Jenet free.

It didn't take Callum long to explain the situation and Deneg remained silent after having asked several questions.

Mallory wanted to demand what he was thinking. Wanted to tell him to hurry up and let them know if he was willing to accept their offer for some of their share in exchange for the statue.

"So," Ryan began. "Should we bring in a couple of the treasure chests so you can look through everything and decide what you want in exchange for the statue?"

Deneg took the statue out of his satchel, leaving the sack behind too. "Are you sure it's a living person?"

"There's one way to find out." Ryan turned to Brodie. "You still have that helmet?"

Deneg took a step back. "You do realise that could be a bad idea. What if she attacks?"

"Why would she?" Brodie asked.

"How would you feel if you'd been imprisoned as a statue?" Deneg asked.

Brodie drew his stiletto, his armour sliding into place. "Then we attack her back."

"The helmet." Ryan held out his hand to Brodie. As soon as he had the helmet, he turned to Deneg. "We can't let you sell the statue if it's a person. Why should another be imprisoned so your brother can go free?"

Deneg stared down at the statue. Sighing heavily, he handed it over to Ryan. "As long as you're willing to part with enough of the treasure that I can have my brother rescued, I will relinquish my claims on the statue."

Ryan placed the statue on the ground. "It's a deal."

Chapter Forty

When a notification appeared in the corner of her vision, Mallory checked, not having expected anything. It was a quest update. *Treasure Hunt: Deneg has agreed that the statue found in the demonic treasure room will be set free if it is a living person and his share of five thousand gold pieces will come out of the rest of the treasure found in the treasure room.*

The wandering soul, who had entered the cave and remained near the exit, came in closer as Ryan put the helmet on the statue's head. He scurried backwards when the statue grew in size, becoming a living person. Her gold coloured hair was braided back from her face and she held herself like royalty, looking down at them.

Brodie looked the warrior up and down. "Wow. You're taller than Ryan."

"My father was a nephilim and my mother a titan."

The warrior held her sword ready, warily watching them as she backed away. "Where is Azerron?"

"We've never met him," Callum said. "So we have no idea where he'd be."

The warrior stopped once she was in a position where none of them were behind her. "Who are all of you and why are you wearing Azerron's armour he likes to wear when he rides Scorch?" The last was said once her gaze was fixed on Brodie.

"Are you Jenet Grayrock?" Mallory wasn't sure what to tell the warrior. Would she do or say something if she learned they'd raided the treasure room?

The warrior inclined her head. "And you are?"

"Mallory." She introduced the rest of those with her. "We returned your helmet so you'd turn into your normal form."

"Why?"

"So you couldn't be sold as a statue." Callum absently patted Smudge, who peered over the edge of the makeshift sling.

"Who planned to sell me?" Jenet kept her sword ready, her gaze roaming between all of them.

"We didn't know you were real," Brodie said. "Just like we didn't know Scorch was real until we put the bridle on him."

"You raided the treasure room?" Jenet asked.

Mallory dreaded answering, but it wasn't like they could avoid such a clear question. Or if they did, that'd be an answer in itself. "We solved the puzzles to earn the keys that opened the treasure room."

"What do you plan to do with it?" Jenet asked.

Mallory glanced at Deneg who remained beside his coffin. "Rescue someone sold to an arena."

Jenet's eyes narrowed. "Can you prove your claims? Or is this a way to make me feel sympathetic towards you?"

Mallory shook her head, Ryan speaking before she could come up with an answer.

"Do you have a way to prove a person's claims? We haven't been in this world long enough to know all the possibilities."

"Do you have a quest for the rescue?" Jenet asked.

Mallory nodded, noticing that Ryan, Brodie and Callum all did the same.

"She wants you to add her to your party and share information with her," Emica said. "If you do, she'll know all your current quests and the levels of anyone who shares information with her. In other words your strengths and weaknesses."

Jenet inclined her head. "That may be, but I'll promise not to use that information against you."

"Will you share your information with us?" Callum asked.

No." Jenet answered immediately, her tone firm.

Mallory glanced at the young wandering soul who'd once again crept close. Would he cause problems? She didn't know, but for now, the greatest threat was the warrior with the sword so she kept her focus on her. "What if only I share information with you? Will you be able to see the information of all those who've shared information with me?"

"No." Jenet lowered her sword, not sheathing it.

"Okay." Mallory took a deep breath, not certain she was doing the right thing. "I'll add you and share information with you. Let me know when you've finished confirming the truth and I'll remove you from the party."

Jenet held out her hand. "When you're ready."

Mallory was tempted to rest a hand on her wand, but doubted that'd be a good idea. She crossed the space between her and the warrior, taking her hand. "Accept party member Jenet Grayrock. Share journal info." She started to lower her hand.

Jenet clasped Mallory's hand tightly, meeting her gaze as she held on, remaining silent.

Mallory didn't know what to say or do. What if Jenet planned to attack them? Or if she could somehow use Mallory to gain information about everyone else. Several times she started to say something, stopping each time Jenet briefly tightened her grip.

"What are you doing? Will it take all day?" Brodie asked. "I'm starving. It's after lunch and we need to find something to eat. Unless I make something with the eggs, oats, flour and honey."

"You can remove me from the party now." Jenet let go of Mallory's hand, waiting until she was no longer in the party before she spoke again. "You tend to do quests that assist people and the only place you have a negative reputation for is in a dark forces village."

"Yes." Mallory studied Jenet's face, but the warrior's expression was neutral. "Do you consider that good or bad?"

Jenet sheathed her sword. "Good. I fought at Azerron's side against the dark forces for many decades."

Brodie frowned. "I thought he was worshiped by people with the dark forces. Why would they worship someone who attacks them?"

"Follows, not worships," Emica corrected. "We don't worship demons."

Brodie shrugged. "Not much difference."

Jenet slowly shook her head. "No. Not Azerron. He hates the dark forces and what they stand for."

Danae took half a step towards the warrior. "The only Azerron I know of has been on the side of the dark forces for the past eighty years."

"What year is it?" Jenet asked.

"It's day sixteen of the second month of the year five hundred and fourteen," Jorgen said.

Jenet momentarily closed her eyes. "What has happened in the past hundred and twenty years? Why would he have chosen to side with the dark forces? That doesn't make sense."

"I'm sorry," Danae said. "All I know is what I've heard. Which isn't much."

"My father might know more." Emica turned to Brodie. "Ask him what he knows about Azerron and why he sided with the dark forces."

"Who is your father that I should listen to what he has to say?" Jenet demanded.

Emica didn't answer immediately. "He's in the service of the Duke."

"Many are in the service of the Duke. What sets your father apart?" Jenet asked.

Again Emica didn't answer immediately. "My father is Captain Hisoki."

Jenet studied Emica for a moment before glancing at everyone else. "These are your retinue, my lady?"

Emica shook her head. "Most of them wouldn't last in my father's employ." She glanced at Brodie. "I'm travelling with them since it's unsafe for me to return to Shadhurst."

"Then wouldn't that make them your retinue?" Jenet asked.

"What is a retinue?" Brodie asked.

Callum laughed. "A servant." His smile remained in place. "And Emica is right, you wouldn't make a good servant."

Brodie glared at Jenet. "I'm no one's servant."

"It's an honourable job." Jenet returned her attention to Emica. "You have a way to contact Lord Hisoki?"

"He prefers captain," Emica said.

Jenet inclined her head. "I would be interested in what he has to say."

Emica turned to Brodie. "Can you ask him what he knows of the demon Azerron?"

Brodie took the duplication paper from his belt pouch as he faced his sister. "I need pen and ink."

"It's in the chest on the wagon." At a noise, Mallory looked towards the exit, surprised to find the young wandering soul was coming inside. She hadn't noticed him leave.

"Adventurers, come. You are wanted," the young wandering soul said, blocking Brodie from entering the tunnel that led to the exit.

Jenet stepped forward, grabbing hold of Mallory's wrist. "Wait. What about my situation? I need to know what happened to Azerron while he had me imprisoned and I want to know your price to set me free."

"There is no price." Mallory tried to pull away from Jenet.

The warrior kept hold of Mallory's wrist. "Have you so many riches that you need no more? I can give you the location of where Azerron kept his golem army. Their hearts have been made from the timber of wandering souls with the captain's being made from knotwood to create an essence golem."

Mallory shook her head. "I didn't mean I wouldn't accept a price to set you free, I meant that we don't expect anything in exchange for freeing you."

"Adventurers, hurry," the young wandering soul urged.

Chapter Forty-One

Mallory tried to take a step in the wandering soul's direction, but Jenet kept hold of her wrist. It was impossible to break her grip. "I need to find out what's wrong." Mallory nodded in the direction of the young wandering soul. "They've already been in serious danger today."

"We haven't finished discussing the matter of my freedom," Jenet protested.

"You're not about to leave me in here unprotected, are you?" Deneg asked. "I need to return to sleep. I've managed to have so little of it today. And there's also the gold I need to free my brother."

"Someone should have stayed with the wagon," Ninette said.

Mallory looked from each of them, not sure what to do. Sometimes their party wasn't big enough to deal with everything that needed to be done.

"I'll stay with Deneg." Callum moved closer to the vampire, facing him. "We can sort out enough money from the treasure to free your brother once night falls. All we need to know for now is that you're happy to let us free Jenet."

Deneg closed the short distance between him and Callum, lowering his voice. "You would stay and protect me, even after everything?"

Callum nodded, meeting Deneg's gaze.

Deneg ran his hand across Callum's cheek. "Thank you, Cal." He smiled, his long canines impossible to miss. "I'll see you when the sun sets." After another smile and a long look at Callum, Deneg returned to his coffin, pulling the lid down and locking it.

"Will you give me the bracelet that was used to bind me to another's will?" Jenet asked.

"Adventurers, will you come?" the wandering soul asked, urgency in its voice.

Ninette took a step towards the exit. "Did you want me to watch the wagon?"

Ryan nodded. "That'd be good."

"We can help her." Jorgen ushered his cousin out ahead of him, ignoring his protests as they followed Ninette outside.

"If you want to see what's wrong with the wandering souls, I'm okay to stay here," Callum said.

Mallory couldn't resist sighing. Even Ryan's grin for her didn't help her dredge up a smile. "Okay." She took a deep breath, glancing at Jenet's hand holding her wrist. "Let me go. If you want to come with us while we find out what's going on, we can talk about the bracelet." She nodded towards the wandering soul. "But before we sort out setting you free, we need to learn what's wrong with the wandering souls."

Jenet slowly released Mallory. "You do know they can take years to tell a person what their problem is."

"If that's the case, then it's not urgent and we'll sort out setting you free." Mallory took another deep breath before she strode towards the exit, following the young wandering soul that hurried ahead of her.

Ryan walked at Mallory's side, slipping his hand in hers. "We've got this." He kept his voice low.

"What else could be wrong with them?" Mallory nodded towards the young wandering soul. "We killed the tree leeches. How many things can go wrong for tree people?"

"Fire?" Ryan suggested.

"I hope not." Mallory couldn't resist glancing over her shoulder to where Brodie walked beside Danae with Fang at his side, Emica and Jenet following them. Was this their fault? Had flames from Scorch's hooves set the forest on fire? She came to a stop when she stepped out of the ruined entrance of the cave and found a wandering soul waited for them.

Brodie stopped on the other side of Mallory. "Think it's the same one?"

Mallory shrugged. It seemed like the same one to her, but she had no idea how to tell them apart. She glanced at the young wandering soul. Other than by height and even that wasn't very useful when numerous ones of the same height were together in the one place.

The wandering soul bowed low. "It is good of you to answer our call again, adventurers."

Mallory breathed in deeply, scanning the area. She saw no fire and smelled no smoke. But that didn't mean anything. The wind could be blowing in the wrong direction to carry the scent to them. "What is the problem?"

"They have returned, adventurers."

Mallory frowned. "Who has returned?"

"A swarm of death has come seeking my people once more."

"A swarm of death?" Mallory had no idea what he was talking about. They talked so strangely. "Your people are dying again?"

"The same death wanders amongst us," the wandering soul said.

"You've got more leeches?" Brodie demanded. He continued speaking when the wandering soul lowered and raised its upper branches. "Didn't we kill all of them?"

"Ones lacking light released them near my people," the wandering soul said.

"Lacking light?" Ryan asked.

"It's what they call the dark forces," Emica said.

Mallory once again scanned the area. "Where are they?"

"You must rid us of the swarm of death again, adventurers. We will reward you for your help."

At the wandering soul's words, a journal notification appeared in the corner of Mallory's vision. She opened her journal and read over the new quest. *Wandering Souls In Danger Part Two: The dark forces are attacking wandering souls through the use of tree leeches. The wandering souls will reward you if you help them.*

"What kind of reward?" Brodie asked.

"It doesn't matter," Ryan said. "We'd help them anyway."

"Yeah, but it's still good to know what the reward

is," Brodie said. "I mean, I'm not expecting treasure, but it'd still be nice to know what we'll get."

"You seek treasure, adventurer?" the wandering soul asked.

Brodie grinned. "Hell yeah."

The wandering soul dipped its branches. "That we can do."

Brodie stared at the wandering soul, open-mouthed. "You have treasure? Where do you keep it?"

"We know the soil, know what is hidden in its depths," the wandering soul said.

"Cool," Brodie said. "All of you?" He glanced at the young wandering soul who had sunk its roots into the ground. "Even the young one?"

"We know our home," the wandering soul said.

"We should get Deneg's coffin back in the wagon before we go after the dark forces," Ryan said. "It's no point getting rid of the leeches again if they're only going to release more of them."

"We should have lunch too," Brodie said. "I'm starving and it's after one."

"The youngling will remain with you and show you where the ones lacking in light are staying," the wandering soul said.

Mallory stepped towards it, half raising a hand

when it started to move away. "Wait. What is the youngling's name?"

"The youngling has not earned a name," the wandering soul said.

"Earned?" Brodie asked. "Like a payment?"

"Names are given to commemorate milestones. Some of my people have many names, others have yet to earn a single one," the wandering soul said.

"How do you earn names?" Mallory asked.

"Through deeds." The wandering soul bowed to them. "Hurry, adventurers. Some of those facing death are ones that faced it before. Their time is limited."

Mallory breathed out heavily as she watched the wandering soul stride away. "I wish they understood time better."

"We'll act like time is running out," Ryan said. "That way we should hopefully be able to save all of them."

"Okay." Mallory again glanced around the area. A fire might have been easier to deal with. She thought of her new spell, water manipulation. A fire certainly would have been easier. "Okay." She said the word again, not feeling any better for having said it or feeling like they were prepared for the quest. "Brodie get Ninette to help you make food. Make whatever it was you were going to make with the oats. We don't have time to hunt."

"Yet you have time to cook and eat?" Jenet asked.

Ryan grinned, glancing at Brodie before focusing his attention on Jenet. "It's safest. Who knows what some might be tempted to eat otherwise." He turned to Mallory, ignoring Brodie muttering that the goblin ale hadn't hurt him as he strode towards the wagon. "I'll get the travellers to help me return the coffin to the wagon."

"I'll help." Emica walked towards the wagon with Ryan.

"I should see if Brodie and Ninette need help with the food." Danae hurried after Brodie, who was nearly back at the wagon.

Jenet waited until it was only her and Mallory, the youngling wandering amongst the trees exploring, before she spoke. "When will you have time to discuss setting me free?"

Chapter Forty-Two

"Now?" Mallory doubted she'd have time to talk later and the warrior didn't deserve to be kept as a statue. It made her think of Pelga who was trapped as a harp. "I don't suppose you know how to break a demonic curse keeping someone as a harp?"

"There are certain shrines in dangerous areas that will do that and powerful demons who can break curses created by those less powerful than they are," Jenet said. "Is that what you wish me to do? Break the curse on someone in exchange for my freedom?"

Mallory shook her head, even though she would have preferred to say yes. "If you were interested in saving Pelga, I'd be grateful, but it isn't something any of us would expect of you. I'd also love to know the words used to stop Scorch from leaving flames where he steps. But it's not a condition of setting you free either."

Jenet studied Mallory. "You do understand the way the world works."

Mallory laughed. "Yeah, I do. But I'm not putting a price on setting you free. That seems too much like selling a person and I don't agree with slavery."

Jenet finally inclined her head. "I believe you mean exactly what you say and to show you how much I trust you, it is 'extinguish spark' to stop the flames, and 'battle trample' to bring them back. The word to remove the mask is Scorch." She paused a moment. "If you would trust me as much as I trust you, I'd see that the curse was broken and Pelga escorted back to her family."

"How do we know we can trust you?" Ryan asked.

Mallory turned to see him coming towards them, along with Jorgen, Esben and Emica, the four of them carrying the coffin.

"There are-" Jenet broke off. "Actually, I don't know if there are people who can vouch for me. I don't know who still lives or who might have changed beyond all recognition. Like Azerron."

"We don't know many people on Ruby Isle let alone on Inadon," Ryan said.

"Were you with any faction?" Emica asked.

Jenet walked beside them as they continued to

carry the coffin towards the wagon. "Gladiators. I worked out of Shadhurst."

"There'd be records there about you," Emica said.

Jenet inclined her head. "More than likely. I completed a lot of quests for them in between helping Azerron take down members of the dark forces. He wanted me to leave the gladiators and work solely with him." She slowly shook her head. "He can't have joined the dark forces. Not after all the years we spent hunting them."

Brodie strode towards them, the duplication paper held aloft. "Hisoki replied." He fell into step with them.

"Did he have any messages for me?" Emica asked.

Brodie stepped back out of the way so they could put the coffin on the wagon. "He said Azerron had a falling out with the commander of the gladiator's faction over imprisoning Jenet Grayrock. He thought it wrong to imprison someone like that. Especially one who'd done so much for the faction."

"What else did my father say?" Emica asked.

"Just asked if you were safe. I said you were," Brodie said.

"That was it?" Emica stepped away from the wagon, the coffin back in its usual place.

Brodie held out the duplication paper. "You can see for yourself."

Emica took the paper, reading it over before handing it back. She glanced around the party, everyone watching her. She faced Jenet. "Was that what you needed to know?"

"There must be more to it than that. I'll need to speak to the commander. Or possibly the steward. They keep track of all the goings on in the faction. Unless things have changed since my time there."

"Does that mean she can do the quest?" Brodie asked.

"I will expect the bracelet in exchange," Jenet said.

"What's it look like?" Brodie asked.

"There are two of them," Jenet said. "They're gold, about four inches wide and have a single gem set in the middle of the band. Mine is blue while the one for Scorch is red. I only need mine."

"How wide is four inches?" Brodie asked.

"About ten centimetres." Callum held up a hand, indicating the size with the help of his thumb and middle finger.

"I think I know the ones you're talking about." Brodie jumped up into the wagon to scratch around in a chest. He held up two wide bands, a gap in the back of them. "This them?"

Jenet nodded. "If you wear the one belonging to Scorch, he'll obey you without question."

Brodie slipped the bracelet with the red gem in it onto his wrist. He again held up the other one. "Does this one make you do what the wearer says?"

Mallory took the bracelet from her brother and handed it to Jenet. "You're free. And we expect nothing in return."

"Should have asked for the location of the army," Brodie muttered. "I bet there's more treasure there."

Jenet slipped the bracelet over her wrist. "I'll break Pelga's curse and draw you a map so you can find the demonic dungeon where Azerron keeps his golem army. He deserves to lose them after the amount of years he had me imprisoned."

Brodie victory punched the air. "Hell yeah. More treasure."

"Adventurers follow now?" the young wandering soul asked hopefully.

"Lunch should be ready. We need to eat. It keeps us running. So we'll have it first," Brodie said. "I made something a bit like an ANZAC biscuit. I'm not sure how it'll turn out, but the raw mix tasted good." He turned to Jenet. "You staying for lunch? There should be enough for everyone."

"You're willing to feed me?" Jenet asked.

Mallory smiled at the shocked tone Jenet used. Not that she could blame the warrior considering Brodie's comments. "We wouldn't send you on your way hungry."

"Adventurers?" the young wandering soul came closer. "Now, adventurers?"

"Soon." Brodie glanced at the young wandering soul in between serving the food with Ninette's help. "You really need a name. Can't you do something so we can call you by a name? Or can we just give you one like we did with Precious? You're both trees."

Mallory took the soft biscuit from Brodie, shuffling it between her hands as it cooled. "Brodie." She put a warning note in her voice. She didn't want him to offend the wandering soul.

"What?" Brodie asked.

Mallory sighed. "Sometimes you're rather clueless." She took a bite of the misshapen biscuit that had cooled enough to eat. "This isn't bad."

"I used up all the eggs, honey and oats. We've only got a kilo of flour left and a hundred and fifty mils of the maple syrup and only fifty mils of cooking oil. We're going to need more stuff," Brodie said.

Ryan took a second biscuit. "We can live off what we hunt and gather. No need to spend money now we're finally earning some. Who knows how long it'll be before we earn a decent amount again."

It wasn't until the meal was nearly finished that they discussed their next plan. They decided Mallory, Ryan, Brodie, Callum and Danae would track down the dark forces while the rest travelled to Longmeadow in the wagon and bought more tree leech mist. Jenet would go with them and remain in Longmeadow when they returned to the cave with the potion, taking Pelga with her.

Chapter Forty-Three

Mallory turned to Jenet. "Do you have enough money to live on until you can start earning some again?"

"Why do you ask?" Jenet dusted the crumbs from her fingers and lap.

"We can give you a handful of silver pieces to help you out," Mallory said.

Jenet stared at her before finally speaking. "If you have need of me, leave a message for me with the gladiator faction in Shadhurst. I owe you for how honourably you've treated me in our dealings."

Mallory wanted to argue that anyone would have done the same, but she remained silent, knowing that many wouldn't have.

"Adventurers?" the young wandering soul asked.

Ryan rose from the log he'd been sitting on. "Yeah. We're just about ready."

They cleaned up and packed the wagon while Jenet gave Mallory a drawing of a basic map that she'd drawn on the back of the letter from Tivon that Mallory had handed over when the warrior had asked for parchment.

Mallory stood beside Ryan, watching as the wagon pulled away from them, leaving the horses and donkey with the wagon since they didn't know where they'd need to go to find the dark forces and if the horses could reach the location. "Do you think everyone will be okay?"

Ryan slipped an arm around her waist, drawing her close. "They'll be fine. Probably better than us since they aren't about to go looking for a dark forces camp and Jorgen is a much higher level than all of us."

"Come now, adventurers?" the young wandering soul asked hopefully.

"Yeah, we'll come now." Mallory drew away from Ryan. "Okay. Lead the way."

Ryan checked his pocket watch as they followed the young wandering soul. "As long as nothing holds them up, they should be back at the cave entrance around six. Not long after dark."

"Let's hope we're done before then too," Mallory said.

They remained silent as they followed the young

wandering soul who occasionally looked back at them, twisting its upper trunk so it could see them. The sound of a bowstring being released nearby had the wandering soul moving swiftly in front of Mallory, an arrow impaling one of its limbs. It cried out when struck.

Mallory grabbed her wand, looking in the direction the arrow had come from. Movement caught her attention and she cast fireball, three arrows and a throwing knife all striking the archer at the same time. Another glance around showed nothing. "Think he was the lookout?"

Ryan lowered his hunting bow. "Possibly. Whatever he was, he was well hidden. Even Fang and Smudge didn't notice him. We should get out of here before more turn up." He faced the young wandering soul. "Are you okay?"

The young wandering soul made soft sounds that were almost a whimper, sinking its roots into the ground.

Brodie stepped in front of it. "Want me to pull the arrow out?"

"Thank you for that." Mallory continued to hold her wand. "You saved me the pain of being struck by an arrow. Want me to see if I can heal you?"

"You will be able to," Danae assured her.

"Wandering souls are one of the less common sentient races, not a creature or beast. If they were an animal, you wouldn't be able to heal them."

"Is that the sort of deed that gives you a name?" Callum gestured towards the arrow.

The young wandering soul bowed its upper branches.

"What sort of name?" Brodie took hold of the arrow. "You look like a pincushion."

"We could call it Arrow," Callum suggested.

Mallory healed the young wandering soul once Brodie drew out the arrow, relieved Danae was right and she was able to heal it considering it wasn't even close to human in form. "Its name should be Shield. That's more accurate than Arrow."

Brodie held up the arrow. "How about Target?"

"What about Spike?" Ryan suggested.

"I like that," Callum said.

"It's okay. But I still think Target is better," Brodie said.

Mallory finished healing the young wandering soul. "What do you think?"

Again the young wandering soul bowed its upper branches. "I am honoured to accept the name Spike, adventurers. Your gift is precious."

Mallory met Ryan's gaze at the word 'precious',

managing not to return his grin. She forced her gaze to return to the young wandering soul. "Okay. Spike it is."

Danae, who stood with her back to them, glanced over her shoulder. "We should keep moving before another one of them finds us."

Spike drew its roots up out of the ground. "My people are pleased with the name."

"I bet they would have liked Target better," Brodie muttered.

Spike started to move forward.

Mallory hurried after Spike, about to put out a hand to stop it. She lowered her hand, not sure if that would offend. "Wait, Spike. We don't want them to see us."

"Hide time?" Spike asked.

Mallory nodded. "Yeah. We need to hide from them."

Spike sank its roots into the ground and closed its eyes, gently swaying in the light breeze.

Mallory drew in a deep breath. "Not like that."

Spike opened its eyes. "Hide good. No one find."

"Ah, yeah." Mallory glanced at Ryan who grinned at her. There would obviously be no help from him when it came to explaining the situation. Not with how amused he was by it. "We need to hide as well as seek." She had no idea if hide and seek was played on Inadon or if wandering souls in particular knew the game, but the terms fit in a way.

"Can only be one. Game works that way," Spike said.

Mallory tried to think of another explanation, Spike's comment answering her earlier thought. "We need to sneak up on them so we can catch them by surprise. Only when we're ready though. We don't want to surprise them too soon."

Spike closed its eyes, returning to swaying gently in the breeze.

"Has Spike gone to sleep?" Brodie asked.

Callum came over to stand in front of Spike. "If I didn't know better, I'd think it was an ordinary tree."

Spike opened its eyes. "Stealth of the rogue."

"Ah, maybe." Mallory could only hope that this time Spike had understood.

Spike glided across the ground, swaying in time with the breeze, each sway taking it forward a fraction.

Callum stared at the young wandering soul. "That is amazing. Even watching, I don't always catch its movements. They could surround a place without anyone knowing."

"Hell yeah! That's what I call stealth," Brodie exclaimed.

"Let's hope it can keep the movement up." Mallory couldn't help worrying since Spike was only a youngling. Not that she knew exactly what that meant other than it was younger than the other wandering soul.

"I'll check the archer to see what we can get," Ryan said. "If we're lucky, it'll be arrows since we're so low."

It didn't take Ryan long to check and he found three arrows and a longbow that he gave to Danae since she was a level three archer.

"Thank you." Danae returned her short bow to her back, keeping hold of the longbow. "This is wonderful. It'll have at least twenty-three damage and between my racial bonus and dexterity bonus, I'll have an extra thirty-four percent damage on the base stats."

"I need to get my last CAS point so I can level up and use a longbow," Callum said. "It'll beat using a short bow."

"We hardly get any drops for rogue," Brodie muttered.

Ryan grinned. "Yeah, we know. It's not fair."

Brodie glared at Ryan. "Shouldn't we be quiet so they don't hear us coming?"

Chapter Forty-Four

Mallory managed not to smile while her brother could see her expression, but the moment his attention was caught by something, her smile escaped. She bet he wouldn't have been hushing anyone if Ryan hadn't been teasing him. He would have been the one they were trying to silence.

They continued to stay well behind Spike, coming to a stop when the young wandering soul stopped gliding forward.

"Think it's found the dark forces?" Ryan kept his voice low.

Mallory shrugged. Before she could say anything, Brodie spoke.

"I'll find out."

Callum grabbed Brodie's arm before he'd taken more than a step, dragging him back. "None of us want to be spotted."

Brodie shrugged Callum's hand off his arm and turned to Mallory. "Make me invisible then."

She didn't trust her brother not to end up in more trouble instead of less. "I'll go." She quickly added to her comment when her brother started to protest. "That way I can recast the spell if I need to."

Ryan interrupted Brodie when he tried to protest again. "It makes sense." He turned to Mallory, wrapping his arms around her waist. "Be careful and call for us if you get into trouble."

Mallory smiled at him. "I think you're mistaking me for my brother." She lightly kissed him before reluctantly pulling away. "I won't be long." Not knowing how close the dark forces were, she cast vanish I on herself before moving away from everyone, heading in the direction Spike had been taking.

After a glance at the young wandering soul, she continued, wishing she knew what was ahead of her. A few minutes later she stumbled, wincing when someone called out, demanding to know who was there. She'd obviously found the dark forces. Or at least one of them. Recasting vanish I, she crept silently forward, barely daring to breathe. She half expected someone to call out and say they'd spotted her.

Crouching behind a shrub, she drew in a sharp breath once she'd finished counting enemies. There were four archers, each with longbows, and six warriors with short swords and shields. She wished now she'd brought the spyglass with her. After watching them for a minute, she decided she needed to know more information and recast vanish I before returning to her party and Spike.

"What did you see?" Brodie demanded the moment Mallory became visible, only metres from them.

"I need the spyglass." Mallory held out her hand to Callum, briefly telling them what she'd seen.

"They have to be at least level three archers," Danae said. "Their health won't be too bad if they're only level three. It's the warriors that might be a problem. Although you'd think they'd have better gear than a short sword and shield if that was the case."

"I won't be long." Clutching the spyglass in one hand and her wand in the other, Mallory returned to the encampment, once again invisible.

She brought the spyglass to her eye, relief rushing through her when she found the archers had twenty-four health and the warriors thirty-nine. It should make it easier to take the archers out before they could attack them from a distance. Something glinting in the sun caught her attention and she used the spyglass to get a better look. Her relief vanished. There were four large glass jars with stoppers and each was filled with small tree leeches. From what she could see, there was somewhere between thirty and fifty in a jar, but they moved around too much for her to count them. They needed to take out the archers and warriors before they could use the tree leeches on more wandering souls.

Recasting vanish I, Mallory backed away, not turning towards where she'd left her party until she'd put a few metres between her and where she'd spied on the archers and warriors. She didn't want to risk alerting them to her presence again. They were already wary.

Reaching her party, Mallory barely had the chance to become visible before Brodie was firing questions at her. She held up a hand, trying to slow him down, needing to interrupt so she could tell everyone what she'd seen. Her words brought silence. "We can't let them get away with this."

"Should we wait until the rest return with the tree leech mist?" Danae asked.

"What if they release the tree leeches?" Callum glanced at Spike. "How many of the wandering souls might die?" He patted Smudge on the head when he made a distressed sound.

Fang echoed Smudge's sound, leaning against Brodie's leg.

"Why would they attack them?" Brodie asked. "Seems pointless."

"For the timber," Danae said. Possibly so they can make golems."

"They plan to create an army?" Mallory asked.

Danae shrugged. "Or sell some of the timber to those who'd find a golem useful. Besides, it isn't only for fighting that golems are used. They can gather resources, do menial labour and complete simple tasks, unless they're essence golems. Essence golems can do anything one of the sentient races can do, including level up and gain revives."

"We're not waiting for everyone to return before we take out the dark forces." Ryan rested his hand on the hilt of the sword hanging on his right. "We can't risk them releasing any more tree leeches. Can't risk the lives of the wandering souls." He glanced at Spike. "Any of the wandering souls."

Mallory returned the spyglass to Callum. "If we take out the archers first, that will be the most powerful attacks gone. A single attack from one of them could take out Callum. We desperately need armour and more health."

"I can stay back and take them out from a distance," Callum said. "Smudge and Fang are the ones we really need to worry about. Maybe we should wait for everyone else so we can take the archers and warriors out even quicker."

"We've got this," Ryan said. "There are four archers and five of us. Danni can take out one on her own with the longbow and Brodie and I can attack the same one since we have the lowest of the range attacks. Then Danni can help us once she's finished with hers." He turned to Brodie. "You're not to try and get a hit in on every enemy. We have to focus on taking the archers out before they can shoot us."

Mallory's grip tightened on her wand. She needed a better healing spell. More than she needed the other spells the mage from Longmeadow was selling. "We are going to use some of the money from the demonic dungeon treasure to outfit ourselves better."

Brodie took out two throwing knives, his armour sliding into place. "Can I get an enchanted stiletto?"

"Maybe." Mallory dreaded to think how expensive they'd be, but all of them needed better gear.

"No help, adventurers," Spike said.

The words startled Mallory. She'd thought the

young wandering soul had gone to sleep with how quiet it was and with its eyes closed. "It's okay if you can't help."

"No. My people. I help. My people fear the death in jars," Spike said.

"Spike, it isn't necessary." Mallory couldn't resist resting a hand on his trunk, not far from his eyes. "None of us want you hurt."

"I help." Spike leaned against her hand.

Mallory nearly lowered her hand at the unexpected weight against it. She kept it in place, remaining still.

Callum joined Mallory, standing at her side and facing Spike. "Actually, you could be a really big help. We need someone to watch our companion animals so they can gain XP while not risking being killed. Only Fang has a revive."

"I will guard the furred ones," Spike stated.

Ryan joined them. "Good. That's settled. Let's get closer so we can get the archers and warriors dealt with before they have the chance to cause any more damage."

Chapter Forty-Five

They remained silent, weapons ready and all of them scanning the area. Mallory didn't know about the rest of her party, but she kept expecting trouble. Such as more archers turning up at the encampment. As they drew close, she signaled for them to slow. If she had more mana, she would have made them all invisible. As it was, she could only turn two of them invisible, but that would mean she might not have enough mana to attack as rapidly as she might need to.

They kept low as they drew near, using shrubs and trees for cover. As soon as they were close enough, Ryan pointed out who was to attack which archer. Once everyone had nodded, he counted upwards by raising three fingers one at a time, swiftly grabbing an arrow from his quiver and firing it at the archer Brodie attacked.

Mallory cast ice shard at the archer she was to

attack, needing to cast it twice more before the archer was impaled by an arrow and dropped to the ground. She didn't have time to be relieved they'd taken out all the archers. A warrior bore down on her, sword in hand. Drawing her own sword, she cast ice shard twice before his sword clashed with hers.

"No!"

At Danae's cry, Mallory glanced towards the half-elf, expecting her to be in more danger than she could handle. One of the warriors dropped to the ground, impaled by another one of Danae's arrows, but not before she could prevent him from smashing a glass jar. Tree leeches took to the sky, flying in the direction of where the ones were feeding on wandering souls. Mallory could do nothing about them, even though she wanted to echo Danae's cry. The warrior continued to attack her and she was forced to defend, getting in a couple more attacks with ice shard.

Danae helped Mallory with her warrior, having already taken out two. "Go after them. Use flame and water manipulation on them. Don't let them join the other ones. The wandering souls might not survive the extra leeches."

Not able to escape the warrior's attacks, Mallory

cast vanish I on herself and stepped to the side, the warrior stumbling when he met nothing.

Ryan finished off his warrior and headed in the direction the tree leeches had taken. "We'll be back as soon as we've dealt with them." He sheathed his sword then broke into a run.

Mallory ran after him, keeping her wand out, scanning the area as she tried to spot the escaping tree leeches. They were nowhere to be seen. Were they too late? Had they already found the wandering souls?

"This way." Ryan veered to the left. "I saw one of them fly in this direction."

Mallory tried to keep up with him, but he was slowly pulling away from her. "What about the rest of them?"

Ryan glanced over his shoulder, not slowing. "They might be ahead of this one."

She tried to run faster, but it was impossible. She was already going as fast as she could.

"They're chasing some younglings," Ryan called over his shoulder.

"Can we get the younglings to come back this way?" Mallory slowed when she saw how little stamina she had left. She didn't want to completely run out of stamina. That didn't sound like a good idea.

"Younglings, draw the tree leeches over here." Ryan paused a moment before he called out again, repeating himself. He stopped where he was and half turned towards Mallory. "They're coming back this way. Are you ready?" He took an arrow out and readied his hunting bow. "I don't know if shooting them will work."

Mallory stopped at his side, her grip tightening on her wand when she saw the younglings running towards them, approximately fifty tree leeches following them. She didn't notice that a couple of tree leeches had already latched on until the younglings drew close. Not knowing what to do about the ones attached, she used flame on the ones that chased the young wandering souls.

A tree leech caught alight, flying into several others and setting them alight too. One of them tumbled to the ground, setting fire to the grass.

Ryan shot two of the tree leeches. "Better put that fire out before it becomes a problem."

Mallory used water manipulation, drawing water from the air to shift it to the fire. Not knowing if she should dump it or slowly release it over the fire, she decided to try dumping it. There was enough moisture in the air that she could take more water from it if that method didn't work.

One of the young wandering souls with a tree leech on it came to a shuddering stop, swaying erratically where it stood, roots snaking across the ground.

"Keep moving or they'll catch up to you." She took several steps towards the young wandering soul, throwing flame at one of the tree leeches following, wishing the youngling would move. She didn't want to accidentally hit it.

"Send flame over here." Ryan crouched by a makeshift firepit, several sticks protruding from it.

"What are you planning?" Mallory threw flame at the firepit, the grasses in it immediately catching fire. She focused on the tree leeches again, trying not to think about how many were on the young wandering souls. She doubted they'd contain much sap.

Ryan rose to his feet, holding one of the burning branches. "Getting rid of the tree leeches." He hurried over to the one who'd stopped. "Let me know if this hurts." He pressed the burning branch against a tree leech, turning to Mallory when it tried to fly away. "I'll burn them off, you finish them."

She nodded, casting flame at the tree leech Ryan

had burned. A grin escaped. It would be a breeze now.

The moment the last tree leech had been killed, Ryan slung his bow on his back. He examined one of the young wandering souls. "Are you okay? I didn't hurt you?"

There was a rustle of branches before the youngling opened its eyes and scurried off, the other ones following.

Ryan stared at the young wandering souls as they disappeared into the forests surrounding them. "We better get back and see how everyone else managed."

Mallory took a step towards where they needed to go, her gaze drawn in the direction the young wandering souls had taken. "Do you think they'll be okay?"

Ryan took her hand, walking towards where they'd left their party. "Yeah. And they'll be even better once we sort out those trying to kill them."

Mallory opened her journal to see how everyone was doing and noticed how many experience points she now had. "I gained sixty-eight XP from those tree leeches."

"Each one is worth two XP." Ryan grinned. "Better hope Brodie doesn't notice."

Mallory couldn't resist laughing. "He'll just have to

get over it." Her laughter faded. "I wouldn't want to farm them no matter how quick I managed to gain the XP. I kept thinking they might turn and come after one of us."

Ryan's hand tightened on Mallory's. "At least we managed to take them out before they could cause too much harm to the younglings." He paused a moment. "And I'm now one XP off my next CAS point which will take me up to character level three."

Mallory pointed out some herbs not far from them. "Maybe you should gather two resources so you can level up. It'll give you another revive and improve your stats."

"Once we make sure everyone else is okay," Ryan said.

She nodded, remaining silent as they continued back to where they'd left the rest of their party. As they approached the encampment, Mallory saw Spike was with the rest of the party, Smudge and Fang following him around as he explored the place.

Mallory and Ryan had barely entered the encampment, bodies scattered throughout it, Callum and Danae searching them, when Brodie opened up one of the glass jars of tree leeches. Mallory opened her mouth to protest. She didn't have the chance.

Brodie dropped an open potion vial into the jar

and shoved the cork back into place. He looked in his sister's direction. "About time you got back. We were able to take everyone out and raid the encampment. Callum and Danae are searching the last couple of bodies."

Chapter Forty-Six

Mallory's gaze remained on the large glass jar Brodie had opened. "What are you doing? Why would you even think about risking the tree leeches escaping?"

Brodie held up another potion vial. This one had a cork in place. "How else am I meant to kill them? We found some vials of tree leech mist." Brodie's mouth opened for a moment before he victory punched the air. "Hell yeah. Look how much XP I just got. A hundred XP for dropping a potion bottle into the jar. I wonder how much XP Jorgen got when he took out the other ones."

"Two XP each tree leech." Ryan glanced around the encampment. "Was there anything of value?"

Brodie gestured towards a pile of canvas and a mixture of items. "We put it all there." He glanced towards the glass jar of dead tree leeches. "They helped me level up. My character level is three now."

He paused a moment. "You have reached level three rogue. You can now wield enchanted throwing knives." Again he paused a moment. "I need enchanted throwing knives to go with the enchanted stiletto you're going to buy me."

"Next level you gain another skill," Callum said. "Sleight of hand. What stats are you levelling up?"

Brodie shrugged. "I haven't decided yet." He glanced at the glass jars. "Who gets the other two jars of tree leeches to kill? It's a pity we didn't get location XP for finding the encampment."

"It mustn't be established enough to count as a location," Danae said.

Ryan stopped in front of the pile Brodie had indicated, glancing over at Brodie. "You've reached character level three. Callum and I haven't."

"You might as well be," Brodie said. "Even if Callum gets a jar full, that still leaves another one."

Danae rose to her feet, holding a second longbow. "What about Ninette? We don't have to destroy them straight away. We can wait until everyone is back."

"We're going to need the wagon to collect all this stuff. We won't be able to carry everything to the cave entrance." Ryan rummaged through the piles. "Four canvas tents, two longbows when you count the one Danni just found, a large cooking pot, a map of Ruby Isle that seems to be the same as the one we already have, twenty arrows, a wooden shield, two bedrolls, a wooden bucket, an axe, two health potions, a short sword, a jar of coffee that looks like it contains six servings, four wooden plates and three pairs of brown trousers."

Brodie held up three potion vials that were full. "We also have three lots of tree leech mist. We'll only need two of them."

Callum took one of the vials from Brodie. "Has it been decided? Should I take one lot out?" He glanced at the glass jars.

Ryan nodded. "Sounds good to me. You've got the lowest character level out of the five of us."

Mallory glanced around the group. "Is everyone happy to wait for Ninette to get rid of the last jar?"

There were murmurs of agreement and nods. Brodie glanced skywards. "When will they be back again?"

"They should be at the cave by six," Ryan said.

"What's the time now?" Brodie asked.

Ryan checked his pocket watch. "Three thirty."

"That's ages away," Brodie complained.

Callum gestured towards a campfire in the middle of the encampment, a cooking pot still hanging over it. "You could finish cooking their soup. You'll probably be hungry before too much longer."

"Not what I meant when I said how long it'd be," Brodie muttered. "What if it's too long for the wandering souls to wait? Should we use the tree leech mist on them now?"

Ryan hurried after Spike, who was still wandering around the encampment, studying everything. "Can you tell us if your people are still okay? The ones with the tree leeches."

Spike stilled, sinking its roots into the ground. "They live."

"How much longer do they have?" Ryan asked.

"They will see the setting sun and beyond," Spike said.

Mallory joined Ryan, standing at his side in front of Spike. "Can you tell us when it's getting too dangerous for them? So we know when they need the tree leeches removed. We don't want any of them to die."

Spike lowered and raised its upper branches. "I will warn you. My people are grateful for your care." It lowered and raised its upper branches once more before returning to exploring the encampment.

Callum uncorked one of the jars and dropped an open potion vial of tree leech mist into it before pushing the cork back into place. He watched the contents of the jar. "I wonder if there's a way to turn these into an XP farm. That was an easy hundred XP. I'm now character level three and I've put my class point in archer. You have reached level three archer. You can now wield longbows." He strode over to the pile of gear and picked up one of the longbows, leaving his short bow behind in its place. "It's nice to finally be improving our gear in a significant way."

Brodie peered into the pot over the fire. "Wish I could get better weapons." He looked up from the pot. "But at least I've got awesome armour. And a great horse to go with it."

"Scorch isn't your horse," Mallory warned.

Brodie picked up a ladle and inspected it before he used it in the pot. "He goes with the armour." He glanced at the bracelet he wore. "Besides, he answers to me." There was another pause as he tasted the food. "We should have kept Bobbi, Scorch and the riding horse with us."

"The armour doesn't make Scorch yours," Mallory said. "And the horses would have been in the way or risked being harmed when we attacked the archers and warriors."

Brodie shrugged, again tasting the food. "This should be ready in about half an hour and I bet they would have been fine. I could have ridden Scorch into battle."

Mallory had no idea what she could do while they waited for the rest of their group to return from Longmeadow. She thought of her leather bound notebook she'd put in the chest, wishing now she'd kept it in her satchel. Maybe she should do that in future for times like this.

The next half an hour passed quicker than expected and Brodie served up the food, finding enough wooden bowls for them to use. Afterwards, he cleaned the five bowls and added them to the pile of gear.

"Did you decide what you're putting your attribute points into?" Danae asked Brodie.

"Yeah, I need more health. I've only got one revive left. So I'm putting two in constitution, one in intelligence so I've now got nothing under five, one in dexterity and one in luck. I think we need a bit more luck with how many enemies we're collecting. I bet Azerron will be angry if he ever finds out we stole his treasure and horse." Brodie paused a moment. "My health is now thirty-six and my stamina is sixty." He turned to Callum. "What are you putting your attribute points into?"

"I've put one point in strength, two in constitution

and two in dexterity," Callum said. "That gives me thirty health and fifty stamina." Callum faced his brother. "You going to gather two resources so you can level up?"

"I'll sort it out later," Ryan said. "We've got other things to focus on for now."

"Where are we heading after we finish up here?" Danae asked. "After we've saved the wandering souls and delivered Deneg somewhere safe."

Callum took out the map of Ruby Isle. "We have a few quests we could do."

They argued back and forth over what their next step should be, finally settling on getting the treasure sold and most of the money banked and buying better gear. Including the spells Mallory wanted. Their discussion lasted longer than they expected and there was just enough time for Mallory and Ryan to return to the cave entrance to meet up with the rest of their group. Callum, Brodie, Danae, Smudge, Fang and Spike remained with the gear, building up the campfire to give them enough light. Mallory was glad of her magelight that allowed them to find their way in the dark to the cave entrance.

The rest of their group was waiting for them when they arrived and Emica explained that Deneg was still asleep, having woken briefly at sunset to say he needed more sleep after his had been disturbed so much during the day. Once everyone was in the wagon, including Kitty who dashed back under the driver's seat, Ryan directed Ninette to where they needed to go. During the journey Mallory explained everything that had happened, finishing with telling Ninette about the jar of tree leeches.

Ninette glanced over her shoulder. "Are you sure? I don't mind if someone else gains the XP."

Chapter Forty-Seven

Mallory smiled at Ninette. "We're sure. You've got the lowest level so it makes sense that you have the XP." She interrupted Ninette's thanks. "Was Jenet happy to be left in Longmeadow?"

"She seemed pleased to see the village again," Ninette said.

"She kept talking about all the changes," Esben said.

Mallory tried to imagine what it would be like to return to the world a century later. She couldn't. She linked her fingers with Ryan. All she could think was that there were so many people that probably no longer lived.

The journey back to the encampment was quiet and while everyone loaded up the gear, struggling to find places for all of it, Ninette used a tree leech mist on the large jar of tree leeches. Danae also stowed her short bow on the wagon since she wouldn't need it now she had a longbow.

"I'm halfway through character level two," Ninette said.

"Then how about I add everyone to the party and we get the quest for the wandering souls finished." Mallory added Ninette first.

Everyone piled onto the wagon, Brodie patting Scorch before he hopped in, and they made their way to the group of wandering souls that were covered in tree leeches. Brodie argued that he should use the potion on them this time. That Jorgen didn't need the experience points. "I can add some points into stealth and then I'd have more time than Jorgen. He said he hasn't levelled his up."

"We should let him have a go," Ryan said. "See if he can manage before we go after the drake eggs."

Mallory wanted to protest. How many times had her brother caused a disaster over the years? She tried not to sigh, reminding herself of the points he had in dexterity. "Okay." She held out a vial of tree leech mist. "Be careful." She looked at the group of wandering souls as they pulled up nearby.

"Hell yeah." Brodie patted Fang on the head when she nuzzled him. "Wait in the wagon, girl. You'll be close enough to get the XP and you'll level up after this."

Ryan grabbed Brodie's arm when he would have rushed ahead. "You need to be invisible first."

"Oh, yeah. I forgot about that." Brodie turned to his sister. "I'm ready."

Getting out of the wagon, Mallory studied her brother. "Are you sure you're up to this?" She really wished it was Jorgen doing the task. The previous time had been without a problem and things often became problematic when her brother was involved.

"Of course I am. Now make me invisible so I can show you."

Still not certain it was the best plan, Mallory used vanish I on her brother, hearing him move away from them. "Activate stealth."

"Stop worrying about me." Brodie's footsteps became silent.

Or at least Mallory hoped they had become silent and he wasn't standing still. Either way, she could no longer hear him. She scanned the area, looking for signs of her brother as the rest of her party came to stand with her, Spike remaining near Scorch who seemed to fascinate the young wandering soul. She was still trying to decide if it was good or bad that she saw no signs of her brother when he appeared in front of her.

"Job done." Brodie glanced over his shoulder. "They should start dying off soon."

"How many do you think are over there?" Esben asked.

"Looks to be about the same as earlier," Jorgen said. "Two hundred."

"Makes sense," Ryan said. "They had two hundred between the four large jars at their encampment."

"Hell yeah." Brodie victory punched the air. "You should see my XP rise. It's jumping up by the second. How do we get to do more of these types of quests? Fang and I got four hundred XP. Your companion animal has reached level three. Your companion now has an increased ability to forage or hunt for food. And I gained three CAS points."

"Adventurers, I thank you for your help."

Mallory spun to see a wandering soul stood behind them. She hadn't heard it arrive. She looked it up and down. Several of the trees nearby looked almost the same as it. She had no idea if they were wandering souls or actual trees.

"Let me offer you this reward for all you've done for my people." It drew a knot of wood from itself, holding it out.

"What's that for?" Brodie stared at the knotwood. "I thought we were getting real treasure."

"It's what essence golems are made from. Golems that can think for themselves and are almost sentient," Emica said.

"It's extremely valuable," Jorgen added.

"It is?" Brodie took a step closer, eyeing the object.

"There is treasure on the path between places. Spike can show you the way," the wandering soul said.

"Path between places?" Brodie asked.

"It's a road," Danae said.

Brodie glared at the wandering soul. "Don't see why they can't just say that."

Mallory took the knotwood from the wandering soul, ignoring the journal notification in the corner of her vision, guessing it was for completing the quest. "Thank you. We're glad we could help."

"Your names, adventurers?" the wandering soul asked.

Mallory introduced each of them, feeling like she should bow to the wandering soul when it dipped its upper branches so they briefly brushed across the ground.

"You will be known as Mallory Protector amongst my people. All of you have earned the name protector." The wandering soul faced Spike. "As have you Protector Spike."

A shiver ran through Spike, rippling through its leaves. "Honoured. Very honoured." Spike's upper branches brushed across the ground.

"Hey, where did all of them come from?" Brodie asked. "And how come I have XP for a new location? And we've got ten rep for the Valley Of Wandering Souls. That's cool. And why does Spike have the name protector first while we have it second?"

Mallory turned to see wandering souls move in close, many of them bowing their upper branches, some of them sweeping the ground with their branches due to how low they bowed.

"Names are listed in order of importance to the individual," the wandering soul made a sweeping bow. "My people are grateful. You are always welcome in our valley." Again it lowered its upper branches before turning and lumbering away.

"You don't want to go with them?" Brodie asked Spike when the rest of the wandering souls followed the one who'd spoken.

"Spike adventurer. Spike travel too."

Mallory stared at the young wandering soul. "You want to come with us?"

Spike slightly lowered its upper branches. "Spike come with. Earn third name."

Ryan chuckled. "I guess we better get back on the road and take Deneg to Longmeadow."

They all piled back in the wagon, except Brodie who swung onto Scorch's back. Spike followed him, wrapping roots around the horse as it examined him.

Scorch snorted, backing away from the youngling, steam rising from his nostrils as he drew out of the light grip of the roots.

After removing all the extras from the party, Mallory checked the notification, finding it was about the quest as she'd first thought, but also the new location, like Brodie had mentioned. She couldn't help smiling at the thought of the location having come to them, rather than the other way around. *Wandering Souls In Danger Part Two: You were rewarded with wandering souls knotwood for your party and Spike will lead you to a buried treasure. You also earned ten experience points each.* Closing her journal, she turned to Ryan. "What are you going to put your attribute points into?"

Ryan didn't hesitate. "Two in strength, two in constitution and one in dexterity. I can now carry a hundred and thirty kilos, have thirty-nine health and sixty-five stamina. I've also put a point into warrior.

You have reached level three warrior. You can now wield enchanted dual swords." He glanced at Brodie with a grin. "Does that mean I get enchanted swords now?"

Laughing at her brother's glare for Ryan, Mallory took out her leather bound notebook, planning to write some of the day's adventures down while they were fresh in her mind and while she had some quiet time. Who knew what they might run into on the way to Longmeadow. Just because the last journey there had been quiet, it didn't mean this one would be too.

"Where are we going after Longmeadow and seeing if we can find the one with the spell that the mage mentioned?" Brodie asked, no longer glaring at Ryan.

Mallory turned to the next blank page in her notebook, glancing at her brother before opening the bottle of ink. "We should go home while we're in Longmeadow. Everyone who stays behind should be safe there."

"I'm not going home," Brodie said. "Besides, I can't go home wearing this mask."

"The word to take it off is Scorch," Mallory said. She also told him the words for turning the flames on and off.

Brodie glared at her. "You can't make me take the mask off."

Ryan chuckled. "We'll have to go home eventually, but we can leave it a bit longer before we do."

Ignoring her brother's long list of things they should do before they returned home, Mallory wrote in the notebook. It didn't take long and she was putting it away at the same time as Emica interrupted Brodie.

"Has my father sent any more messages?"

Brodie took out the duplication paper, reading it over. "He said that Rass and Zorla have left the capital and he hasn't been able to find out where they're going."

Mallory closed her eyes at the news, opening them when Ryan took her hand. She met his gaze.

Ryan lightly squeezed her hand. "We're getting stronger and better equipped every day. Next time we face him we'll beat him just like we've done every other time."

Her worries eased and a smile slowly formed. "Yes, and we'll keep levelling up and getting better so he'll never win against us." She leaned against Ryan's side, looking at the road ahead of them. Maybe they should do some levelling up on the way to Longmeadow while they waited to learn where the treasure was buried. They could all do with some experience points. Even after all the ones they'd recently gained.

Final Stats

Character weight does not include any backpacks, satchels, their contents or items carried by livestock.

Mallory

Character Level: 5
Health: 42
Stamina: 70
Mana: 60
Weight: 5kg 269g/90kg

CAS XP: 120/155
Available CAS Points: 3
Available Class Points: 0
Level Progress: 5:7/10

Attributes

Strength: 9
Constitution: 14
Intelligence: 12
Wisdom: 12

Dexterity: 5
Charisma: 5
Luck: 6

Class

Mage: 2
Warrior: 3

Class Skills
None

Spells

Fireball: 0
Health I: 0
Poison Dart I: 0

(Expand For More Details)

Weapon and Armour Affinity

Wand: 1 (+1% damage)
Cloth Armour: 0
Short Sword: 0

(Expand For More Details)

Crafting

Alchemy: 1
Apothecary: 50
Wheelwright: 1

(Expand For More Details)

Reputation

Global: 0
Local Areas:
Ruby Isle
(Expand For More Details)

Buffs and Negative Stats

Necklace: doubles healing done
Silver bracelet: +1 mana every 15 secs
(Expand For More Details)

Available Revives 5

Mallory

Spells Expanded

*All attack spells have +37% damage to base attacks.

Level 0

Fireball: 0
Mana cost: 3
Cooldown: 2 seconds
Damage: low 3, normal 5, critical 7
Duration: Instant

Flame: 0
Mana cost: 5
Cooldown: 3 seconds
Damage: low 4, normal 6, critical 8
Damage Over Time: 4 every 2 seconds
Duration: Non-flammable materials 6 secs,
flammable materials until runs out of fuel

Ice Shard: 0
Mana cost: 3
Cooldown: 2 seconds
Damage: low 3, normal 5, critical 7
Duration: Instant

Lightning Strike: 0
Mana cost: 3
Cooldown: 2 seconds
Damage: low 3, normal 5, critical 7
Duration: Instant

Mend I: 0
Mana Cost: 17
Cooldown: 5 seconds
Area Of Effect: 1cm2
Duration: Instant

Level 1

Beacon: 0
Mana Cost: 15
Cooldown: 5 seconds
Area Of Effect: to be cast on a
solid surface
Duration: 10 mins

Health I: 0
Restores health to target
Mana Cost: 6
Cooldown: 3 seconds
Area Of Effect: +1HP to target within 2m
Duration: Instant

Poison Dart I: 0
Mana Cost: 6
Cooldown: 3 seconds
Damage: low 4, normal 6, crit 8
Damage Over Time: 5 every 3
seconds
Duration: 3 secs

Mallory

Spells Expanded 2

Level 2

Lightning Trap: 0
Mana Cost: 10
Cooldown: 5 seconds
Damage: 10
Duration: damage on contact

Shrink I: 0
Mana Cost: 20
Cooldown: 10 seconds
Area Of Effect: cast on the object,
living creature or sentient being
the castor wishes to shrink
Duration: Permanent.

Vanish I: 0
Mana Cost: 25
Cooldown: 5 seconds
Area Of Effect: causes target, within
a 2m range, to vanish
Duration: 1 min

Water Manipulation: 0
Mana Cost: 12
Cooldown: 5 seconds
Area Of Effect: relocate up to five
litres of water up to a distance of
five metres
Duration: Instant

Level 3

Magelight: 0
Mana Cost: 20
Cooldown: 10 seconds
Area Of Effect: creates a ball of light
near caster
Duration: 15 mins

Weak Reanimate: 0
Mana Cost: 20
Cooldown: 5 seconds
Area Of Effect: reanimate one of the
dead level 3
Range: 2m
Duration: 1 min

Teleportation Link I: 0
Mana Cost: 30
Cooldown: 1 minute
Initial Area Of Effect: Cast at a location the
castor wishes to return to
Initial Duration: Instant
Delayed Area Of Effect: Recast to return to
the initial location, transporting the
castor, companion animal and gear worn
or carried by the castor
Delayed Duration: 1 hour

Mallory

Weapon and Armour Affinity Expanded

Dagger (and enchanted): 1 (+1% damage)
Wand: 1 (+1% damage)
Cloth Armour: 0
Unarmed: 0

Chain Mail Armour: 0
Short Sword (and enchanted): 0
Shield (and enchanted): 0
Dual Swords: 0

Crafting Expanded

Alchemy: 1
Apothecary: 50
Bard: 0
Bartering: 0
Brewer: 0
Cooking: 0

Diplomacy: 0
Enchanting: 0
Fishing: 0
Hunting: 0
Husbandry: 0
Languages: 0

Mason: 0
Potter: 0
Sailing: 0
Scribe: 0
Sculptor: 0
Shipwright: 0

Smithing: 0
Thatcher: 0
Weaver: 0
Wheelwright: 1
Woodcutter: 0

Reputation Expanded

Ruby Isle:
Buckneth 22
Cutthroat Harbour -17
Delten 2
Jenlea 0
Mer Point 10

Seacoast 2
South Peak Mine 5
South Point 2
Surith 5
Valley Of Wandering Souls 10

Velkden 42
Wayholt 10
Wildebay 10
Wrentville 1

Buffs And Negative Stats

Necklace: doubles healing done
Silver bracelet: +1 mana every 15 secs
Mage cloth armour hooded jacket: -1 dam when attacked, +1 mana every 5 secs
Gold ring: +1 mana every 10 secs

Ryan

Character Level: 3	CAS XP: 29/128
Health: 39	Available CAS Points: 17
Stamina: 65	Available Class Points: 0
Mana: 20	Level Progress: 3:0/10
Weight: 10kg 536g/130kg	

Attributes

Strength: 13	Dexterity: 7
Constitution: 13	Charisma: 5
Intelligence: 5	Luck: 6
Wisdom: 4	

Class / Spells

Class	Spells
Warrior: 3 Class Skills None	None

Weapon and Armour Affinity / Crafting

Weapon and Armour Affinity	Crafting
Chain Mail Armour: 0 Short Sword: 1 (+1% damage) Shield: 1 (+1% damage) (-1% damage taken) Dual Swords: 0	Hunting: 10 Wheelwright: 1 (Expand For More Details)

Reputation / Buffs and Negative Stats

Reputation	Buffs and Negative Stats
Global: 0 Local Areas: Ruby Isle (Expand For More Details)	None

Available Revives 4

Ryan

Crafting Expanded

Alchemy: 0
Apothecary: 0
Bard: 0
Bartering: 0
Brewer: 0
Cooking: 0

Diplomacy: 0
Enchanting: 0
Fishing: 0
Hunting: 10
Husbandry: 0
Languages: 0

Mason: 0
Potter: 0
Sailing: 0
Scribe: 0
Sculptor: 0
Shipwright: 0

Smithing: 0
Thatcher: 0
Weaver: 0
Wheelwright: 1
Woodcutter: 0

Reputation Expanded

Ruby Isle:
Buckneth 22
Cutthroat Harbour -17
Delten 2
Jenlea 0
Mer Point 10

Seacoast 2
South Peak Mine 5
South Point 2
Surith 5
Valley Of Wandering
Souls 10

Velkden 42
Wayholt 10
Wildebay 10
Wrentville 1

Brodie

Character Level: 3
Health: 36
Stamina: 60
Mana: 25
Weight: 6kg 709g/60kg

CAS XP: 48/132
Available CAS Points: 5
Available Class Points: 0
Level Progress: 3:4/10

Attributes

Strength: 6
Constitution: 12
Intelligence: 5
Wisdom: 5

Dexterity: 10
Charisma: 8
Luck: 7

Class

Rogue: 3

Class Skills
Stealth: 0 (30 seconds,
1 hour cooldown)

Spells

None

Weapon and Armour Affinity

Stiletto: 1 (+1% damage)
Throwing Knives: 2
(+2% damage)
Leather Armour: 0

Crafting

Bartering: 15
Cooking: 10
Wheelwright: 1

(Expand For More Details)

Reputation

Global: 0
Local Areas:
Ruby Isle
(Expand For More Details)

Buffs and Negative Stats

None

Available Revives 1

Brodie

Crafting Expanded

Alchemy: 0
Apothecary: 0
Bard: 0
Bartering: 15
Brewer: 0
Cooking: 10

Diplomacy: 0
Enchanting: 0
Fishing: 0
Hunting: 0
Husbandry: 0
Languages: 0

Mason: 0
Potter: 0
Sailing: 0
Scribe: 0
Sculptor: 0
Shipwright: 0

Smithing: 0
Thatcher: 0
Weaver: 0
Wheelwright: 1
Woodcutter: 0

Reputation Expanded

Ruby Isle:
Buckneth 22
Cutthroat Harbour -17
Delten 2
Jenlea 0
Mer Point 10

Seacoast 2
South Peak Mine 5
South Point 2
Surith 5
Valley Of Wandering
Souls 10

Velkden 42
Wayholt 10
Wildebay 10
Wrentville 1

Callum

Character Level: 3
Health: 30
Stamina: 50
Mana: 25
Weight: 8kg 416g/80kg

CAS XP: 50/128
Available CAS Points: 27
Available Class Points: 0
Level Progress: 3:0/10

Attributes

Strength: 8
Constitution: 10
Intelligence: 5
Wisdom: 5

Dexterity: 12
Charisma: 5
Luck: 8

Class

Archer: 3

Class Skills
None

Spells

None

Weapon and Armour Affinity

Hunting Knife: 1 (+1% damage)
Studded Leather Armour: 0
Longbow: 0

(Expand For More Details)

Crafting

Wheelwright: 1

(Expand For More Details)

Reputation

Global: 0
Local Areas:
Ruby Isle
(Expand For More Details)

Buffs and Negative Stats

Silver Ring: +2 damage to bow attacks

Available Revives 2

Callum

Weapon and Armour Affinity Expanded

Short Bow (and enchanted): 1 (+1% damage)
Hunting Knife: 1 (+1% damage)
Studden Leather Armour: 0

Sling: 0
Slingshot
Longbow: 0

Crafting Expanded

Alchemy: 0	Diplomacy: 0	Mason: 0	Smithing: 0
Apothecary: 0	Enchanting: 0	Potter: 0	Thatcher: 0
Bard: 0	Fishing: 0	Sailing: 0	Weaver: 0
Bartering: 0	Hunting: 0	Scribe: 0	Wheelwright: 1
Brewer: 0	Husbandry: 0	Sculptor: 0	Woodcutter: 0
Cooking: 0	Languages: 0	Shipwright: 0	

Reputation Expanded

Ruby Isle:	Seacoast 2	Velkden 42
Buckneth 22	South Peak Mine 5	Wayholt 10
Cutthroat Harbour -17	South Point 2	Wildebay 10
Delten 2	Surith 5	Wrentville 1
Jenlea 0	Valley Of Wandering Souls 10	
Mer Point 10		

Danae

Character Level: 3
Health: 33
Stamina: 55
Mana: 25
Weight: 6kg 702g/70kg

CAS XP: 87/128
Available CAS Points: 10
Available Class Points: 0
Level Progress: 3:0/10

Attributes

Strength: 7
Constitution: 11
Intelligence: 5
Wisdom: 5

Dexterity: 12
Charisma: 5
Luck: 8

Class

Archer: 3

Class Skills
None

Spells

None

Weapon and Armour Affinity

Hunting Knife: 1 (+1% damage)
Studded Leather Armour: 0
Longbow: 0

(Expand For More Details)

Crafting

Alchemy: 9
Bartering: 1
Cooking: 1
Glassblowing: 5

(Expand For More Details)

Reputation

Global: 0
Local Areas:
Ruby Isle
(Expand For More Details)

Buffs and Negative Stats

None

Racial Bonus

Archer +10% damage
Mage capable of using spells
one level above class level

Available Revives 2

Danae

Weapon and Armour Affinity Expanded

Short Bow (and enchanted): 1 (+1% damage)
Hunting Knife: 1 (+1% damage)
Studded Leather Armour: 0
Sling: 0

Slingshot
Enchanted Arrows
Longbow: 0
Unarmed: 1 (+1% damage)

Crafting Expanded

Alchemy: 9	Diplomacy: 0	Mason: 0	Smithing: 0
Apothecary: 0	Enchanting: 0	Potter: 0	Thatcher: 0
Bartering: 1	Fishing: 0	Sailing: 0	Weaver: 0
Brewer: 0	Glassblowing: 5	Scribe: 0	Wheelwright: 1
Clothier: 0	Husbandry: 0	Sculptor: 0	Woodcutter: 0
Cooking: 1	Languages: 0	Shipwright: 0	

Reputation Expanded

Ruby Isle:
Buckneth 4
Cutthroat Harbour -17
Delten 2
Jenlea 0
Mer Point 10
Seacoast 2

Simria 22
South Peak Mine 5
South Point 2
Surith 5
Ursen 0
Valley Of Wandering Souls 10

Velkden 42
Wayholt 18
Wildebay 10
Wrentville 1

COMPANION ANIMALS' FINAL STATS

Smudge 8HP (Callum)

2896XP/3000XP

Items: 1GP owed from Mallory

Wearing: None

Abilities: +25% movement speed

Fang 6HP (Brodie)

33833XP/4000XP

Items: None

Wearing: Leather collar (made from belt) with revive ring tied to it (plain gold band)

Abilities: +25% movement speed

Free Ebook

Subscribe to Avril's newsletter and receive a free ebook. This ebook is exclusive to those on her mailing list. To find out more about this offer visit:

www.avrilsabine.com/free-ebook

*

We value your privacy and will not sell, rent, exchange or loan your email address to third parties. Your information is confidential and you are under no obligation to remain on the mailing list and can unsubscribe at any time.

To The Reader

If you enjoyed this book, why not consider leaving a review to help other readers discover it too? Reader engagement is one of the few ways that lets an author know readers want more books in a particular series or genre. So leave a review and tell friends, not only about this book but also about other ones you've enjoyed, so you can continue to enjoy books by your favourite authors for years to come.

Dreams are meant to be lived,

Avril, Storm and Rhys.

Acknowledgements

Thanks to the usual crew who helped make this story what it is and thank you to all those readers who've told us how much they're enjoying the series and that they're looking forward to future Guardians Of The Round Table stories. We're currently working on the seventh book. So there are certainly more to come.

About The Authors

Avril is an Australian author who lives with her family on acreage in South East Queensland. She writes mostly young adult and children's speculative fiction, but has been known to dabble in other genres. She has been an avid gamer since she was ten, which was the year she discovered Dungeons & Dragons and was given a Commodore 64.

Storm has a wide range of interests from gaming and blacksmithing to cooking and sewing. It's not unusual to find him cooking at any hour of the day or night, particularly after a long gaming session.

Rhys loves books and gaming and has thoroughly enjoyed combining two of his favourite things. He has been running tabletop gaming sessions for the past few years and enjoys creating characters and doing in depth worldbuilding.

Titles By Avril Sabine

Stories about strong characters and characters who discover their strengths.

SERIES

Assassins Of The Dead- Young Adult Fantasy/ Paranormal

Book 1: Dark Blade

Book 2: Dragon Touched

Book 3: Society Against Vampires

Book 4: King's Request

Dragon Blood- Young Adult Urban Fantasy (with elements of romance)

(5 book series)

Book 1: Pliethin

Book 2: Wyvern

Book 3: Surety

Book 4: Knight

Book 5: Mage

Dragon Mage- Young Adult Urban Fantasy (with elements of romance)

(Series two of Dragon Blood series)

Book 1: Promise

Dragon Blood Chronicles- Young Adult Urban Fantasy (with elements of romance)

(Companion stand alone series to Dragon Blood)

Book 1: Oath

Book 2: Betrayed

Guardians Of The Round Table- Young Adult Fantasy LitRPG

(Co-written with Storm and Rhys Petersen)

Book 1: Dexterity Fail

Book 2: Goblin Boots

Book 3: Singed Feathers

Book 4: Frog Mage

Book 5: Crystal Mine

Book 6: Cursed Harp

Rosie's Rangers- Young Adult Western Steampunk

(6 book series)

Book 1: Justice

Book 2: Vengeance

Book 3: Treachery

Book 4: Accused

Book 5: Wanted

Book 6: Corruption

Mark Of Kings- Children's Fantasy

(Upper middle grade/preteen)

(4 book series)

Book 1: The Arena

Book 2: The Island

Book 3: The Assassin

Book 4: The King

STAND ALONE SERIES

Demon Hunters- Young Adult Urban Fantasy/ Horror (with elements of romance)

Book 1: Blood Sacrifice

Book 2: Retribution

Book 3: Tainted

Book 4: Premonition

Book 5: Cursed

Book 6: Feud

Book 7: Extrication

Plea Of The Damned- Young Adult Urban Fantasy/Paranormal

(6 book series)

Book 1: Forgive Me Lucy

Book 2: Forgive Me Aiden

Book 3: Forgive Me Jena

Book 4: Forgive Me Kobe

Book 5: Forgive Me Marti

Book 6: Forgive Me Dawson

Realms Of The Fae- Young Adult Urban Fantasy (with elements of romance)

The Sword (short story in Like A Girl Anthology)

Heart Of Stone

Book 1: A Debt Owed

Book 2: Marked By The Hunt

Book 3: The Magic Collector

Book 4: An Unexpected Betrayal

Book 5: Imprisoned By Iron

Fairytales Retold (Short Stories)

Snow-White And Rose-Red

The Twelve Brothers

The Light Princess

Beauty And The Beast

Sleeping Beauty

Aschenputtel

The Golden Bird

The Frog Prince

The Death Of Koshchei The Deathless

Myths And Legends Retold (Short Stories)

Ion, Son Of Apollo

Sir Gawain And The Maid With The Narrow Sleeves

Princess Ilse, The Giant's Daughter

YOUNG ADULT NOVELS

Young Adult Fantasy (with elements of romance)

Elf Sight

Earth Bound

Young Adult Urban Fantasy

Stone Warrior (with elements of romance)

The Jungle Inside

Young Adult Contemporary (with elements of romance)

Through Your Eyes

The Ugly Stepsister

Perfect Little Princess

Young Adult Contemporary/Paranormal

Whispers In The Dark (with elements of romance and same sex relationships)

Over Too Soon (with elements of romance)

Young Adult Sci-Fi

Experiment X-One-Six (Urban Sci-Fi/Superheroes)

An Endless Dawn (Post Apocalyptic Sci-Fi)

CHILDREN'S BOOKS

Dragon Lord (Preteen/early teens) (Fantasy)

The Irish Wizard (Upper middle grade) (Urban Fantasy)

SHORT STORIES

Urban Fantasy

Eternally Late

Dealings With Joe

Glimpses (short story in That Moment When Anthology)

Contemporary

The Brat Next Door

Fantasy LitRPG

(Set in the same world as Guardians Of The Round Table Series)

Tales Of Inadon 1: The Disc (Co-written with Storm and Rhys Petersen) (short story in Game On! Anthology)

Post Apocalyptic Sci-Fi

Compulsive Directive

NONFICTION

A Year Of Weekly Writing Exercises (Creative Writing)

Cooking For Families With Allergies (Cooking) (Co-written with Storm Petersen)

Tell Me A Story, Grandma (Memoir)

For the most up to date details on available titles visit:

www.avrilsabine.com/books/bibliography

Guardians Of The Round Table Series

To learn more about this series visit:

www.avrilsabine.com/series/gotrt

Find maps, more stats and details about the next book.

BOOKS AVAILABLE IN THE GUARDIANS OF THE ROUND TABLE SERIES

Book 1: Dexterity Fail

Book 2: Goblin Boots

Book 3: Singed Feathers

Book 4: Frog Mage

Book 5: Crystal Mine

Book 6: Cursed Harp

Book 7: Treasure Seeker

BOOKS SET IN THE SAME WORLD AS THE GUARDIANS OF THE ROUND TABLE SERIES

Adventurers Guild Handbook (Lore Book)

Legend Of The Ancestral King (Lore Book)

Lost And Powerful: Myths Of Misplaced Staves (Lore Book)

Disclaimer

This is a work of fiction. Names, characters, businesses, places, events and incidents are either the products of the author's imagination or used in a fictitious manner. Any resemblance to actual persons, living or dead, or actual events is purely coincidental. The opinions expressed or beliefs held are those of the characters and should not be assumed to be the opinions or beliefs of the author.